SILENT KILLER

Shawn hadn't moved. He was staring back towards the snack bar, looking for the vanished mime. "There was something wrong with that mime," Shawn said.

"By definition," Gus said.

"No, something else," Shawn said, still looking back where they'd last seen the mime. "Something I noticed but didn't register until after we left."

There was a long moment of silence. Then Gus spoke quietly. "You mean like he had a gun pointed at my head?"

"I think I would have noticed that a little quicker," Shawn said. "No, it was—"

"Shawn!"

"Yes?"

"The mime has a gun pointed at my head."

Shawn turned back to his partner. The mime stood in front of Gus, his white-gloved hand leveling a gleaming pistol at Gus' forehead.

"Please," the mime said. "Don't make me kill you."

THE PSYCH SERIES

Call of the Mild
Mind Over Magic
A Mind Is a Terrible Thing to Read

psych
THE CALL OF THE MILD

William Rabkin

AN OBSIDIAN MYSTERY

OBSIDIAN
Published by New American Library, a division of
Penguin Group (USA) Inc., 375 Hudson Street,
New York, New York 10014, USA
Penguin Group (Canada), 90 Eglinton Avenue East, Suite 700, Toronto,
Ontario M4P 2Y3, Canada (a division of Pearson Penguin Canada Inc.)
Penguin Books Ltd., 80 Strand, London WC2R 0RL, England
Penguin Ireland, 25 St. Stephen's Green, Dublin 2,
Ireland (a division of Penguin Books Ltd.)
Penguin Group (Australia), 250 Camberwell Road, Camberwell, Victoria 3124,
Australia (a division of Pearson Australia Group Pty. Ltd.)
Penguin Books India Pvt. Ltd., 11 Community Centre, Panchsheel Park,
New Delhi - 110 017, India
Penguin Group (NZ), 67 Apollo Drive, Rosedale, North Shore 0632,
New Zealand (a division of Pearson New Zealand Ltd.)
Penguin Books (South Africa) (Pty.) Ltd., 24 Sturdee Avenue,
Rosebank, Johannesburg 2196, South Africa

Penguin Books Ltd., Registered Offices:
80 Strand, London WC2R 0RL, England

First published by Obsidian, an imprint of New American Library,
a division of Penguin Group (USA) Inc.

First Printing, January 2010
10 9 8 7 6 5 4 3 2

For Rufus R. and the woman who loves him

Prologue

Henry Spencer's head was about to split in two. Part of it was due to the horrible high-pitched whine coming from the backyard. But mostly it was caused by the even more horrible low-pitched whining from the woman on the other end of the phone line. She'd started complaining the second he picked up, and she hadn't stopped to take a breath in five minutes.

Finally there was a pause in her tirade. Maybe she needed air. Maybe she'd keeled over from a stroke. Henry didn't care. He saw his opportunity and he seized it.

"You want to sue, I'll see you in court, lady!"

He slammed down the phone receiver, then picked it up and slammed it down again. It didn't help. His head still throbbed.

This wasn't the first time Henry had been threatened with a lawsuit. Half the creeps he'd arrested in all his years on the Santa Barbara police force had screamed police brutality and vowed to take him to court.

But it was the first time he'd been threatened with a lawsuit because of something his son had done. Or, rather, not done.

Henry massaged his pounding skull, then shouted, "Shawn!"

There was no answer, of course. And the whining kept getting louder.

Henry stalked through the kitchen and and flung open the screen door. Shawn was standing in the middle of the lawn, a radio-control box in his hand.

"Watch out!" Shawn said.

"I'm not the one who—" Henry's sentence was cut off as a model airplane crashed into his stomach, knocking the wind out of him.

"Well, that's just great," Shawn said, flipping a switch on the control box. "You killed it."

"Then half my work is done." Henry pulled air into his lungs, then picked up the airplane and looked it over. It was a nice model, finely detailed. These things weren't cheap. "Where did you get this?"

"I bought it," Shawn said.

"With what money?"

"Money I earned," Shawn said.

"Would that be money you earned taking care of Mrs. Calloway's garden?" Henry said.

"Why do you ask?"

"Because she just called," Henry said. "Apparently she paid you in advance for your work, and now all her flowers are dead because you never showed up to take care of them. She wants to sue you."

"Good luck to her," Shawn said. "It's not like I have any assets, thanks to a medieval allowance policy around here."

Shawn turned the control box upside down and banged on the bottom. The plane in Henry's hand gave a cough and a shake, and the propeller kicked over. Henry grabbed it and held it in place until the toy stopped struggling.

"Maybe I should have said she wants to sue me," Henry said. "But the lawsuit isn't the important part. Hell, if she was stupid enough to pay you in advance, she shouldn't be allowed to own plants anyway. But you said you'd take care of her garden and you killed it."

"It was a weasel," Shawn said.

"Oh, that's good," Henry said. "You took care of her flowers, but a weasel destroyed them."

"I'm not talking about a rodent," Shawn said. He walked over to his father and tried to pry the plane out of his hands. Henry didn't let go. "I'm saying I didn't lie. I told her I would take care of her plants to the best of my ability. Well, this *was* the best of my ability. That's a weasel."

Henry stared at his son, wondering as he had so many times before exactly what he had done in a previous life to deserve this. "You want to go into court and explain this weasel to a judge?"

"It's the truth," Shawn said.

"A weasel is not a legal defense," Henry said. "If anything, it's going to make a judge really angry. He'll find a way to put you in juvie just for smarting off to him."

Henry was pleased to see that Shawn actually looked a little nervous. "What should I do?"

"I only see one way out of this," Henry said. "And that's another weasel."

"But you just said—"

Henry held up a hand to cut him off. "It's a very special weasel, guaranteed to get you out of trouble. But you have to promise to do exactly what I say, or it's not going to work."

"What is it?" Shawn said suspiciously.

"Promise first."

Shawn struggled to find a way around the requirement. Then he smiled. "I promise."

"Right. Because I am an idiot. You have to tell me exactly what you're promising, or it's no deal."

Shawn's smile vanished. "I promise to do exactly what you say."

"Good call, son." Putting down the plane, Henry led Shawn to the garage and threw open the door. He poked around in his tools and came out with a long pole topped with three sets of rotating tines. "There you go."

He thrust the tool out to Shawn, who took a step back. "I thought you said you had a weasel for me."

"I do," Henry said. "This is the Garden Weasel. I want you to use it to dig up Mrs. Calloway's garden, and then I want you to replace everything that died. Is that clear?"

Shawn thought this over for a long time. Then he broke out into a grin. "Yes, sir!"

Shawn took the Garden Weasel and ran down the driveway. Henry looked after him, wondering what had just happened. He had laid down the law for Shawn, and Shawn had agreed to it. Why had he seemed so triumphant? What had Henry missed?

Inches away from Henry's feet, the airplane's propeller kicked twice, then started to spin. The plane taxied down the driveway. Henry dove for it, but it took off and rose out of his reach.

And then Henry knew. Shawn hadn't agreed to do the work. Shawn hadn't agreed to do any work. He had simply acknowledged the clarity of his father's demands. It was another one of Shawn's weasels.

The airplane's whining filled the air again. But this time Henry didn't complain about the headache it brought on. He wanted to be in as bad a mood as possible when Shawn came home. Then he'd teach him all sorts of uses for a Garden Weasel.

Chapter One

It was the same dream that had tormented Gus since he was seven. He was lost in the woods, whacking through thick undergrowth with only a sliver of moon to light his way. Shawn had been next to him just a second ago. Now he was gone. Gus wanted to call out for him. Or for help. Or for his mother. But he didn't dare make a sound.

Something was hunting him. Gus didn't know what. He couldn't see it. But he could hear it. Crashing through brush and snapping branches as it plunged towards him. Closer and closer, until Gus could hear its ragged breathing. Feel the hot breath on the back of his neck.

Then Gus did scream. Scream and run, run blindly, barely feeling the low branches flay the flesh from his body, tripping, stumbling, until he saw the chasm opening up beneath him.

This was the worst part of the dream. Gus could see the plunge just ahead of him, the cliff falling off hundreds of feet down to a roaring river far below. There was plenty of time to stop or turn away. But no matter how hard he willed his feet to change direction, they kept pounding inexorably towards the cliff's edge. He pummeled his thighs, tried to throw himself to the ground, to grab hold of a tree—anything to slow himself down. Nothing worked. His feet kept propelling him forwards. Even as he felt his left foot—it was always the left that went first—take that fatal, final step with only open air beneath it, he could not stop. His right foot followed its mate off the edge, and for one moment Gus was suspended in air.

That's when he woke up every time.

Every time until now.

Because try as he might to persuade himself that he was only dreaming, Gus knew this time it was different.

This was real.

The branches tearing at his arms, the jagged rocks digging into his feet, the pain in his lungs as he gasped for breath— they were all real. At least it wasn't night, as it was in the dream, but the thick trees were so dense they nearly blocked out the sun completely. Gus really was in the wilderness, and there was some Thing after him. He could hear its hot, rough breath coming through the forest towards him.

And where was Shawn? He was the one who had talked Gus into taking this descent into hell. He was the one who had said that a little fresh air would be good for them. And yet he was also the one who couldn't make it through the opening scene of *Cliffhanger* without suddenly realizing he'd forgotten to ask for extra fake butter on his popcorn and running out of the auditorium, not returning until any pretense of a realistic depiction of death in high places had been replaced by that pressing issue of how to find a hundred million in stolen government cash at the top of a mountain.

Shawn had been right by Gus' side when they first entered this savage place. What happened to him? How had he disappeared? Had the Thing that was chasing Gus gotten him first? When it finally caught up with him, would Gus see shreds of his best friend's mangled flesh snagged on its gleaming fangs? Or had Shawn simply taken a wrong step and plunged the way Gus did in his dreams? Gus had a vision of Shawn's broken body sprawled out over a bed of jagged rocks, and for a brief moment envied him the quickness of his death.

This was it, then. The end. The fate that he'd been dreaming about for so many years. It was finally coming true, just as the Oracle or the Norns or the Magic 8 Ball had been trying to tell him since he was a little kid. If he had paid attention to those dreams, if he had followed the warnings, would he be facing his doom today? No doubt he would, Gus knew. He'd read enough Greek tragedies and seen enough *Twilight Zone* episodes to know that trying to avoid your fate only brought you to it faster.

Gus couldn't run anymore. His breath was coming in shallow gasps, his feet had been numb for so long he might as well have been running through Marshmallow Fluff, and all his muscles were cramping so hard no one would ever be able to straighten out his corpse. And still the Thing was coming through the woods towards him.

He took a deep breath and stepped away from behind the tree that had been holding him up. The creature's puffing breath had changed to a bellow. The Thing was close. The sound reached a crescendo, and Gus caught his first glimpse of the Beast as it blasted through the brush.

Chapter Two

It was as black as tar, and its skin was as shiny hard as a massive beetle's. One bright eye in the middle of its face blasted light at Gus.

Gus crouched down in a fighting stance, trying to understand what he was seeing. What was this Thing coming for him? He had expected a bear, or a dire wolf, or even a saber-toothed tiger. But this was long and low, stretching back for what seemed to be thirty feet. And most disturbingly of all, it bore a rider. This wasn't a wild Thing at all, but a beast of war, trained for combat and for killing. No wonder that in all the times he'd dreamed this moment, Gus had never seen what was chasing him. The image would have been too frightening not to wake him up.

And yet, there was a familiar aspect to the creature. Somewhere beneath all the panic signals his brain was trumpeting out to his nervous system, Gus' rational mind was running through a catalog of images, trying to connect one to the Thing that was rushing towards him blasting steam out of an infernal blowhole.

There was no time for that, however. The creature was almost on him. Gus crouched down and prepared to leap away from the hideous black teeth that tore along right above the steel rails.

Rails? Gus thought, but before he could use that final image to solve the puzzle, a hand grabbed his shoulder and yanked him off his feet. Gus fell sideways, staggering to keep his balance, and the monster roared on.

"Dude, if I'd known you wanted to ride the little train so bad, I would have bought you a ticket."

Gus felt his heart rate slow to near-fatal tachycardia as he turned to see Shawn, body unbroken and flesh unsnagged. If he shared any of Gus' terror he was hiding it behind the brick of pink popcorn he was trying to cram into his mouth.

"Train?" As the word left Gus' mouth, the image flashed in his head, and he realized that the Thing that had terrified him so completely was not a creature after all. The rest of reality rushed into his mind like the passenger cars following the locomotive.

The wilderness Gus and Shawn were standing in was actually the Camellia Forest, part of a large public garden. The trees towering above him were some of the thirty-four thousand plants in the seven hundred camellia varieties that had been spread out over twenty acres of prime suburban landscape outside Pasadena. Just past the steel tracks Gus could see the bright colors of the International Rosarium glinting in the sunlight, and beyond that the rest of the one hundred and fifty acres of park.

"Yes, Gus, it was a choo-choo," Shawn said. "More precisely, it was the Descanso Gardens Enchanted Railroad, a one-eighth-scale replica of an actual train, and a major highlight for the young and young at heart, according to the garden's brochure. What did you think it was?"

"I knew it was a train," Gus said as reality replaced the fantasy landscape that his dream-induced panic had instilled in him. "I was waiting to hop a boxcar."

"I can see why you'd want to do that," Shawn said. "The three-dollar ticket price does seem steep for a five-minute ride, and it's not like they have a dining car. Although this pink popcorn they sell at the snack bar goes a long way towards making up for that."

Shawn held out the remaining piece of pink brick to Gus, who broke off a chunk and nibbled at it sullenly.

"We're on a case," Gus said. "You were handling the officials. I wanted to speak to the denizens of the demimonde, to see if they had any insight on the subject."

"So you thought you'd hop a freight, gain the confidence of the local hobo community, see if they'd open up to you?"

"Exactly," Gus said, finally feeling the terror draining out of his muscles.

"That's a good idea," Shawn said. "Except, of course, for the fact that the boxcars on this train are so small the three-year-olds ride on top. But maybe there was a mouse inside who could have given you the inside squeak."

"You can laugh if you want, but I was pursuing every possible lead to try to recover our client's property. What were you doing?"

"Nothing as clever as riding the really, really little rails," Shawn said. "I was checking out the lost-and-found department."

"I'm sure that was useful," Gus said.

"Compared to straddling a miniature railroad waiting to be struck down by some forest-dwelling monster, maybe not."

Gus glared at him, then grabbed another chunk of the pink popcorn. "Fine. I took a wrong turn on the nature trail. The sun was too hot. I left my water bottle in the car. I guess I got a little dehydrated, and from there disorientation is only moments away. I didn't want to take this stupid case to start with."

That was true, but it didn't have anything to do with Gus' fear of the wilderness. It had to do with his fear of monsters.

In the years since they'd established Santa Barbara's premier psychic-detective agency, Shawn and Gus had caught murderers, blackmailers, grave robbers, serial killers, oil well bandits, and seal slayers, and Gus had stared them all down with a quick grin and a clever retort—at least in his memory he did.

But there had been a handful of cases when they had had gone up against ghosts, dinosaurs, and mummies, and those were the ones that still kept Gus up at night. Even though they all turned out to be fakes, the idea of fighting slavering supernatural beasts from beyond hell was simply something Gus preferred to leave to others.

There was only one thing he dreaded more than the idea of going up against monsters.

And that was working for one.

Chapter Three

Ellen Svaco didn't have dripping fangs, her hair wasn't a nest of hissing vipers. Her arms weren't pus-filled tentacles.

But the instant she walked through the doors of the beach bungalow that housed Psych's offices, Gus knew she was a monster. And not just any monster, but the worst kind.

Ellen Svaco was the sort of monster who would call a second-grader up to the blackboard and make him stand there until he correctly spelled the fiendishly difficult name of California's state capital no matter how many times he had already failed and no matter how many of the other students were laughing at him and no matter that the lunch bell had already rung. Gus had met one such ogre before, and the encounter had scarred him so badly it took many years before he could bring himself to say the word "Sacramento" without a shudder and a stutter.

Like that other creature, Ellen wore her graying hair tied back so tightly it stretched every centimeter of her skin across the contours of her skull. Her shapeless shift looked like it came from the sale rack at the Mormon Fundamentalists' thrift shop. She could have been forty or four hundred or anywhere in between.

"My name is Ellen Svaco and I'm looking for a detective named Spenser." She said the name in a tone that made it sound like she was referring to a skunk that had crawled under her house to die. "With an 's' like the poet. At least that's what I was told."

Shawn barely glanced up from the newspaper photo of Detective Carlton Lassiter he was busy defacing with a ballpoint pen. "Whoever said that is playing some kind of joke on you," he said as he added eyeballs to the ends of the springy antennae he'd drawn on Lassiter's forehead. "There is no 's' in 'poet.'"

Gus saw the skin around the woman's eyes tighten in irritation and felt his hand shooting up in the air. He tried to stop it before his fingers had cleared the desk, but he had spent so much of his school years saving Shawn from academic self-immolation that it had become a reflex as impossible to restrain as jerking his leg when the rubber hammer hit his knee or fleeing from a movie theater when they started showing a trailer for any movie where Eddie Murphy played more than two roles.

"Edmund Spenser, author of *The Faerie Queene,* is considered one of the most important Elizabethan poets," Gus said.

"That's nice for him," Shawn said. "But can he fit all one hundred and twenty different colors of Crayons in his mouth at the same time? Because I can."

That was true, as Shawn had proven only the night before. Gus saw the skin around the woman's eyes tightening even further. He felt his pre-adolescent terror of any teacher's disapproval rising in his chest.

"This is Shawn Spencer, and he is a detective," Gus said. "How can we help you?"

The woman glared at Gus. "I'm having a very hard time believing that you are a walking weapon, the physical incarnation of street justice, and the unstoppable id to Spenser's superego," she said.

"It's amazing how many people have that same problem," Shawn said. "I told him not to stop shaving his head."

"I think there's been some kind of misunderstanding," Gus said.

"More like blatant misrepresentation," the woman snapped. "Are you or are you not Hawk?"

"My name is Burton Guster. Most people call me Gus."

"Which is a kind of hawk," Shawn said.

"It is not," Gus said.

"Gus the Hawk. I remember you showed it to me on some flag when you thought you wanted to be a flexitriloquist."

"First of all, the bird on the flag of the Azores is the Goshawk, not Gus the Hawk," Gus said. "And a scholar who studies flags is a vexillologist."

"Then what's a flexitriloquist?" Shawn said.

"There's no such thing. You just made it up."

"I'm pretty certain I saw an ad for it on Craigslist," Shawn said. "Are you sure it isn't someone who can throw her voice while she does Pilates?"

Ellen Svaco let out the kind of sigh that could paralyze a class of second-graders within seconds. "But you're Spenser?" she said to Shawn.

"With a 'c,' like the shell," Shawn said. "Or should that be like the saw?"

The woman breathed silently for a moment, and Gus had the sudden desire to find the nearest elementary school so he could report to the principal's office.

"I can't believe that policeman lied to me," she finally said. "He said this Spenser was America's finest detective, his street-smart sidekick was as lethal as he was loyal, and for proof I had to look no further than a seemingly endless series of fictionalized accounts of their cases."

For the first time, Shawn looked interested. "And how exactly did this come up in conversation?"

"I went in to see the police about a very serious matter," she said. "It was serious to me, in any case. Apparently the detective in charge thought it was some kind of joke."

"Did this detective have a handlebar mustache, thick glasses, and eyeballs on stalks protruding from his head?" Shawn said.

"Of course not."

"Well, if he did," Shawn said, slipping the newspaper across the desk to her, "would he look something like this?"

She gave the paper a quick glance, as if years of practice had taught her to see pictures through layers of defacement. "That's him."

"Lassie sent her here?" Gus said. "Why?"

"Because he knows when a case is too big for him," Shawn said. "He realizes that there are some things that are so explosive, so filled with pitfalls and dangers that a mere policeman can't be expected to handle them."

"Or he's trying to get back at you for having Papa Julio's Casa de Pizza deliver seventeen pineapple-and-anchovy pizzas to his house."

"Or that," Shawn conceded. "I guess we'll know when Ms. Svaco tells us what her case is about."

"Why should I tell you anything?" she said. "I have no idea who you are, and I have no intention of being the butt of some policeman's practical joke."

"As I said, this is Shawn Spencer and I'm Burton Guster," Gus said. "We are Psych, Santa Barbara's premier psychic-detective agency."

Ellen Svaco stared at Gus as if he'd just shot a spitball at her. "Psychic detectives? You people must really think I'm an idiot."

She turned and walked towards the door, her sensible pumps thwocking hollowly on the linoleum. Gus felt a huge sense of relief to see her go—until he glanced over at Shawn and saw that his partner was studying her carefully as she walked away. Studying her in the way Gus knew meant that he was observing all sorts of tiny details that no one else would ever notice, details that Shawn would put together to tell a story about her. Just as her hand hit the doorknob, Shawn grabbed his forehead with both hands and let out a moan.

"Murder!" he wailed. "Murder most foul!"

Chapter Four

Ellen Svaco froze at the door. When she turned around, Gus was surprised to see there were no actual icicles hanging off her ears. "Excuse me?"

"That's what you should have said if you wanted the police to take your case," Shawn said. "An accusation of murder always gets their attention."

"But there is no murder," she said.

"Are you sure?" Shawn said. "Because that would be a hell of a case. Especially if you were the victim."

"If I'd been the victim of a murder, how could I go to the police?"

"I have no idea, but it's a great way to start a story," Shawn said. "Gus, take a note in case someone ever wants to write a seemingly endless series of fictionalized accounts of our cases."

"Maybe the fictional version of you won't be an idiot," Ellen said, turning back to the door.

"Yes, but would the fictional version of me know how to find your necklace?"

For the first time since she came through their door, Ellen Svaco didn't appear to be suffering from stomach pains.

"What about my necklace?" she said dubiously, almost exactly at the same time as Gus.

"Not much," Shawn said. "Just that you ordered the head

detective of the Santa Barbara Police Department to find it for you."

"I did go to the police station to request help in finding my necklace."

Gus sighed and settled back in his seat. It looked like they were getting a client. "Where was the last place you saw it?" he asked.

Shawn held up a hand to stop her before she could respond. "If she knew that, she wouldn't have come to a psychic-detective agency," Shawn said. "A regular detective is perfectly capable of asking the same questions your mother did every time you lost your mittens."

"I grew up in Santa Barbara," Gus said. "I never had any mittens to lose."

"Which made your perpetual search for them even more pathetic," Shawn said, then turned back to Ellen Svaco. "I don't want you to tell me anything. I just want you to think about the necklace. Think about how much it means to you, about all the good times you've had together."

She looked like she was about to say something, but Shawn gave her a calming shush and she stopped herself, closing her eyes. Shawn studied her carefully and he *saw*. Saw the small scratch on the side of her neck. Saw the four red stripes of rash on the back of her hand. Saw the smudge of chalk dust high on her forehead and the small brown spot on her blouse. He pressed his fingers to his temples and bowed his head.

"I'm sensing something," he said. "A banana."

"A banana?" Ellen Svaco sat back up in her chair.

"Not just a banana," Shawn said. "A giant banana, hurtling through the world at amazing speeds, filled with songs of joy. Does that mean anything to you?"

It did to Gus—that they were going to be here all day while Shawn played silly games with the new client. "Sometimes the visions take a while to coalesce," Gus told her. "He just gets random images at first, and eventually they come together into a coherent whole. So maybe we could call you tonight and—"

"That's what we call the school bus," Ellen said. "On Monday I took my second-grade class on a field trip to—"

"No, wait," Shawn said, again pressing his fingertips to his temple. "I see a magical land of enchantment. A place of peace and happiness where no voice is ever raised in anger and everybody loves everyone else."

"She took them to Fairyland?" Gus said.

"Nicer than that," Shawn said. "Canada."

"It was only a half day," Ellen said. "And I'd be fired if I took the kids out of the state, let alone the country."

"No, not Canada." Shawn scrunched his eyes shut even more tightly. "*La* Canada. You took them to the Descanso Gardens outside Pasadena."

She stared at him suspiciously. "How do you know that?"

"That's where the necklace is," Shawn said. "You left it there, and a little piece of your soul with it. That's what was communicating with me."

For a moment a pleased expression almost appeared on Ellen's face, but she managed to banish it before it resolved into a smile. "You must think you're pretty clever," she said. "Now I'm supposed to write you a check and go off happy?"

"I'll make you a deal," Shawn said. "You pay us in cash, and we won't care what your mood is."

"Meanwhile, all you've said is that my necklace is somewhere within a hundred and fifty acres of public gardens, not including the parking lot. So when I can't find it, you can still say you solved the big mystery."

"We'll recover your necklace," Shawn said.

"We will?" Gus said.

"And we will bring it to your doorstep. I might even bring it across your doorstep if you promised to open the door when I got there."

Ellen made a show of thinking it over then scrawled an address across the top of Shawn's newspaper. "Just put it in the mail along with your bill. But don't even think about sending the bill without the necklace. I've got every state licensing agency on my speed dial."

Gus waited until she'd left the bungalow, and made sure the door was closed, before he said anything. By the time he was certain they were alone, Shawn was rooting around on Gus' desk.

"I don't know what that little piece of her soul is telling you, but the necklace isn't on my desk," Gus said.

"No, but these are." Shawn held up Gus' keys, then tossed them to him. "If we hurry, we can get to La Canada before lunchtime. There's a new burger stand I've been dying to try."

"It's going to take us at least two hours to get to La Canada from here," Gus said. "And besides, we had lunch an hour ago."

"Which means we'll be ready for another one as soon as we grab that necklace," Shawn said as he headed towards the door.

"I'm not going anywhere until you tell me why you're so sure it's there. And if I hear the word 'soul' one more time I'm going to throw up."

Shawn sighed and turned around. "We could save an awful lot of time if you'd just watch my eyes when I'm observing. Then you could see what I see. Pretty soon you could think like I think."

"And right after that I could commit myself," Gus said. "How did you know about the field trip?"

"She had a strange rash—four short stripes on top of her hand and one across the heel of her palm," Shawn said. "At least it was strange until you knew what it was. It was the shape of four little fingers and one thumb clutching her hand."

"She's allergic to children?"

"Only if they've been picking a bouquet of pretty green and red leaves," Shawn said.

"The kid got poison oak on his hand and then grabbed Ellen Svaco's?"

"Exactly.

"But poison oak grows all over Southern California. How did you know this happened at Descanso Gardens?"

"I didn't know," Shawn admitted. "But I did read the *Santa Barbara Times* today."

Shawn refolded the newspaper and handed it to Gus. On the bottom of the page was a small article about a group of parents who were furious because their children had gone on a field trip to Descanso Gardens and come back covered in poison oak. A couple of them had even been sent to the hospital.

"Maybe she should have been watching her kids a little more closely instead of worrying about her necklace," Gus said.

"I think she was watching the kids," Shawn said. "In fact, I think that's how she lost the necklace. There's a scratch on her neck that looks like it was made by a chain—that's how I figured out she had lost the necklace. I'd guess she saw one of her students playing in poison oak, she rushed over to pull him out, and her necklace chain caught on a tree branch and snapped off. Now all we have to do is locate that patch of poison oak, find the nearby tree, and the necklace will be waiting for us there."

"Why?"

"Because it's an inanimate object, so there's very little chance it will get tired of waiting for us and head out on its own."

"No," Gus said. "Why are we doing this? She's a nasty bat, the case is a dog, and there are a million other things I'd rather spend my afternoon on. So why are we driving to La Canada?"

"Because Lassie sent her over to us."

"Yeah, to get rid of her and piss us off."

"Exactly," Shawn said. "And it's really going to annoy him if we not only take her case and solve it in hours, but also get paid for doing it."

Gus had to admit there was a certain logic to Shawn's reasoning. And he'd been curious about the new burger place in La Canada, too. Besides, the sun was out and the sky was bright blue; it was a great day for a long drive.

Apparently he wasn't the only one who thought that way. Because as Gus eased the Echo out of its parking spot in front of the Psych office, a black Town Car three spaces down started up—and stayed exactly three car lengths behind Gus and Shawn all the way into La Canada.

Chapter Five

Shawn's plan was flawless—at least in the confines of the Psych office. Because from their perspective in that cozy bungalow on the beach, there was only one stand of poison oak in the entire hundred and fifty acres of Descanso Gardens, and it was surrounded by chain-link and crime scene tape. But this was July in the San Gabriel Valley, and the noxious weed was spreading faster than the army of professional gardeners could stamp it out. Shawn and Gus were going to have to check every tree near every stand of the stuff—and hope that Shawn's analysis had been correct.

They split up so they could cover more ground, and all had been going fairly well until Gus started searching the nature trail. That winding path took him out of the tree cover and up a steep hillside into the region's natural chaparral. By the time Gus realized how hard the sun was beating down on him, he was already becoming dizzy and disoriented. And for some reason, the idiot who designed that part of the gardens decided that drinking fountains were not to be considered part of nature. As the blasting sun, untempered by the lovely ocean breezes he would have been enjoying back in Santa Barbara, leached the moisture from his body, his heat-exhausted brain brought him back into his standard nightmare.

Now, with the giant camellias providing blessed relief from

the blazing sun, Gus could feel the last wisps of fever dream retreating from his mind. That left only his irritation.

"Would it make you feel any better if I told you the snack bar also sells root beer slushies?" Shawn said with what was as close to an expression of concern as he would get unless his friend had been run over by the train.

"What would make me feel better is finding that stupid necklace and getting out of this hellhole," Gus said.

"Heckhole," Shawn said, gesturing at the many small children running on the paths around them. "And it just so happens I'm the magic wish fairy today."

Shawn held out the hand that wasn't clutching the sticky plastic pink popcorn wrapper. Lying across his palm was a heart-shaped gold locket about an inch across. A broken gold chain dangled off the end. He pressed a latch by the locket's left ventricle and the front popped open. Inside were facing photographs of an unbelievably homely middle-aged man and a slightly younger, if even homelier, woman. The photographs were badly trimmed to fit inside the uneven space, revealing a shiny green surface behind them.

"So you can see where she gets her fine looks from," Shawn said.

"At least it's done," Gus said. "Was it where you thought it would be?"

"First place I looked," Shawn said. "It was at the lost and found."

Gus stared at him. "You went straight to the lost and found desk?"

"Of course," Shawn said. "Why search if there's a chance someone else has already found it?"

"You let me hunt for hours in the blazing sun."

"I couldn't be sure."

"But you *were* sure," Gus said. "After you got it back. And you still let me stay out there."

"It was for your own good," Shawn said. "Immersion therapy. To help you get over your irrational fear of being lost in the wilderness. This stupid dream is crippling you. And believe me, I know how bad a recurring dream can be."

"If you did, you wouldn't have done this to me," Gus said.

"It's not like I've been taking it easy," Shawn said. "I had my own version of immersion therapy."

"You did?"

"Yes. I had to get over my irrational fear of ice-cream sandwiches," Shawn said. "It took a lot of tries, but I think I'm almost there. Want to help me finish it off?"

Gus tried to stay angry, but the thought of ice cream pushed everything out else out of his brain. And after they'd emptied the snack bar's freezer chest, he felt so happily sated that he couldn't bring himself to darken the mood with even well-deserved negativity.

Shawn, apparently, didn't have the same problem. Gus looked up over his last bite of ice-creamy goodness and was about to propose they move on to the burger stand when he noticed Shawn staring off into the distance, looking troubled.

"Is something wrong?" Gus said.

"Is something wrong?" Shawn repeated. "Oh, yes, my friend, there's something wrong. Something very, very wrong."

"Oh, yes, my friend?" Gus said. "You mean it's something so bad you're required to talk like a character in one of those *Raiders of the Lost Ark* rip-offs Tom Selleck used to star in?"

"It's worse. It's the return of an evil so malevolent, so hideous, the entire civilized world cheered when it was finally vanquished from the earth at the end of the eighties."

"The Soviet Union has reestablished itself in a public garden?"

"Even worse than that," Shawn said. "Look."

With a mounting sense of dread, Gus turned slowly to see what Shawn was talking about.

Shawn was right. As horrifying as the Beast prowling through Gus' heat-induced hallucination had been, this was worse. Its face was waxen white, its lips bloodred, its eyes ringed with thick black. Gus' first instinct was to run screaming out of the snack bar area; his second was for a frontal attack. Before he could decide between fight and flight, though, he noticed that the creature was slamming its blue-and-white-striped appendages uselessly against some kind of invisible barrier.

"It's trapped in the box," Gus said.

"For the moment," Shawn agreed. "But that's not going to last long. Before we can do anything, it will be out of the box and then it will start walking into the wind. And after that, well, you know what happens."

Gus did. Once the wind stopped blowing, the demon would turn its bereted head on the innocent people in the garden and start to imitate them. But this wouldn't be just any imitation. It would be vicious caricature, emphasizing the least attractive aspects of its victims. Or, far more likely, emphasizing whatever set of moves it had been taught in mime class that week.

"Should we alert security?" Gus whispered.

"It's apparently neutralized the guards." Shawn pointed down at the second beret lying at the mime's feet. It was dotted with coins, mostly pennies, but also the occasional nickel or dime, along with a single quarter. One lone dollar bill was tucked into the brim, obviously placed there by the mime itself to plant the idea of donating paper money in the minds of its viewers. "To haul in that much cash, it must have been here for hours."

"Without us noticing it?"

"It's very quiet," Shawn said. "Which is what we should be. Let's put our trash in the wastebasket and walk out of here."

"But if we leave first, he'll target us for sure."

"Just look straight ahead and keep walking," Shawn said. "Whatever happens, keep walking."

Gus didn't need Shawn to tell him that. He still remembered that terrible day on the Santa Barbara Pier fifteen years ago when he had been targeted for mockery by a particularly cruel mime. By the time he escaped into the crowd, Gus had witnessed such a vicious deconstruction of his walk that he was paralyzed by self-consciousness and unable to get out of bed for a week.

Balling up their trash and tossing it in a receptacle, Shawn and Gus walked slowly but determinedly away from the snack bar, past the bathrooms, and towards the exit. As they rounded the ticket booth, Gus noticed that Shawn wasn't next to him anymore.

"He's gone," Shawn said.

Gus stopped walking, but refused to turn his head to see Shawn behind him.. "You looked back?"

"No," Shawn said. "Not really. More of a glance. A glimpse, maybe."

"That's what they all say, right before they turn into a pillar of salt."

"Better than being a pillar of Jell-O," Shawn said.

"Yeah?" Gus said. "Wait until it rains and see which pillar lasts longer."

"How many times do I have to tell you?" Shawn said. "There's more to life than how long you can stand out in the rain without melting."

"If there is, I haven't come across it," Gus said, still refusing to cast a backwards glance. "Can we go now?"

Apparently not. Shawn hadn't moved. He was staring back towards the snack bar, looking for the vanished mime. "There was something wrong with that mime," Shawn said.

"By definition," Gus said.

"No, something else," Shawn said, still looking back where they'd last seen the mime. "Something I noticed but didn't register until after we left."

There was a long moment of silence. Then Gus spoke quietly. "You mean like he had a gun pointed at my head?"

"I think I would have noticed that a little quicker," Shawn said. "No, it was—"

"Shawn!"

"Yes?"

"The mime has a gun pointed at my head."

Shawn turned back to his partner. The mime stood in front of Gus, his white-gloved hand leveling a gleaming pistol at Gus' forehead.

"Please," the mime said. "Don't make me kill you."

Chapter Six

There was another long, silent moment.

"I thought you weren't supposed to talk," Shawn finally said.

"Put your hands up," the mime said through clenched teeth. "I don't want to hurt you, but I will."

"Absolutely." Shawn's arms shot up in the air. Gus' followed quickly.

"Now turn around and walk towards the bathrooms."

Shawn and Gus turned around, their hands high in the air. Shawn waved his back and forth, trying to attract some attention.

"You're never going to get away with this," Gus said. "There are dozens of witnesses."

"And they're all staring right at us," Shawn said, waving his hands wildly. With each wave, another few people turned towards them.

Gus and Shawn exchanged a look; then Gus shouted to the throng of parents, kids, and gardeners who were staring at them from the snack bar area. "Help! He's got a gun!"

Gus didn't know what to expect. Best-case scenario would be a squad of beefy, well-armed security experts descending on them. Second best might be dozens of cell phones dialing 911 at the same instant. He would have settled for one irate mom with a canister of pepper spray on her keychain.

What he didn't expect was what happened. The crowd was still for a moment. Then they burst into laughter.

"Don't laugh," Gus commanded them. "This is serious. He could kill us!"

But the crowd only laughed harder.

"Has this whole town gone crazy?" Gus asked Shawn.

"Look behind you," Shawn said.

Gus risked a glance over his shoulder. The mime had hidden his gun under his shirt. To the crowd of onlookers, it might well have been his finger. His painted face was alternating between a mask of furious anger and an impressively accurate impersonation of Gus' fear.

"I so do not look like that," Gus said.

"Really?" Shawn said. "This man is holding us at gunpoint, and you're worried that his imitation of you is too mean?"

The killer mime said something urgent and harsh. It sounded like "ash oon." Shawn and Gus turned back to look at him and saw that as he said the syllables again, his ruby lips were locked into an evil scowl. Because of course he couldn't let his audience see him speaking.

"Ash oon?" Shawn said. "I'm afraid we don't know what that is."

There was a click from under the mime's shirt. He had cocked the pistol.

"But if you wanted us to step into the bathroom, we could do that," Shawn said.

As the crowd cheered them on, Shawn and Gus marched towards the public restrooms, a low, wide building faced with river rock and brown-painted wood.

"Inside," the mime hissed. Shawn pushed the door open and led Gus in. The mime followed them inside and slid a latch locked behind them, as the faint sounds of applause came through the walls.

The bathroom was surprisingly clean for a public facility in midsummer. The linoleum floor was shiny and dry; the three stalls' white paint was fresh and unmarked by graffiti. All the discarded paper towels had somehow made it into the receptacles. And the room deodorizer was a mild clove scent.

Still, there were many other places Gus would have preferred to be. And none of them contained gun-toting mimes.

"Take off your clothes and throw them on the ground," the mime said.

Shawn winced. "My mother always told me not to take off my clothes for strange men in a public restroom."

"Then I'll shoot you," the mime said. "If I have to kill you to protect Rushmore, I will."

"I know some people really love that movie," Shawn said, "but this seems a little over the top. And can you really tell me that Olivia Williams would have ever forgiven that idiot kid after he almost killed Bill Murray?"

"Stop it!" the mime shouted. "Get undressed now!"

"I don't see a back door in this building," Gus said. "Once you pull that trigger, everyone outside will know you're not an adorable mime."

"If such a thing exists," Shawn said.

"How long do you think that latch will hold out once the police bring the battering ram?" Gus said.

"I've got six bullets in my gun," the mime said. "Two for you, three for him, and one left over for myself. The latch will hold out long enough for that."

"How come I get three and he only gets two?" Shawn said.

"Take off your clothes," the mime said. "I won't tell you again."

"What do we do?" Gus whispered to Shawn.

Shawn stared at the mime. Then he lowered his gaze and pulled off his T-shirt.

"You, too," the mime snapped at Gus.

It took Gus a lot longer to get down to his boxers than it did Shawn, who had apparently dressed with exactly this scenario in mind. Even his shoes were slip-ons, which he slipped off in less than a second. Everything Gus was wearing seemed to have more buttons than he remembered, and his fingers slipped and fumbled with every one. Somehow the laces on his standard brown dress shoes had been tied into triple knots, and it took what felt like hours for him to undo them. After a few more hours, Gus stood next to Shawn, dressed only in his boxer shorts, his bare feet adhering to the linoleum.

"I didn't say get ready to go swimming," the mime said. "All your clothes."

Gus wanted to sneak a look at Shawn to see what he was going to do. But he didn't dare. He was afraid he'd find courage in his friend's eyes, and then he'd refuse to do what the mime was demanding, and then they'd both be dead. He bent down and quickly stripped off his shorts, covering himself with both hands as he straightened up.

"Now kick them over here," the mime commanded, and Gus did. Out of the corner of his eye he saw a blur of movement that must have been Shawn also following the order. The mime scooped up all the clothes with his free arm, then gestured with the gun. "Into the stall."

"Could we go into separate stalls?" Shawn said. "Because they're really only meant for one person, and I don't think we should be doing a lot of touching in our present condition."

The mime didn't answer. He lowered the gun to where Shawn had strategically placed his hands.

"You know, one stall sounds fine," Shawn said. "It'll be much warmer that way."

Shawn and Gus scurried into the middle stall and slammed the door shut behind them. Gus turned the latch firmly, locking them in.

"Oh, yeah, that will do a lot of good," Shawn said. "No one's ever gotten through one of these before."

"You want me to leave it open?"

Shawn didn't. Each stood pressed against a stall wall, trying to pretend the cold metal wasn't lowering their body temperatures with every passing second.

"Are you almost done with our clothes out there?" Shawn finally called out.

There was no answer.

"Maybe you could finish up with our underwear first?" Shawn suggested hopefully.

Still no answer came.

"What do you think he's doing out there?" Gus whispered.

Shawn pressed his eye to the crack at the edge of the door and tried to peer out.

"One of two things," Shawn said. "Either he's taken our clothes and woven them into a cloak of invisibility, or he's gone."

Shawn pulled open the stall door and stuck his head out. The mime was gone. And so were their clothes. Shawn checked every stall and tore through all the trash cans, but the mime hadn't left them so much as a sock.

"What do we do now?" Gus said.

"We're taking him down." Shawn bolted to the door.

"You can't go out there," Gus said as Shawn reached for the door handle.

"Watch me."

"It's not me who's going to be watching," Gus said. "It's all the moms out there with their little kids."

"So what do you suggest? That we just stay in here until everyone has gone home and we can slip out without anyone seeing us?"

"That's not a bad idea," Gus said. "But my car keys were in my pants pocket. So even if we do get out of here, we've got to walk through one of the San Gabriel Valley's least progressive suburbs stark naked. How long do you think we'll last out on those mean streets without any clothes?"

"I'm still waiting for a suggestion."

"There are a lot of people out there," Gus said. "Sooner or later, most of them are going to need to use the bathroom. And when they come in, we can beg them for a piece of clothing. It may take some time, but we can piece together enough clothes to walk out of here."

"Because most people who come to a public garden wear an extra pair of pants just in case."

Gus fumed. Of course Shawn was right, but that didn't make it any more pleasant to have his only idea shot down.

"Maybe if we wish really hard, the magical elves will hear us and weave us a new set of clothes," Gus said.

Shawn beamed as if Gus had said something brilliant. "That's it," he said.

"Elves are it?"

"Not elves," Shawn said. "We'll make our own clothes."

Chapter Seven

When Gus was four years old, his mother dressed him up as Cupid for a Valentine's Day party. He wore a fluffy cotton diaper, a pair of wings, and a halo. And nothing else. She paraded him through a houseful of adults, all of whom cooed over the adorable little cherub.

For the rest of his life, Gus treasured that memory. Not because he enjoyed the evening; it was as miserable an experience as anything he'd ever suffered. But from that night on, no matter what happened to him, no matter how great the humiliation, he could always think back and tell himself, "At least it wasn't as bad as being Cupid in a diaper."

That thought never failed to make him feel better. When he was in first grade and spilled water down his pants, giving the entire school the impression that he'd wet himself, he took solace in the knowledge that this moment was less embarrassing than parading around in a diaper and wings. When he mistimed a kiss aimed at Santa Barbara High School's third-string cheerleader Missy Summerland at a victory rally and ended up locking lips with a wide receiver, he knew that this was not as bad as being naked Cupid. Even the time that he and Shawn gave a lengthy and thorough reveal to a baffling case only to be informed that a different suspect had confessed hours before, Gus comforted himself with the thought that at least he wasn't wearing a diaper and wings while presenting the conclusion.

But that memory could do him no more good. Because he'd finally experienced something more humiliating than that Valentine's Day appearance. And it involved diapers, too.

These weren't the fluffy, opaque, completely secure diapers his mother had dressed him in. No. These were made out of flimsy paper toilet seat covers. Flimsy, near-translucent paper toilet seat covers.

Shawn had emptied the dispensers from all the stalls and both men had done their best to wrap the covers around their midsections in such a manner that they'd stay up on their own. But without tape or pins, there was no way to keep them together, and Shawn and Gus had to walk out of the men's room clutching wads of paper to their fronts and backs. If there was a single person in the Gardens who didn't stare at them until they were out of sight Gus never noticed him.

The humiliation might have been terminal for Gus. Fortunately, the burning sun had heated the asphalt path almost to the melting point, and he could use the agony he felt every time he set down one bare foot to take his mind off the embarrassment.

Beyond the mortification of both soul and flesh, there was one other major problem Gus was wrestling with: What were they going to do once they reached his car? He supposed they could use a brick to smash one of the windows, if there happened to be any bricks lying around the parking lot, but smashing wouldn't get the car started. That was, if the mime hadn't used Gus' keys and driven off in the Echo.

He hadn't, which was the first good thing that had happened to Gus all day. But when they got to the parking lot, Shawn didn't go to the Echo. Instead he started looking in the trash barrels that stood outside the park's wrought-iron fence. The first two were empty aside from trash. The third, however, held their clothes.

"How did you know they'd be here?" Gus said as he pulled his underpants on under his tissue paper diaper.

"I sort of figured that not even a mime would risk life in

prison to steal some clothes he could buy at Goodwill for under a buck," Shawn said, slipping on his jeans before he stepped into his shoes.

"Then what was that all about?"

Shawn dug in his pockets. "Not my wallet," he said, fishing it out and flipping through it. "Or any of the four dollars left inside it." He checked Gus' pants before tossing them to him. "Or your wallet, or your car keys."

"This doesn't make any sense at all," Gus said. "Could it all have been some bizarre mime initiation ritual?"

Shawn dug in his pants again, and his face turned grim. "The necklace is gone," he said. "We've been set up."

Chapter Eight

The freeways on the drive back to Santa Barbara were nearly empty, the sky was a vivid blue, and dolphins were dancing in the waters off the Pacific Coast Highway. But Gus didn't notice any of that. His foot was jammed down on the accelerator and his eyes locked on the road ahead.

In the passenger seat, Shawn snapped shut his cell phone in frustration. "I can't believe Lassie hung up on me again."

"When he understands what's happening, he'll listen."

"That's the problem," Shawn said. "Before he can understand, he has to listen first. And as soon as I start to tell him the story, he bursts out laughing and hangs up."

"If you tell him we were held up at gunpoint—"

"In a public men's room by a killer mime who stole our clothes." Shawn finished Gus' sentence for him. "Last time I tried that he put me on hold, then forwarded my call to Papa Julio's Casa de Pizza."

"What did he say when you mentioned Ellen Svaco?"

"One word," Shawn said. "Who?"

Gus tried to make sense of this. Had Lassie simply forgotten he'd sent the teacher to see them, or did this suggest something more ominous? "There's got to be something we can do."

"You can start by getting off the freeway here."

Gus had been so agitated he hadn't noticed they were almost at the Los Carneros Road exit into Isla Vista. Giving his rearview a quick scan, he tore across four lanes and flew down the ramp, slamming on the brakes for the stop sign at the bottom. Making sure there was no cross traffic, he turned left onto Los Carneros and headed into town.

"Maybe we've got this all wrong," Gus said. He could see the traffic light at Hollister straight ahead. It was red. He gunned the car, figuring to make the next green. "How do we know this was a setup?"

"Do you really have to ask?"

Gus checked to make sure Shawn was wearing his seat belt. He was. Which meant there was no point in slamming on the brakes to watch him go flying through the windshield. Instead he pressed his foot on the accelerator as he turned right through the green light onto Hollister.

"Are you asking if I have to ask why anyone would send us to a public garden to be held up by a mime?" he said through clenched teeth.

"It was a rhetorical question," Shawn said. "Because the answer is so obvious to anyone who's been paying attention."

"I guess I've been a little distracted," Gus said. "Little things like being kidnapped do that to me."

"You should work on that," Shawn said. "You let the bad guys know they can throw you off with a little gunplay and you'll never have a moment's peace."

"That's good to know," Gus said in a close approximation of the tone his mother used to use when she caught him feeding his brussels sprouts to the dog. "Thank you so much for the advice."

The light ahead was turning yellow. Gus floored it and made a fast left onto Storke Avenue.

"It's the least I can do," Shawn said. "As an experienced private detective, I have a duty to train the generation that's going to follow me."

"You've been a private detective for five seconds longer than me," Gus said. "And that's only because you said my fly was unzipped when we were walking up to the licensing window, and I stopped to look, so you got your license first."

"Which is why I feel I should share my experience and knowledge with you," Shawn said. "So let's walk through what we already know."

Gus didn't want to walk through anything, but he knew he'd never get any answers unless he played along. "Ellen Svaco lost her necklace, so she went to the police to ask them to find it," he said. "They wouldn't help, so she came to us. We did find it, but then it was stolen by a gun-wielding mime."

"Very good," Shawn said. "You've got it all exactly right. Except for one small detail."

"What's that?"

"All of it," Shawn said.

Gus turned right onto El Colegio Road and immediately slammed on the brakes. There was an unbroken line of cars in front of him. He cursed to himself, remembering why he hated coming to Isla Vista. Home of the University of California–Santa Barbara, and situated along some of the most beautiful coastline in California, Isla Vista needed to cram tens of thousands of penniless college students into some of the world's priciest real estate. That meant packing dozens of people into apartments barely big enough for one, which gave the town a population density somewhere between that of Lower Manhattan and central Beijing. And since rents even for those cramped spaces were so high, very few of the students could afford a car. That meant the streets were flooded with alternative modes of transport—all ridden by people who sincerely believed that traffic laws applied to everyone on the earth except them.

Fortunately the address Ellen Svaco had given them wasn't too much farther, and they'd have to cover only a few blocks of the town's main business district before they'd turn right, so there would be no need to cut across lanes of traffic. But Gus knew it could easily take fifteen minutes to go a quarter mile through the area, and there was no other way to get there.

Gus resisted the urge to punch the pedal and simply shove the other cars out of his way and tried to put his adrenaline rush to work understanding what was going on.

"I was there for all of it," he said. "I remember it as if it happened today. Because it did."

"Lassiter had no idea who Ellen Svaco was," Shawn said. "She never went to the police. She told us that story to manipulate us into helping her."

"Why all this intrigue? She lost her necklace on a field trip."

The car inched forward.

"I don't think it was lost," Shawn said. "I don't think she'd ever had it. And I have a feeling if we asked at her school, we'd discover that the Descanso Gardens field trip was her idea. But it wasn't really a field trip."

"Then what was it?"

"A handoff," Shawn said. "She brought the kids there as cover so she could collect the necklace."

"From the tree?"

"From the lost and found," Shawn said "I'm sure someone turned it in a few days before."

"Why so long?" Gus said. "And why the lost and found? Why not just give it to her?"

"Whoever had it must have been worried he was being followed," Shawn said. "He couldn't take a chance on meeting Ellen Svaco in person. And then something happened—maybe he caught a glimpse of whoever was following him. He panicked. He ran—but first he stopped by Descanso Gardens and turned the necklace in to the lost-and-found booth. Somehow he let her know it was there."

"So why didn't she just go pick it up?" Gus said as the car moved forward another couple of inches.

"She must have thought there was a chance she was being followed, too," Shawn said. "If she was, it might seem suspicious for her to zip off to La Canada a day after her contact disappeared from around there."

"That's why you said the necklace had been there a couple of days."

"You can't just slap together a school field trip in an afternoon," Shawn said. "And she needed the cover."

"So she went to Descanso Gardens, but she didn't pick up the locket."

"Something made her suspicious," Shawn said. "I'd guess it was having her other necklace stolen."

"There's another one?"

"Yes, but this one is just a regular necklace," Shawn said. "Remember there was a scratch on her neck? I thought that was from her snagging the chain on a tree. But what if whoever was following her got a little ahead of himself and tried to steal her necklace—only it was the wrong one?"

"So she sent us," Gus said.

"Only they followed her to our office, and then they followed us the rest of the way," Shawn said.

"Who is 'they'?" Gus said. "Was the mime in league with Ellen Svaco or against her? And who or what is this Rushmore he claimed he was protecting?"

"Those are three of the questions we're going to ask her." Shawn drummed on the dashboard like Desi Arnaz with a bongo. The traffic in front of them moved forward, and Gus saw they'd reached Ellen's street. He made a hard right turn onto a treelined residential boulevard and pressed the accelerator to the floor. Within seconds they'd reached Ellen Svaco's address, a small bungalow a block from the ocean. The were three shallow steps leading up to a small porch in front of the door. And on the porch, facing the door, was a man.

If you had only one word to describe the man, it would be "average." Average height. Average weight. Average suit. The only remarkable thing about him was his hair, which looked like it had been designed for the Romulan incarnation of Mr. Bean.

His hair and the gun he held in his right hand.

Chapter Nine

Shawn jumped out of the car and ran up to the house, with Gus following. The average-looking man tensed at the sound of the car door, but when he spun around to see who was coming, he dropped his gun to his side.

"Lassie!" Shawn called to Carlton Lassiter, head detective of the Santa Barbara Police Department. "What are you doing here?"

Lassiter scowled. "You called me repeatedly," he said. "You begged me to come here."

"And you refused. You thought it was a prank."

"I did," Lassiter said. "But if I have to choose between the chance you'll make a fool of me and the possibility of helping a citizen in danger, I'll risk my dignity every time."

It was a straight line like none Lassiter had ever given Shawn. But Shawn was so pleased at the help that he let it pass.

"What changed your mind?" Gus asked.

"It wasn't the fifteen subscriptions to *Guns and Ammo* you two took out in my name," Lassiter said. He pointed down at the door latch. "It was that."

Shawn and Gus followed his gaze.

"The door is open," Shawn said.

The door was indeed unlocked and slightly ajar.

"Maybe she's expecting us," Gus said.

"This is a beach community and a college town, full of drifters and druggies," Lassiter said. "No one leaves their door unlocked in a place like this."

"She's an elementary school teacher," Gus said. "Maybe she doesn't have anything worth stealing."

"At least nothing that wasn't already stolen from us," Shawn said.

Lassiter gave him a sharp look. "You will be making a full report."

"Right after we see what we're going to be reporting," Shawn said.

Lassiter nodded curtly, then rapped on the door with the barrel of his gun. "Ms. Svaco?" he said. "Police."

There was no answer from inside. He rapped again. Still no answer.

"Ms. Svaco?"

The only sound was the crashing of the waves against the shore a block away.

"Don't just stand there, Lassie," Shawn said. "We've got to do something."

Lassiter nodded, then holstered his gun and pulled out a cell phone.

"I meant do something useful," Shawn said.

"I am doing something useful," Lassiter said. "I'm calling Judge Napoli to request a warrant to enter the premises."

"That's a good idea," Shawn said. "We'll meet you inside when you've got the paperwork figured out."

Shawn reached for the door, but Lassiter positioned himself in front of it. "I can't let you do that, Spencer," he said.

"We called you for help."

"And I came," Lassiter said. "But if you request official police help, it comes with official police rules. Rule number one is you can't search private property without a warrant."

"Unless we've got a really good reason," Shawn said.

"Not unless," Lassiter said. "Not despite. Not because. Not even if."

"There is such a thing as an exigent circumstance," Shawn said.

"Technically true," Lassiter said. "If I had reason to believe there was a crime in progress or a person in imminent danger, I would be able to go through this door. But I've already walked around the property, and the blinds are down on all the windows, so I couldn't see inside."

"Isn't that suspicious?" Shawn said. "Who keeps their blinds closed on such a nice day?"

"People have a right to protect their privacy," Lassiter said. "I have no reasonable expectation there is anything seriously wrong."

"Not even a mime pulling a gun to steal the necklace Ellen Svaco hired us to retrieve?" Shawn said.

"I can't guarantee what a judge would call reasonable," Lassiter said, "but I'm pretty sure that's not even close."

Shawn and Gus exchanged a frustrated look. Then Gus straightened up. "Say, Shawn," he said, "did you hear that?"

"Why, yes," Shawn said. "Yes, I did."

"I didn't hear anything," Lassiter said.

"Listen harder," Gus said. "It sounded like a cry."

"A cry for help," Shawn said.

"A cry for help from inside that house," Gus said.

Lassiter squinted his eyes and listened so hard they could see his ears moving. After a long moment he opened his eyes again. "Nope," he said. "Nothing."

"Listen harder," Shawn said.

Lassiter scowled, but he put on his listening face again. After a moment, a tiny voice floated on the wind. "Help me! Help me!"

"That time you had to hear it," Shawn said.

Lassiter's eyes flashed open. "I heard Guster doing the voice of the guy at the end of *The Fly*," he said. "And I'm sorry, but the constitution doesn't allow me to break into a private home even if I believe a half-man, half-insect is about to be eaten by a spider."

"It doesn't?" Shawn said. "You'd think the Founding Fathers would have planned for that kind of thing."

"Don't you ever watch TV, Lassie?" Gus asked.

"What I do in my private time is none of your concern."

Lassiter scowled again and raised his cell phone to his face. "If I want to find Judge Napoli while he still remembers his own name, I've got to start calling bars now."

"What half-fly here is saying is that there's a clever little police trick we've picked up from watching some of your better shows," Shawn said. "We all agree we hear a scream coming from inside the house, and then we've got our exigent circumstance."

"Unless there's no one inside," Lassiter said. "And then we're stuck explaining under penalty of perjury how we heard an empty house screaming for help."

"What, you've never seen *The Amityville Horror*?" Shawn said.

Lassiter turned to his phone in disgust.

"I can't think why we don't call the police for help more often," Gus said.

"Lassie's just doing his job," Shawn said. "Say, I think your shoe's untied."

"It is?" Gus said.

"I believe so," Shawn said. "You might want to check it while I take a step forward to press our case with Detective Lassiter."

Gus crouched down on one knee. Shawn took a step forward and stumbled over him. He fell forward, right into Lassiter, pushing him backwards. Lassiter tried to right himself, but tripped over the door's threshold and tumbled back. The door flew open under his weight, and he crashed to the floor inside the bungalow with Shawn on top of him.

Lassiter shoved Shawn off him and got to his feet. "All right, get out of here," he commanded. "Right now."

"I don't know, Lassie," Shawn said. "It looks pretty exigent to me."

Lassiter knew he wasn't supposed to be in here, and now that he was, it was incumbent upon him to get out as quickly as possible. But the cop in him couldn't resist one look around. Ellen Svaco didn't seem to have too many possessions—the furniture was all assemble-it-yourself quality, the wall decorations were unframed posters of famous paintings, her TV was a small, fat desktop tube model, and the major design element was lots and lots of old books.

It wasn't the meagerness of the house's contents that grabbed their attention. It was the fact that every bit of it was scattered across the bungalow's floor. Furniture was smashed into pieces, the posters were torn in shreds, the TV was a mess of wires and plastic.

Gus joined Shawn and Lassiter in the ransacked bungalow.

"Ms. Svaco?" Lassiter called out, but there was no answer.

"Maybe she wasn't here when they broke in," Gus said.

"She was here." Shawn pointed towards a door leading to the bathroom. Gus saw a small pink hand lying palm up on the ground.

Lassiter did a broken-field run across the demolished room until he'd reached the hand. He signaled for Shawn and Gus to stay back, but they were right behind him. By the time they were halfway there, they could tell there was no point in going any farther. Ellen Svaco lay sprawled lifelessly across the white tile, an angry red line across her throat where someone had garroted her.

Even knowing it was useless, Lassiter took her wrist and felt for a pulse. Her icy skin told him everything he needed to know.

"She's dead," he said.

Chapter Ten

G us stared down at the body and tried to put together the steps that had led them here. Ellen Svaco had come to them looking for a necklace she'd lost in the park. After that, nothing made sense. There was an armed mime, a walk of shame in tissue paper diapers, and now a dead client. Not to mention a near case of heatstroke and wilderness-induced panic attack and hallucination.

For one happy moment Gus let himself speculate that he was still hallucinating. He wasn't in Isla Vista at all, but still back in La Canada, wandering on that sun-blasted nature trail; he had dreamed everything that happened afterwards. It made a kind of sense, as most of his non-wilderness-related nightmares involved a spell of public nudity, and the toilet-cover diapers Shawn had made for them were humiliating enough to show up in one of his worst dreams.

But no one else in the house was acting like it was a dream. Shawn was carefully studying the room, while Lassiter, kneeling by the body, was barking orders into his cell phone. When he was sure no one was looking at him, Gus glanced down casually and made sure that his clothes were firmly in place. They were. This was reality.

Lassiter snapped his cell phone shut and stood up, seeming to notice for the first time that Shawn and Gus were still in the room.

"You two, out," he snapped.

"Make that three."

Gus, Shawn, and Lassiter all wheeled around to the front door. The man standing there was over six feet tall with the bleached blond hair and ropy muscles that come from a lifetime of playing beach volleyball. His uniform seemed to have been designed to show off his physique—short khaki pants that exposed most of his thighs and a baby blue polo shirt that was tight across the pecs and featured the stencil of a badge and official logo Gus couldn't make out from across the room. A holstered gun hung off his thigh.

"Stand down, Officer," Lassiter said. He reached into his breast pocket for his ID. But before he could get his hand near his lapel, the blond man had his gun out and leveled at the detective.

"Don't move!"

"It's going to be hard to get out if I don't move," Shawn said.

The blond man shifted his gun sights to Shawn, then back to Lassiter.

"You know, sometimes I can go for an entire week without having a gun pointed at me," Shawn said. "Now it's two in one day. Go figure."

"Officer!" Lassiter's bark brought the blond man's attention—and his gun—back in his direction. "I am Detective Carlton Lassiter of the Santa Barbara Police Department. I am reaching very slowly into my pocket to pull out my ID."

"You just make sure it's nice and slow, 'Detective,'" the man said.

"Now that's impressive," Shawn said.

"What's that?" Gus said.

The man kept his attention focused on Lassiter.

"Most people would feel the need to use air quotes to put that much condescension around the word 'detective,'" Shawn said. "Blond guy did it with his voice alone."

Very slowly, Lassiter reached into his breast pocket and pulled out a wallet, then let it fall open to reveal his badge and ID. "I've identified myself," Lassiter said. "Now you."

"Officer Chris Rasmussen, Isla Vista Foot Patrol," the blonde said. "All my ID is right here on my chest." He patted the insignia on his polo shirt. "We small-town law enforcement personnel don't get a pretty tin 'badge' like they give the big-city police folk."

Now it was Gus' turn to be impressed. "You're right," he said to Shawn. "I know both of his hands were occupied, but I could swear I saw air quotes."

"Now that I know who you are, maybe you could tell me what you're doing in this house?" Rasmussen said. He lowered the gun to his side, but he didn't holster it.

"These two men are private detectives who have occasionally helped out the Santa Barbara Police Department," Lassiter said.

"Occasionally?" Shawn said.

"That's fair," Gus said. "We don't solve *all* their cases."

"Just the hard ones," Shawn said.

"Silence!" Lassiter snapped, then turned back to Rasmussen. "They called me suggesting that the occupant of this house, one Ellen Svaco, might be in jeopardy. When we got here, the door was open—"

"And it sounded like David Hedison was about to be eaten by a spider," Shawn said.

Lassiter glared at Shawn, then stepped aside, giving Officer Rasmussen a view into the bathroom. "Unfortunately we were too late. I've called it in, and the forensics team will be here in a few minutes."

Rasmussen's gaze flickered as he saw the body, but it hardened again as he turned back to Lassiter. "So you got a call and you just hoofed it on down here without a care in the world."

"My 'care' was for the victim," Lassiter said.

"That was pretty good, too," Gus said to Shawn.

"Worth a one-handed air quote at best," Shawn said. "I've heard Lassie much more condescending than that."

"Was there some other 'care' I should have been concerned with?" Lassiter said.

"Much better," Shawn said to Gus.

"Something we small-town law folk call jurisdiction," Rasmussen said. "If you have reason to suspect a crime has taken place on my streets, you call me first."

"You're kidding, right?" Lassiter said.

"Try me."

"Listen, McCloud," Lassiter said. "This isn't Dogpatch and it isn't Hazzard, although if it were, you'd certainly have the shorts for it. This is still Santa Barbara County—"

"That's right," Rasmussen said. "Santa Barbara County, not city. You've got no jurisdiction here."

"There's a dead woman two feet behind me," Lassiter said. "I hardly think the question of which law enforcement agency catches her killer is of primary importance."

"Funny, that's not what your people said when my hot pursuit crossed your precious city limits," Rasmussen said. "That time, jurisdiction was important enough to throw me in jail overnight."

Lassiter stared at him in astonished recognition. "You were the idiot who went screaming down State Street at ninety miles an hour?"

"It's called hot pursuit for a reason," Rasmussen said.

"You weren't even in a police car," Lassiter said. "Just some crummy old Mustang."

"We're the Isla Vista Foot Patrol," Rasmussen said. "It would look bad if we had official vehicles, so when need arises we volunteer our private cars."

"As I recall, the 'need' in this case was some punk spray-painting a street sign," Lassiter said. "And that was your excuse for jeopardizing countless innocent lives."

"We take our laws seriously here," Rasmussen said. "Which is why I'm taking over the investigation of this apparent homicide."

"This is my case," Lassiter said.

"This is my jurisdiction," Rasmussen said.

"I'm not leaving," Lassiter said.

Rasmussen raised his gun. With his free hand, he pulled his cuffs off his Sam Brown belt.

"In that case," he said, "you're under arrest."

Chapter Eleven

"Put your hands on your head," Rasmussen barked at Lassiter.

Lassiter stared at him coldly and didn't budge. Rasmussen stared back. Each man was frozen, waiting for the other to make the first move.

"Shawn!" Gus hissed. "We've got to do something."

"Yeah, let's go," Shawn said. "I'm getting hungry again."

"We can't leave Lassie," Gus said. "He's only here as a favor to us."

Shawn thought this over and reluctantly came to the same conclusion. With a heavy sigh he stepped between the two policemen. "I've seen this scene in a hundred movies, and it never makes any sense. You're both on the same side."

"He's right," Gus said. "You both want the same thing."

"Well, not all the same things," Shawn said. "Officer Rasmussen clearly desires a tan that will put George Hamilton to shame, while Lassie aspires to the subtler shades of your average mushroom. But I think we can all agree that what you both want most of all is to find the person who killed Ellen Svaco."

"Stay out of this, Spencer," Lassiter said.

At the sound of the name, Rasmussen's head swiveled over to Shawn. "Spencer?" He stared. "I thought I recognized you. Are you Shawn Spencer of Psych?"

"So my fame has traveled all the way to Isla Vista," Shawn said. "My master plan is working. Soon they'll know Psych even as far away as Oxnard."

Rasmussen walked over to Shawn, holstering his gun as he went. "It's an honor to meet you."

"Well, thanks," Shawn said.

"Your father is my hero," Rasmussen said, giving Shawn's hand an enthusiastic pump. "The greatest cop this state has ever seen. I used to read about him in the papers. Sometimes I even wish he could have been my dad."

"There were times I wished exactly the same thing," Shawn said.

"He's the reason I became a police officer," Rasmussen said. "If only I could work a case with him my life would be complete."

"Hard to imagine such a rich life isn't complete already," Gus said.

"Indeed," Shawn said. "Too bad my dad is retired."

Outside the bungalow a black crime scene van pulled up to the curb.

"But of course, no one ever really leaves the Santa Barbara Police Department," Lassiter said. "I talked to Henry just the other day and he was saying how much he missed the life."

Rasmussen wheeled back to Lassiter as if he'd forgotten the detective was there.

"He did not," Shawn said. "He loves being retired. He can spend all his time figuring out ways to torture me."

"May I speak to you for a moment, Shawn?" Lassiter said. His voice was mild, but his eyes flashed sparks as he walked over to him.

"Hey, I told you to freeze," Rasmussen said. "And you need to freeze right now."

"No," Lassiter said. "I don't think you'll want to explain to Henry Spencer why you shot his protégé."

"You are so not my father's protégé," Shawn said as Lassiter came up with him. "And having put in many years as his unwillingly designated protégé, let me say how lucky that makes you."

"Spencer, I need your help," Lassiter said. "The forensics team is right outside. If this jackass wants to make a fuss, he can tie them up for hours before they get to the body."

"He can't seriously stop your investigation, can he?"

"He can slow it down, and that's almost as bad," Lassiter said. "This woman was in your office this morning, and now she's dead. I am not going to let that stand, and I don't believe you are, either."

Shawn glanced over at Gus, who nodded his agreement. "I'm sure my father would love to help out on this case," Shawn said loudly.

Rasmussen lit up like a kid who'd just seen Santa slide down his chimney. "Really?"

"Only as a personal favor to his protégé, of course," Shawn said. "It would have to be an SBPD case all the way."

"A joint task force," Rasmussen said.

"With Santa Barbara in lead position," Lassiter said.

"Done." Rasmussen put out his hand.

Lassiter ignored it and marched to the door, where the first members of the forensics team were assembling. "Body's in the bathroom. Get me something fast."

"And make sure I get copied," Rasmussen called as they filed past him. "When are we meeting with Henry Spencer?"

Lassiter turned back to Shawn. "Yes, Shawn, when are we meeting with Henry Spencer?"

"Meeting?" Shawn said.

"To work on the case."

Shawn gave him a blank look. "I thought we were just saying that to get this yokel to let your guys in."

"I think he'll notice if Henry isn't actually involved in the case," Lassiter said. "And he can still make plenty of trouble if we need to do any more investigating in Isla Vista."

"I really don't think this is a good idea," Shawn said.

Lassiter sighed irritably. "Then it's just like it's one of yours. Look, Henry doesn't actually have to do anything. He's just got to show up."

Shawn looked for a way out, but couldn't find an opening. "I'll try to get him to your office tomorrow morning."

"I'll be there at eight sharp," Rasmussen said.

"Good, you can make the coffee," Lassiter said. "We'll start at nine."

Shawn and Gus squeezed past the entering investigators and headed back to their car.

"I don't believe this," Gus said. "What a day."

"Tell me about it," Shawn said. "We start out looking for a necklace just to annoy Lassie, and we end up facing multiple murders."

"Multiple?" Gus asked. "Who died besides Ellen Svaco?"

"Me," Shawn said. "Because when I tell my dad that I volunteered him to work a case with Lassie and this idiot, he is going to kill me."

Chapter Twelve

Henry Spencer raised the sticks high above his head. And waited. He'd torn the sleeves out of his sweatshirt to give his arms complete freedom, and tied a bandanna around his forehead to keep the sweat out of his eyes, and pulled on jeans that hadn't fit in ten years because—well, he wasn't quite sure why they'd told him to do that. But this was the moment he'd been dreaming of for weeks, the instant he'd rehearsed in his head time after time. Around him, the three others waited, poised just like him, waiting for the computerized keyboard to finish its preprogrammed run. Then they'd all kick in.

Henry Spencer had never wanted to be a rock star. He'd never yearned to be onstage with a Stratocaster between his legs and thousands of fans screaming at his every move. He'd never learned to pick out the opening notes of "Stairway to Heaven" on the display model in the guitar store or stood in front of his mirror practicing the front-footed stance unique to rock gods and Jack Kirby superheroes.

In his teens, in fact, Henry was almost completely oblivious to music. While his high school buddies were rocking around the clock or shaking their money maker or getting their groove thang on, Henry was doing his homework or attending practice for whichever sport was in season. He was vaguely aware that there were such things as radios, and that they tended to blare out their noise wherever he happened to be, but none of it made any more impression on him than the sound of traffic in the distance.

It wasn't that Henry disliked music. It was just that it was a distraction, and Henry never had time for anything that would take him away from his chosen path.

At least until that path reached its end.

Although Henry liked to think of himself as the same driven man he'd been before he retired, his mind and body were beginning to rebel against the decades of discipline. He told himself that it was important he continue to rise every morning at five seventeen, but his physical self knew there was no actual reason to wake before the sun, and his hand had started to hit the snooze before his training could stop it. When he set out for a quick six-mile jog, his legs began to suggest it might be nicer to stroll before they'd hit the halfway mark.

Henry was mature enough to expect the physical changes age was inevitably bringing, but the mental ones were a continual shock. And none was more shocking than what happened the day he was cruising the manager's specials at the Food Giant looking for a discounted steak that was still hours away from its expiration.

He noticed the song playing over the sound system.

Except that he didn't just notice it. He *recognized* it. Recognized that it was called "Me and You and a Dog Named Boo" and that it concerned a young man who traveled across the country in an old car, without any destination in mind. Henry tried to tell himself that he must have noticed the song in his teens because its philosophy of aimless wandering annoyed him so much, but that didn't explain why he had just caught himself humming the tune. And it didn't explain why his foot was tapping under his shopping cart, or why he suddenly knew that the song's singer would end up in Los Angeles only to feel that restless urge to hit the road again.

Even though the minutes were counting down until his manager's special steak would expire, Henry stayed in the aisle until the song ended and the next one began. To his shock, he realized he knew this song, too. Even though the lyrics made no logical sense, Henry was now aware that he'd long felt great sympathy for a balloon seller named Levon whose only sin was the sincere desire to be a good man.

This was an astonishing discovery for Henry, and he prowled the aisles for an hour, filling his cart with enough groceries to keep him through Christmas as he allowed the sound system to ferry song after song from the depths of his subconscious to the front of his brain.

That shopping trip sent Henry on a six-month odyssey through the annals of pop history. He worked thoroughly and methodically, just as he had when he was investigating murders for the Santa Barbara Police Department. He started by Googling pop charts for the years he was in high school—years, his half hour of scientific research assured him, when pop music has its greatest impact on the human mind—and then plugged those titles into the search box of the iTunes store, playing the free thirty-second sample of each song. If he found he knew the next word after the snippet ended, he'd shell out the ninety-nine cents for the whole thing. By the end of the first week, his computer was bulging with pop hits of the sixties and seventies. He bought himself a tiny iPod and took it along on his runs, and discovered that the pleasure of the music convinced his legs to keep moving.

As his quest went on, Henry found himself moving away from top-40 singles. Apparently the radios blaring in the background of his youth went in for album cuts as well. And this is where his life changed.

The album was called *Who's Next,* and he had downloaded it because he recognized a song about what it's like to live without ever being truly understood—didn't this exactly match what he'd felt in his teens? If he'd just bought the single he might have listened to it a few times and moved on to "Dark Water" or "Joy to the World." But he was doing albums now, so he hit the song that followed "Behind Blue Eyes."

There was no chance that the teenage Henry Spencer would have put up with "Won't Get Fooled Again." An anthem blasting all authority as corrupt was simply not something he would have been ready to accept as he dreamed of a life in blue.

But as an adult, Henry was secure enough in his beliefs that he didn't need to engage a thirty-five-year-old pop song in a political argument. He was caught immediately by the opening guitar chord's transition into that hypnotic synthesizer riff, and then the crash as the bass, guitar, and drums all kicked in at once. He knew this song. He'd heard it over and over and over again, and somehow he'd never noticed it until this very moment.

It wasn't until the time counter hit the seven-and-a-half-minute mark that Henry realized he was in trouble. He'd been listening while he was washing the dinner dishes, shuffling his feet roughly in rhythm with the tune, when the guitar, bass, drums, and vocal all dropped out again, leaving only that hypnotic, repeating synth line. Henry was scrubbing a plate when Keith Moon's drums kicked in.

The plate hit the surface of the water and sent suds flying as Henry's hands pounded along with the drums. Before he knew what he was doing, he had air-drummed the end of the song.

Henry wheeled around to make sure no one was watching him, although he knew he was alone in the house. What was he doing? He took a deep breath, turned back to the dishes, and vowed never to let this happen again.

But it did. And not just with The Who. If he didn't keep strict control at all times, his hands would start banging out the rhythms of almost any song. And when he came across Phil Collins' "In the Air Tonight," he knew that no amount of self-control would keep him from drumming the break.

It didn't take Henry long to understand what was happening: His hands were living the adolescence he'd never allowed them in his youth. And the only way to stop them would be to quit music. Go back to his sound-track-free existence, marching only to the beat of his own internal metronome.

He could do it. He knew he still had the strength. But as soon as he realized that, he understood something else: He didn't want to. He liked the tunes that filled the empty spaces in his head.

As a lifelong soldier in the fight between chaos and order, Henry knew the most important rule of battle: Either you fight

with everything you've got, or you surrender. Anything in between does nothing but cause harm to everyone involved.

So Henry surrendered to adolescence. Not permanently, of
course, and not in ways that anyone would ever know about.
He decided to take one great plunge into a second childhood,
knowing that he would climb out feeling refreshed and rejuve-
nated, and never needing to do it again.

He signed up for a Rock and Roll Fantasy Camp. He'd
spend five days in the hills outside Ojai learning to drum from
the masters. Not Keith Moon, of course, or John Bonham—
drummers, it appeared, tended to have shorter shelf lives than
the manager's specials at Food King. But there were plenty of
aging stars who would teach him. And when it was all done,
he'd have it out of his system, and no one would ever have to
know.

In any other context he probably would have felt nothing
but pity for his fellow campers, all middle-age men grasping to
retrieve a tiny bit of their youth. But this week wasn't about
judgment; it was about living out a fantasy he'd never even
known he had. So for today, Ralph the Lawyer and Fred the
Developer and Sid the Dentist were actually Pete and Rog and
the Ox. And Henry—for this one shining moment, Henry was
Keith Moon.

The doodling synthesizer beats were accelerating. Ralph was
warming up his shoulder for the windmilling guitar chords. Fred
was swirling his long blond hair—or the long blond hair that
existed in his mind, anyway. Sid clutched the fretboard of his
bass as if it were about to blast out of his hands.

And Henry was ready. Sticks poised, waiting to slam down
on the shining-white drum heads. He'd practiced the solo in his
head for months, and now it was almost time.

He raised the drumsticks high over his head. He could feel
the rhythm rising in his blood. The moment was now.

And then there was silence.

The synthesizer stopped just before it reached its crescendo.
The musicians all looked up, confused, like shuttle astronauts
whose liftoff had been aborted without warning.

Henry glanced over at the side of the stage. At the skinny

young man who was bending over the synthesizer. Please, no, he prayed, although he knew this one was never going to come true. Please don't let it be him.

Shawn flipped one last switch and turned to face the band. "I'm sorry," he said. "Were you guys listening to that?"

Chapter Thirteen

The cabins at the Rock and Roll Fantasy Camp were small and Spartan; the campers' fees went to paying the guest instructors, or at least their coke dealers, therapists, and ex-wives, and not for luxurious accommodation. This didn't bother Henry when he checked in. The cabin was plenty big enough for one.

But now it held Henry, Shawn, and Gus, along with Henry's fury and his embarrassment, and it was feeling mighty cramped. Shawn's throat was too close to Henry's hands to be certain they wouldn't attempt revenge for their thwarted celebration. Henry almost regretted ripping the sleeves out of that sweatshirt; right now unlimited freedom for his arms seemed to be an invitation to filicide.

Fortunately Shawn had made that difficult by spreading himself over Henry's single bed. Gus was still an available target, having wedged himself into a corner between a dresser and the cabin's sole window, but there was no more point in blaming Gus than there had been at any point in his lifelong friendship with Shawn. Gus was a passenger.

"I'm going to ask you one more time," Henry said, trying to keep his voice as calm as possible. "What exactly are you doing here?"

"I've decided I haven't embarrassed myself and my family

enough in life, and thought this was a great way to look like a total tool," Shawn said. "Oh, no, wait. That's you."

Henry's hands clenched into fists. With great mental effort, he forced them to relax. "Have you considered I might be here to investigate a case for a friend?"

"I'm sure you are," Shawn said. "The case of the missing youth. Or is it the mystery of the lost hair?"

"I realize this is terribly unpleasant for you," Henry said. "If only there was some way you could have avoided it. You know, like by staying away."

"How could I, when you were practically blasting out press releases across the country?"

"I didn't tell anyone about this," Henry said.

"You told MasterCard," Shawn said.

"What did you do?" Henry said, his anger rising even further. "Hack into my credit card account?"

"Shawn wanted me to," Gus said. "But I told him no. There are layers of security, traps for hackers who try to break in. I heard of one guy in Michigan who thought he could get into—" He saw the look on Henry's face and stopped himself. "Besides, I said. That would be wrong."

"Not to mention illegal," Shawn said. "So we broke into your house and found your last bill. You really do need to use that shredder."

"I can think of a use for it right now," Henry said.

"Anyway," Shawn said, "we've come here to save you money and embarrassment."

"That will be a first," Henry said.

"Technically it will be two firsts," Gus said.

"Which is what makes this such an exciting opportunity for you," Shawn said. "We're here to give you a chance to relive your glory days. And I mean your real glory days, not the song. Which is not only the worst song on *Born in the USA,* but the worst song Springsteen ever wrote, and possibly the worst song ever written by anyone in the world besides Diane Warren—"

"Hey," Gus interrupted, "I warned you about ragging on 'Unbreak My Heart.'"

Shawn ignored him. "—and which I'm sure the Hairless Four, or whatever your band calls itself, is going to do next."

"The only glory days I'm thinking about are those wonderful ones when I was childless," Henry said.

"I mean the days when you were important," Shawn said. "When you still had a purpose in life and didn't have to dress up like Jennifer Beals in *Flashdance* just to make it through another dismal day. I'm offering you a case."

Henry stared at his son. For all his questionable tactics, Shawn was smart. He knew how to get people to do what he wanted. And if Henry could generally see through him, at least he usually sounded like he was offering him something he'd genuinely desire. This time, not so much.

"You want to hire me to work for Psych?" Henry said. "Do you think I'm starving in a gutter?"

"If you were, you'd probably be dressed better," Shawn said, then hurried to the meat of his offer before Henry could respond. "The Santa Barbara Police Department wants you back."

Henry was happy being retired. Henry was happy not having to deal with the bureaucracy, and the lowlifes, and the long hours behind a desk, and the longer hours out in the field. Henry didn't want to go back to work.

At least that's what he told himself. But there was a part of him, deep down, maybe even deeper down than the place where all those songs were hiding all those years, that was jumping for joy at the offer. There was just one small problem.

"And they sent you because all their phones are broken and they've forgotten how to drive?" Henry said.

"It's not really an official SBPD case," Shawn said. "Well, it is, but the Isla Vista Foot Patrol doesn't agree, and they're ready to rumble to fight for their turf."

Now Henry was completely lost. Shawn saw the confusion on his face and launched into an explanation that, after many false starts and corrections from Gus, finally approximated what had happened over the previous day.

"So you volunteered me to help you out on this one," Henry said. "Without asking."

"I'm asking now," Shawn said.

"No, you're not," Henry said. "You're doing everything but asking. You're trying to trick me into doing what you want instead of honestly asking for my help."

"Would that help?" Shawn asked.

"What?"

"Honesty," Shawn said. "Sincerity. Heart."

"I don't know," Henry said. "Since you've never actually tried anything that radical before, it's hard to say what would happen if you did. But I can guarantee that nothing else is going to work."

Shawn nodded thoughtfully as he took this in. Then he turned away from Henry and faced the wall. When he turned back, the trademark smirk was gone from his face. He stared at his father with deep, grave eyes.

"Ellen Svaco came to Psych for help," Shawn said. "I didn't realize the kind of trouble she was in. If I had, she might still be alive. I can't do anything about that, but at least I can help catch her killer."

Henry thought about this. "I'll help," he said. "On one condition."

"I'm not going to sit in for you on the great rock and roll swindle," Shawn said. "But I will troll the retirement homes for your replacement if that will make you feel better about breaking up the band."

"It's not that," Henry said, "and it's not negotiable."

"Everything's negotiable," Shawn said.

"Not this," Henry said. "If I'm on this case, you're off it."

Chapter Fourteen

Shawn stared at his father as if he hadn't heard him correctly. "You do understand that this is my case."

"I understand that it was," Henry said. "Now you've got to ask yourself what's more important: that this woman's murderer be brought to justice, or that you're the one who does it."

"How about this," Shawn said, thinking quickly. "I'll stay on the case, but Gus will promise not to be involved."

"Hey!" Gus protested from his corner.

"Like you weren't looking for a way to get on this without me," Shawn said.

"Only so I could work as a mole, passing you information from the inside," Gus said.

"Which is why I wasn't going to let Gus in, either," Henry said. "This case is too dangerous."

This was so outrageous that Shawn bolted up from the bed. And while he didn't necessarily mean to thrust his face right into his father's, the cramped quarters of the cabin meant that some portion of his anatomy had to be pressed up against Henry, so he made necessity his accomplice.

"Dangerous!"

"You've been on the case less than one day and you've already had two guns pointed at you," Henry said. "At some point, one of those is going to go off."

"Do you realize how many murderers I've gone up against?" Shawn demanded. "I went face-to-face with a serial killer who'd been terrorizing Santa Barbara for years when you were on the force, and I won."

"And I'm always pleased to read about your exploits in the paper," Henry said. "Well, most of the time, anyway."

"Then what's the problem?" Shawn said. "Just think of this as getting the paper a day early. Except if I were you I wouldn't use this information for my own personal gain, like betting on horse races or anything, because that never works out well."

"I think that's only if some strange metaphysical force sends you the paper so you can use it to protect innocent people from fates they don't deserve," Gus said.

"It's fair to say that I'm as strange a metaphysical force as any of us is going to see," Shawn said. "So is this settled? We'll work the case from different sides: You help the police, and Gus and I will do it the smart way. We'll call you for the summation."

Shawn headed for the door. At least he would have headed for the door if there had been an inch of space between Henry and the bed for him to squeeze through. But there wasn't, and Henry didn't move out of his way.

"I told you, it's not negotiable," Henry said.

"Why?"

Henry's hard grimace softened. "When you were little, I used to worry about you all the time. When you missed curfew, when you slipped out your window in the middle of the night, when you were just a few minutes late for dinner, my heart broke at the thought that something might have happened to you."

"You certainly hid it well," Shawn said. "Under all that yelling and nagging."

"Do you really think that was hiding it?" Henry said. "The point is, once you moved out of the house, I stopped worrying."

"That was a mistake," Shawn said. "What I was doing then was much worse than anything I did while I lived with you."

"I knew that," Henry said. "But you were an adult. It wasn't my job to worry like that anymore, so I stopped. It's the same with your detective work. As long as I don't know about it until you've finished a case, it's none of my concern. But if I have to watch you putting yourself in danger, it will be just like you're twelve years old again. And I don't think anyone wants that."

"Not if you're going to make me go to bed at eight thirty," Shawn said. "I'm still trying to see the second half of the *A-Team* episode where they went to Africa. They were caught by cannibals and put in a cauldron over a fire, but before I could find out what happened to them, you unplugged the TV and turned off the lights. For all I know they were eaten decades ago."

"It turned out the cannibals weren't really cannibals," Gus said. "It was all a plot by—"

"Don't tell me!" Shawn said.

"The episode's been on DVD for five years," Gus said. "If you cared that much, you could have seen it a hundred times by now."

"It's not the same," Shawn said. "If there isn't at least one commercial with Jacko urging me to knock a battery off his shoulder, I can't watch it."

"And I can't watch you putting yourself in danger," Henry said. "It's as simple as that."

Shawn shot Gus a pleading look over Henry's shoulder. Gus shrugged helplessly. Shawn turned back to Henry. "I've got to do this," he said. "Please."

"It's a hard lesson to learn and a hard way to learn it, but you don't owe this woman anything, son," Henry said. "She asked you to find her necklace. You did. What happens in the rest of her life—even her death—is simply none of your business."

"She was our client," Shawn said. "When a man's client is killed, he's supposed to do something about it. It doesn't make any difference what you thought of her. She was your client and you're supposed to do something about it. 'And it happens we're in the detective business. When one of your organization gets killed, it's bad business to let the killer get away with it, bad all around, bad for every detective everywhere.' "

For a moment Henry seemed impressed by Shawn's passion for the profession. But something about the words nagged at him.

"'Partner,'" Henry said as the memory fell into place.

"Yes!" Shawn said. "We'll be partners."

"No," Henry said. "It's 'when a man's partner is killed he's supposed to do something about it.'"

"Is that what's bothering you?" Shawn said. "Because I promise if Gus is killed I'll stick with that case, too."

"Thanks," Gus said. "Really means a lot."

"It's from *The Maltese Falcon*," Henry said. "You want me to let you stay on this case because of some speech by a fictional detective."

"I can't think of a better reason, can you?"

"No, and that's the point," Henry said. "Now, if you're not going to step off this case, there's a dentist, a lawyer, and a real estate developer who can't finish their song until I play my drum solo."

Henry took the two steps back to the cabin door.

"You win," Shawn said. "We're off this case."

"Not good enough," Henry said, slipping out into the dimming Ojai sunlight. "Too much wiggle room."

"I promise that as long as you are working with Lassiter on this case that neither Gus nor I will do anything to investigate, explore, probe, scrutinize, deconstruct, interrogate, or in any other way examine the circumstances surrounding the violent slaying of our former client, the late Ellen Svaco," Shawn said.

For a moment Henry looked convinced. Gus was almost convinced himself. There were only two ways he could see for Shawn to weasel out of the promise, which was at least three fewer than Shawn usually built into such a sentence.

"I accept," Henry said after brief consideration.

"Excellent," Shawn said.

"Except for two things," Henry said. "The deal is binding for as long as I'm on the case, no matter what level of involvement or noninvolvement Carlton Lassiter shares in it. And since we don't have precise information at this moment on the exact manner of this woman's death, you will apply the same interdiction to any consideration of any eventuality that led to it, violent or not."

Gus was impressed. These were two of Shawn's best weasels, and Henry had spotted both of them. No wonder Shawn hadn't been able to talk himself out of a grounding since he turned eleven.

But Shawn seemed to be taking his defeat in stride. He put out his hand for his father to shake. "You really won't get fooled again," he said. "They need you at the police station in the morning."

Henry took his hand. "We'll do right by you, son."

"Just make sure you change first."

Henry glanced down at his sweat-soaked rock and roll clothes. "I don't know," he said, "I'm getting to like this look."

The cabin door banged shut and Henry was gone. Gus moved out of his corner, finally feeling free to fill his lungs more than halfway. "What do you want to do now?" he said. "Because if you don't have any plans, there's a bookstore in town with a tree growing in the middle of it. I've always wanted to see that."

Shawn stared at him as if he'd suggested they pass the afternoon at a Wiggles performance. "Are you kidding?" he said. "We've got work to do."

"On what?"

"On our case."

Gus replayed the last few minutes of the conversation in his head. Shawn's promise seemed as unweaselable as the nondisclosure agreement Gus' pharmaceuticals employer had made him sign before they admitted to him that there really was no such thing as restless elbow syndrome and that the only reason they'd sold so much of their drug to treat the disease was a long series of "seminars" in Hawaii they'd paid doctors to attend.

"You just promised your father that we wouldn't have anything to do with Ellen Svaco's murder," Gus said.

"And we won't," Shawn said.

"But that was our case," Shawn said.

"Never was," Shawn said. "No one hired us to investigate that."

"Then what?"

"Ellen Svaco hired us to get her necklace back," Shawn said. "That's the case we're working on."

Chapter Fifteen

Gus and Shawn drove in silence back to the Psych offices. Gus assumed Shawn was lost in thought about how to find whoever was behind the theft of the necklace. But he couldn't stop thinking about what would happen when Henry found out that he and Shawn were still working on the case. Because, despite Shawn's rationalizations, Gus knew they were deliberately flouting the agreement.

It wasn't until they were back in the office and Shawn was firing up the computer that Gus raised the point. "If your dad finds out that we're working on this case, he's going to be really mad."

Shawn didn't even look up from the computer. "I already told you; it's not the same case."

"Yes, as weasels go, this is as close to a ten as you've ever come," Gus said. "But we both know that's only going to make him even madder. All I'm saying is let's make sure we stay out of the way of the official investigation."

"We will be out of their way," Shawn said. "Because Lassiter will be running his investigation his way and we'll be doing ours the right way. Odds are we'll never cross paths. Now come help me hack into the police department's computer."

"Shawn . . ."

"Okay, okay," Shawn said. "It's not like we'd learn anything that way, except that Lassie hasn't won a game of solitaire in five years. What I really need you to do is to hack into the computers of the Descanso Gardens lost-and-found department. If we're lucky they have a camera positioned above the booth to record the face of anyone dropping off or claiming an item."

That was a task Gus didn't mind tackling. Unfortunately there was one small problem he couldn't solve.

"It seems that the Descanso Gardens lost-and-found department doesn't have a computer," Gus said after some time of fruitless searching. "Or, if they do, it's not online."

"How about the snack bar?" Shawn said. "Can you get into their computer?"

"Why?"

"I want to know if they've restocked their ice-cream sandwiches yet," Shawn said. "If we're going to have to schlep all the way down there again, I want to know there's at least going to be a tasty treat at the finish line."

Gus dropped into a guest chair. "This is crazy."

"I know, I know," Shawn said. "It's much cheaper to buy our own ice-cream sandwiches at the supermarket and bring them with us, instead of paying the ridiculous markup they charge at tourist traps like Descanso. But even if we bring a cold bag, they're still going to be pretty melty by the time we get to La Canada."

"I don't understand why we're going to La Canada in the first place," Gus said. "Do you really think the killer mime is still out there, waiting for someone else to walk by with a necklace for him to steal?"

Shawn was about to respond, but just before the first word left his mouth he cut it off.

"What?" Gus said.

"You're right," Shawn said. "Why La Canada?"

"Well," Gus said, suddenly wondering if he'd been too hasty, as he always did when someone actually took his advice. "There might have been someone who saw the mime and can help us identify him. Better yet, we could get the names of all the people who paid their admission with credit cards that day, track them down, and see if they took any pictures that have the mime in them."

"That's not what I meant," Shawn said. "Obviously we'd go to La Canada because that's where the crime happened. The question is why did it happen there?"

"Because that's where the necklace was?"

Shawn let out a deep sigh. "I'm going to try this one more time," he said.

"Why?" Gus said.

"Why what?"

"Why are you going to try one more time?" Gus said. "Why are you going to drop one more vaguely suggestive clue phrased as an open-ended question? Why don't you just come out and say what you're thinking?"

"It's called the Socratic method," Shawn said. "It's a form of teaching that involves asking questions to stimulate thought and debate. Although why Professor Kingsfield would name an entire method after some obscure alternative rock band from New Jersey is beyond me. Why are you staring at me?"

Gus was staring at Shawn—staring with a mixture of awe and horror. "How is this possible?" he said finally.

"What's that?"

"How can one body contain such a mixture of arcane knowledge and sheer ignorance?" Gus said.

"That's what they say about the Internet, and it's doing all right," Shawn said. "Didn't you have a point a while back?"

"I didn't have a point," Gus said. "I was hoping that you did, and if that was indeed the case you would share it with me rather than asking a bunch of rhetorical questions."

"Then how will you ever leave here thinking like a lawyer?" Shawn said.

"I'm about to leave here thinking like a pharmaceuticals sales-man," Gus said. "Not to mention a former detective."

"Okay, okay," Shawn said. "Let's work this through together."

"You already worked it through on your own," Gus said. "Just tell me so we can get on with our lives."

"Just tell you?"

"Yes."

"Without any questions at all?" Shawn looked troubled.

"I'm sure you can handle it."

"I can't say I share your confidence, but I'll try," Shawn said. He took a breath. "Okay, here's what I was getting at. The backstory, if you will. All the stuff that happened before we got involved. Some of which took place in La Canada. The question is—"

"Not an appropriate part of speech for this conversation," Gus said.

Shawn glared at him. "You're supposed to be my sounding board."

"I'm supposed to be your partner," Gus said. "You treat me as your sounding board. You say things to me so you can hear them echoed back to you louder."

"The sounding board is a vital part of any stringed instrument," Shawn said. "It doesn't matter how brilliant a fiddler is if you can't hear him because his violin doesn't have an f-hole."

"I'm tired of being the f-hole in this partnership," Gus said. "Now, give."

Shawn fidgeted in his chair. He stood up and crossed the room, then crossed back. "Okay, here's how I see it," he finally said. "There was a locket."

"With you so far."

"Someone had that locket." Shawn grimaced. "And then that locket . . . Can't I just use a couple of rhetorical questions here if I promise not to wait for an answer?"

Gus gave him a stony stare. "Keep going."

"The someone who had that locket was supposed to pass it on to Ellen Svaco for reasons we don't know," Shawn said. "The someone brought it to La Canada and dropped it off at the Descanso Gardens lost and found."

"But why come to La Canada in the first place?" Gus said. "Why not come straight to Santa Barbara if it was meant for Ellen Svaco?"

"Aha!" Shawn leveled an accusatory finger at Gus. "Now you're doing it."

"Yes, but my question was sincere," Gus said. "I wasn't laying a trap so I could demonstrate the superiority of my thinking."

"Is that really what you think I do?"

"That's a question," Gus said.

"You can't solve a mystery without asking questions," Shawn said. "Because the solution to any puzzle lies in the correct phrasing of the problem. If you don't pose the right questions, you can never reach the right answers. So when I throw my questions at you, it's not a challenge to your intelligence. It's me trying to frame the case in the proper context."

Gus thought this over, then let out a sigh. "I'm going to regret this, but go ahead."

Shawn beamed. "Okay, first question: Why was the locket in La Canada?"

Gus waited. Shawn drummed his fingers on the desk. Tapped his feet on the chair leg. Cleared his throat. "You need to answer," he said.

"Why?" Gus said. "If this is an exercise in the proper framing of the puzzle, why do you need me to answer? Just keep on with the questions."

Shawn stared down at the desk. "I need you to say something stupid."

"Uh-uh," Gus said.

"It doesn't mean I think you're stupid," Shawn said quickly. "But if you don't give me the wrong answer, I don't think I can come up with the right one."

"What if I give you the right answer?"

"Okay," Shawn said. "What if?"

"Are you saying I never come up with the right answer?" Gus demanded.

"That's not to say that it couldn't happen," Shawn said. "That would be like saying Jay Leno will never tell a funny joke."

Gus glared at him. "What if I give you the right answer at this very moment?"

"Then I will give you all the credit for solving the case," Shawn said. "I will put your name on the door. I will tell people you're my partner and not my assistant even when you're not in the room."

Gus decided to let this pass. "Okay," he said. "Let's start with the locket. Describe what you saw."

Shawn closed his eyes and thought back. The locket was a simple gold-plated heart on a chain. It was clearly old, as the plating had rubbed off in one spot, but so cheap it would never be considered an antique. Inside it were facing pictures of two homely people, hand-cropped badly enough so that some of the green plastic backing showed behind them.

"Green plastic," Shawn said. "That's it."

"That's what?"

"That's not how this works," Shawn said. "You were going to give me the right answer."

"I was," Gus said. "But now you've figured it out. And there's no way you can keep yourself from telling me about it."

"Watch me," Shawn said.

For a moment, the two of them sat in silence. Then Gus got up and gave Shawn's desk chair a shove, sending him rolling away from the desk. He stood over the computer and typed into a search engine.

"Let's see," Gus said as a Web site popped up in response. "Fun facts about La Canada Flintridge. One: While the 'Canada' part refers to the Spanish word for gorge or ravine, 'Flintridge' refers to nothing at all, since there is no flinty ridge here. Two: It's the USA's eighty-fifth most expensive city to live in. Three: Kevin Costner's ex-wife owns a restaurant here which is locally famous for its breakfasts."

"That's it," Shawn said. "Clearly this is all part of the global conspiracy to get Cindy Costner's pancake recipe."

Gus ignored him and kept reading. "Four: There's a decades-long feud between La Canada and neighbor Pasadena over which city should be listed in news stories as the location of the Jet Propulsion Laboratory. Five—"

"Don't stop now," Shawn said. "I want to know more about the pancakes."

"JPL is in La Canada," Gus said, quickly typing in the search engine again. "It's less than five miles from Descanso Gardens."

"Amazing," Shawn said. "If only we had thought to ask why this all happened in La Canada."

But Gus wasn't going to take the bait now. Because he had the answer. "And that backing in the locket wasn't plastic," he said. "It was silicon."

Chapter Sixteen

There was a lot Gus didn't like about being a detective. The danger, for one. Although being threatened with imminent doom might sound exciting, after the first couple of times it began to get really old. And then there were the hours. Gus never had a problem with working hard, but he did like to know exactly when he could expect to knock off for the day, and that was rarely the case in an investigation.

For all the inconveniences, though, there were some things about the job that he loved enough to put up with anything. Best of all was the moment when a baffling mystery revealed itself into a crystalline, perfect solution.

This, unfortunately, was not one of those times.

Both Shawn and Gus were fairly certain that they had solved at least one part of the crime. The necklace was being used to smuggle a computer chip full of information out of the Jet Propulsion Laboratory. And it was a safe bet that whatever that information was it had some sort of national security implications, since it seemed improbable that Ellen Svaco would have been killed simply so someone could find out what the weather was like on Mars.

Beyond that, however, they were stumped.

Clearly, Ellen Svaco had been some kind of courier. She was supposed to have picked up the chip and then delivered it somewhere else. But there was no way to tell whom she was working for, or why they might have chosen an elementary school teacher for the job. Had she even known what she would be transporting? The fact that she had hired Psych to retrieve it from the lost and found suggested she'd known that someone else was after it, but nothing more than that.

And then there was the mime. He had been desperate to get the necklace—desperate enough to risk a daring daylight robbery. But who was he? They briefly considered the idea that he was the JPL employee who had smuggled the chip out of the lab in the first place and then had developed second thoughts. But while that seemed to simplify things at first, it quickly led to far greater complications. Because if he had put the chip in the locket, then he was probably also the one who'd left it at the lost and found. Which meant he would have known where it was—and the mime hadn't. If he had, there would have been no need to disguise himself and wait for Shawn and Gus to retrieve the necklace before taking it away from them. He could simply have asked for it at the booth.

And then there was the "Rushmore" he'd insisted he was protecting. A Google search of the word turned up multiple references to the mountain, the movie, and a Manhattan condo tower, but none of them seemed to have anything to do with purloined jewelry, public gardens, or the art of mime.

No matter how many times they turned their few facts over, they kept coming back to Ellen Svaco at the center of the mystery. Which was entirely unacceptable, because Ellen Svaco was the one part of the puzzle they weren't allowed to investigate.

If this had been a normal case, Shawn and Gus would have dived into Ellen Svaco's private life. They would have searched her house and car. They would have gone to her funeral to see who else showed up to mourn—and which of the mourners didn't seem particularly sorry to see her go. They might even have attempted to go undercover as substitute teachers at her school.

But each of those routes led almost inevitably to a single roadblock: Henry Spencer. Shawn had learned the fundamentals of detective work at his father's knee—or sometimes across his father's knee, if Shawn had been the subject of Henry's investigation—and the instincts that would be driving Shawn would also be driving his father. Shawn had promised Henry he'd stay out of Ellen's murder, and unless he could figure out a retroactive weasel, he was stuck with the pledge.

The remaining pathways were much less appealing. The only obvious one was to knock on JPL's front door and ask if they happened to be missing a microchip or two, and if they might happen to know what was on it. But it seemed unlikely that the guard at the front gate would be willing or able to share that information with a couple of guys who happened to walk up to him. In a normal situation they'd try to come up with a way to get into the lab posing as scientists or journalists or any other kind of "ists," but JPL had made national news a few years back for forcing its longtime employees to sign waivers allowing government inspectors to dig into every aspect of their lives from birth onwards. It seemed unlikely that a pair of private detectives could slip into the facility by claiming they'd left their ID badges at home.

That left the mime as the sole loose end they might be able to pick up. But this presented a few problems as well. Like the fact that he was a mime. His face had been completely covered by makeup, his hair by a beret, and his hands by white gloves. Even if they had any idea where to start looking, they'd never be able to identify him unless he hadn't bothered to de-mime himself in the intervening hours.

Shawn and Gus spent the evening trying to find a way into the case, stopping once only long enough to send out for pizza and then again to tear the office apart collecting change when the deliveryman arrived and they realized they didn't have enough cash to cover the check.

By midnight they were both halfway to sleep and no closer to a solution. An hour later Gus was looking for his car keys and declaring he was going home as soon as they'd made a little more progress. Fifteen minutes after that he was snoring on the office couch.

Not that he was slacking, Gus told himself as his eyes fluttered closed. The thorniest problems are never solved in the conscious mind; the solutions have to bubble up from the subconscious. And what better way to access his subconscious than to let it have free rein for a couple of minutes? If he napped for just a couple of minutes he would certainly wake up with the answer on the tip of this tongue.

He'd used that argument with himself in the past, and it had never worked. He'd wake up a few hours later barely able to remember which member of En Vogue he was about to marry in his dream, let alone a solution to any problem that was plaguing him when he drifted off.

But this time turned out to be different. Because this time when he woke up, the solution was right there. Only it wasn't on the tip of his tongue. It was on Shawn's.

"I've found the mime," he said.

Chapter Seventeen

The sun had crested the hills east of Santa Barbara, the fog had retreated to the horizon, and the ocean was sparkling in the morning light. The waves off Hendry's Beach should have been filled with surfers finishing up their predawn runs.

But the few surfers who were here were out of the water, pressed up against a line of crime scene tape thirty feet back from the berm. Beyond the tape a small battalion of uniformed officers and red-jacketed lifeguards patrolled the sand, keeping the crowd of onlookers away from the wet-suited divers who were emerging from the surf. The only onlooker allowed inside the police perimeter was an ancient man in an electric wheelchair, who sat at the waterline staring sadly out to sea.

Shawn and Gus made their way through the crowd to the tape.

"You still haven't explained what we're doing here," Gus said.

"Because sometimes words aren't enough," Shawn said. "A strong visual can convey all the meaning of pages worth of verbiage in so much less time."

"Does that include all the time since you woke me up to tell me you'd found the mime?" Gus said. "Because it's been more than two hours, and you can fit a lot of words into one hundred and twenty-seven minutes."

"Don't forget, a chunk of that time was spent eating breakfast," Shawn said. "You wouldn't want me to talk with my mouth full. That would be rude."

"In between bites, I'm sure you could have squeezed in an answer to a simple question or two," Gus said. "Like 'what do you mean you found the mime?' "

"You've got a point," Shawn said. "That would have taken only six words: 'I mean I found the mime.' Or I could have answered your follow-up question, 'Where is the mime?' That would have been only three words."

"And if you had taken a break between bites of your breakfast burrito, which three words would you have used?"

"In regard to the mime's current location?" Shawn jerked his thumb towards the divers emerging from the surf. "In the water."

He lifted the crime scene tape and ducked under it. Just as Gus joined him on the other side, a uniformed officer stepped in front of them.

"Hey!" the officer said. "Didn't you see the tape?"

"Of course I saw it," Shawn said. "That's why I ducked under it. If I hadn't noticed it, I'd probably still be stuck in place, trying to figure out why I couldn't move forward."

The officer put a beefy hand on Shawn's shoulder. "Did you happen to notice the words written across the tape?" he said.

"He didn't bother," Gus said. "Because a strong visual can convey so much more than any number of words."

"And a patrol car can convey your ass straight to jail if you don't step behind the tape," the officer said.

Gus glanced down the beach and saw that two other officers had noticed the disturbance and were on their way to assist. He and Shawn had met a lot of cops in the years since they'd been working as private eyes, but the ones patrolling this scene didn't seem to be among them. Not surprising, since the officer blocking their way had a deep tan and premature wrinkles strongly suggesting he had been working beach patrol for many years, and try as they might to get beachfront crimes, Psych's cases rarely brought Shawn and Gus down to the ocean.

"Maybe we should do what the officer suggests," Gus said.

"That would be the prudent course of action," Shawn said.

"You've got that right," the officer agreed.

"Unfortunately, we're not prudes," Shawn said. "We're private detectives, and we've been asked to meet our client on this very beach at this very time."

"Are you, now?" the officer asked, although the question mark seemed to Gus to be more of a rhetorical device than an indication of true curiosity.

"We are now," Shawn said. "We also were then. And we still will be ten minutes from now, which is more than I can say for you and your present job as a police officer if you prevent me from speaking to my client, who happens to be one of the richest and most powerful men in Santa Barbara."

There was a flash of uncertainty on the cop's face. An officer on beach patrol spends his life confiscating beers, finding lost children, and putting out bonfires. None of these activities brings him in contact with the elite of Santa Barbara, who either own their own beach or know someone who does, and therefore he is rarely threatened with the force of the local political establishment. This cop didn't seem particularly intimidated by Shawn's warning, but he was intrigued enough to signal his fellow officers to back off a step.

"Are you threatening me?" the officer said.

"Of course not," Gus said before Shawn could answer.

"I don't threaten people, Officer," Shawn said. "My lawyer does. Of course most of the time the person he's threatening is me because I haven't paid my bill. But the point remains, that scrunched-up old geezer in the wheelchair is my client, and if you don't let us through to see him, all sorts of bad things are going to happen."

"Like what?" the officer said.

"Well, for one thing, a late-model automobile is going to rise up out of the bay like the *Red October*," Shawn said. "And do you really want to hear Sean Connery trying to sound Russian? Wasn't the Spanish accent in *Highlander* painful enough for you?"

Up until this moment, Gus had been feeling pretty good about the new day. As frustrated as he was by Shawn's refusal to explain what they were doing at the beach, the idea that he really had found the mime promised that today would be substantially better than the previous one. But now the officer was fingering the snap on his holster, and Gus was beginning to anticipate a second day of staring into gun barrels.

The other two uniformed officers joined them at the tape. One of them was as tanned and lined as the first, but the other, Gus was pleased to see, was both pale and wrinkle-free.

"What's going on here?" the pale cop said.

"These two clowns claim they're private detectives," the first officer said.

"Actually, only this clown claimed to be a private detective," Shawn said. "The other clown is too much of a chicken to have said anything, and in fact is wishing that I had never woken him up this morning."

"Really?" Gus said. "You think it's better to be a clown than a chicken?"

"People rarely coat clowns in batter and drop them into boiling oil," Shawn said.

"There's always a first time," Gus said.

The pale officer looked at Shawn, then at Gus. "I've seen these two around crime scenes before," he said. "I think I even escorted them off one once at the instruction of Detective Lassiter, but he had me bring them back right after. So what is it you want here?"

"I was trying to ward off disaster," Shawn said. "But it looks like I'm too late."

A dozen yards beyond the surf's edge, the bay had begun to boil. At least that's what it looked like to Gus. The surface of the water was bubbling; waves seemed to be breaking far from shore. And then the waters parted and a shiny black object bobbed to the surface. As the water poured off it, Gus could see it was a long Town Car floating on an enormous inflatable raft.

"I'm warning you, if Alec Baldwin steps out of that thing, no one tell him he's been replaced by Harrison Ford," Shawn said. "And for heaven's sake, don't mention the name Ben Affleck."

Chapter Eighteen

Gus stared at the floating car, amazed. Not so much at the car itself, of course. He'd lived in Santa Barbara long enough to understand what he was seeing here. The car had driven off the cliffs that towered above this beach and fallen into the water. A team of rescue divers had been sent in to bring it up. They would have spent the last hour painstakingly stretching the uninflated raft underneath the car's tires. And then, when the vehicle was situated exactly in its center, they would have inflated the raft. The buoyancy would have brought it, and the car, up to the surface, where it could be towed to shore.

No, what amazed Gus was not the way the police were able to get a car off the bay's floor. It was that Shawn knew it was going to happen. More precisely, it was that Shawn knew it was going to happen and hadn't bothered to mention it to him.

"Do you have something to do with that car?" the pale officer asked.

"Only to the extent that it's registered to the law firm of Rushton, Morelock, and Weiss," Shawn said. "And that Oliver Rushton is sitting down at the water's edge waiting to find out what it was doing in Peter Tork's locker."

"He means Davy Jones' locker," Gus explained quickly, before any of the officers could start using the clubs they carried on their belts.

"I never liked Davy Jones much," Shawn said. "He was always too pretty for me to believe him as a struggling musician. Plus, how big a star could he have been if he had time to play Marcia Brady's school dance—and for free, at that?"

The pale officer studied Shawn again, and then jerked his thumb back at the man in the wheelchair. "If Oliver Rushton is waiting for you, then you'd better go see him," he said. "But I'm keeping my eye on you."

"You really believe this guy?" one of the other beach patrol officers said. "Maybe we should escort him down."

"Believe me, if Mr. Rushton doesn't want to talk to him, we'll know pretty fast," the pale officer said. "And if he does, you don't want him to know the name of the cop who kept them apart."

The tanned officer grimaced, but he moved aside and let Shawn and Gus walk down the beach towards the man in the wheelchair.

"What are we doing here?" Gus whispered to Shawn as soon as they were out of the cops' earshot.

"You know as much as I do," Shawn said. Then he slapped himself on the forehead. "Oh, no, you don't. Because while I was doing intensive research, you were sleeping."

"The only kind of intensive research you've ever done is copy off my test paper," Gus said.

"Not entirely," Shawn said. "Remember when we had to do that book report on *The Three Musketeers* and you wouldn't let me read what you had written?"

"Because the time before, you copied my report and turned it in first, so I got blamed for stealing from you," Gus said.

"That was the first time I had to do my own intensive research," Shawn said. "And it taught me a valuable lesson I still follow today."

"You were so worried, you stayed up half the night flipping channels," Gus said. "And by sheer luck you found a station showing a movie of *The Three Musketeers,* so you wrote your report on that, which might have worked, except you kept referring to D'Artagnan as Logan and speculating about why the

Sandmen didn't take out Cardinal Richelieu, since he was clearly over thirty."

"Exactly," Shawn said. "Which is what I did last night. Only without the whole *Three Musketeers* movie thing, which is too bad because I was hoping to pick up a few fancy fencing moves. But, instead, I came across a report on the early-morning news about a high-speed car chase that ended with a Town Car flying off the palisades and into the ocean."

"That explains what the car is doing in the water," Gus said. "And it explains why the police are here. But it doesn't explain why you thought this had anything to do with the mime."

"During the chase, the police were able to run the Town Car's plates and discover that it was registered to the law firm of Rushton, Morelock, and Weiss. Which, if you were extremely familiar with the firm and didn't feel like using its entire name every time it came up in conversation, could easily be abbreviated as Rushmore."

"No, it couldn't," Gus said.

"I'm pretty sure it could," Shawn said. "Let's see—you take the first part of Morelock. That's the 'More.' And then you slap that together with the first part of Rushton. That gives you 'Rush.' You put them together and you get something like— wait for it—More Rush. No, better still: Rushmore."

"But that's not how law firms abbreviate their names," Gus said.

"Why not?"

"I don't know why not," Gus said. "Maybe it's because the senior partners like to hear their names said out loud. If Rushton, Morelock, and Weiss is too long, they'll just call it Rushton Morelock."

Out in the water, Gus could see divers tying nylon ropes to eyes in the raft. One of the divers gathered all the ropes together and started swimming towards the shore.

"Are you sure about that?" Shawn asked.

"I've read every one of John Grisham's books," Gus said. "And that's how they do it."

"Well, then, there are two possibilities," Shawn said. "One

is that John Grisham isn't always right—which you have to admit seems a lot more plausible after that book about the football player who went to Rome and ate pizza."

"What's the other one?" Gus said.

"That we're about to make a mortal enemy out of one of the most powerful men in Santa Barbara," Shawn said.

Chapter Nineteen

The man in the wheelchair didn't seem to notice Shawn and Gus as they came up behind him. His eyes were fixed on the spot in the water where the Town Car bobbed on the waves. But before they were within a dozen feet of him, he spoke out in a voice that was cragged with age and grief.

"I said I wanted to be alone," he said, without looking around to see who was coming up behind him.

"And I said I wanted my breakfast burrito with no meat, but when Patty the waitress brought it, it had more bacon in it than anything else," Shawn said. "And you know why that is? Because Patty knows that when I say 'no bacon,' what I mean is stick in as much of the pig as can possibly fit inside a tortilla, including the snout and the trotters."

Now the man did turn around. If he was surprised to see Shawn and Gus, he didn't betray it with even the slightest look. Typical, Gus figured. A guy like this probably hasn't been surprised by anything since Pearl Harbor.

"And which part of the pig are you?" he said, giving them a long, appraising look.

"I'm Shawn Spencer," Shawn said. "I'm a private detective. And this is my henchman, Bertie O'Myrmidon. Or he's my myrmidon, Bertie O'Henchman. I keep getting that confused."

Normally Gus would have jumped in and given his real

name at this point in the conversation. But one look at Rushton
suggested he might be better off if the old man didn't know
who he was. Even confined to an electric wheelchair that had
sunk an inch into the sand, he seemed to tower over Shawn
and Gus. His hand-tailored gray suit, his perfectly symmetrical
fingernails, his shoes cobbled from the hides of several endan-
gered species—all these announced his great wealth. But there
was something else about the man, something money couldn't
buy, that exuded power.

Up the beach, a winch started up with a loud whine, and the
raft began to float in towards the shore. The old man turned
back to watch its approach.

"I've hired and fired the best private detectives in the country," Rushton said. "I've never heard of you."

"Yes, you have," Shawn said.

If he thought he could do it without Rushton's noticing, Gus
would have kicked Shawn. Or at least held his head under the
water until he stopped struggling. Until this moment they had
been doing just fine without antagonizing one of the few men
in Santa Barbara whose name scared even your average beat
cop. He didn't know what kind of enemy Rushton would turn
out to be, but he wasn't so curious he felt compelled to do the
research.

"You overestimate yourself, Mr. Spencer."

Gus winced. Bad enough he was rich and powerful; he had
to have a good memory as well.

"Not at all," Shawn said. "Guy like you wants to hire and
fire the best, first he's got to make sure they're really the best.
Which means studying all the competition, just in case there's
some new best guy you could brag about firing instead."

Gus had the strong sensation that if Rushton lifted his arm
and spoke the right word, lightning would flash down out of
the clear blue sky and strike Shawn dead. Or, with Shawn's
luck, miss him and strike Gus dead instead. But when he sidled around the wheelchair to get a glimpse of the old lawyer's
face, Gus thought he could see a trace of a smile there.

"Maybe you're right," Rushton said. "That doesn't explain

what you're doing here, unless you've tracked me down simply to give me a baseline for comparison."

"We're here for the same reason you are," Shawn said. "Because while we know the truth, we're still hoping against hope that it's actually some unlucky joyrider in that Town Car, and not one of your closest and most dedicated employees."

The raft had reached the shore a few dozen feet away from them. Rushton didn't waste a glance on Shawn. He hit a lever on his armrest and the wheelchair powered out of its rut, cutting two deep lines in the sand as it headed towards the Town Car.

"What are you doing?" Gus whispered to Shawn as they followed Rushton's chair.

"Same thing we've been doing since yesterday," Shawn said. "Looking for a necklace."

By the time they reached the Town Car, one of the police divers was already reaching for the handle on the driver's-side door. Gus noticed that before he pulled it he glanced at Rushton, and waited until the lawyer gave him a curt nod of approval.

The diver yanked on the door handle and jumped back as salt water flooded out of the interior and soaked into the wet sand. As he jumped back to keep his shoes from getting soaked, Gus saw that there was a man belted into the driver's seat. His white shirt and khaki slacks were, not surprisingly, soaked through; his dark hair was plastered to his head.

One of the cops stepped in Gus' line of sight, so he didn't have a chance to get a good look at the dead man's face. But he saw enough to be pretty sure it wasn't covered in white makeup, and there was no doubt its owner wasn't wearing a blue-and-white-striped shirt, white gloves, and a beret. If this man was their mime, there didn't seem to be an easy way to prove it.

Rushton wasn't having any similar problems making his identification. He stared at the body in the Town Car, and even though his expression didn't seem to change, Gus could feel his sorrow.

"That's him," Rushton said. "That's Archie Kane."

There was commotion at the police tape, and Gus glanced up to see a team of paramedics struggling to wheel a stretcher down the soft sand. Before they could reach the Town Car, Shawn stepped up to its open door.

"Do you mind?" he said to the cop stationed there.

The officer was about to tell Shawn how much he did mind when he noticed the look on Rushton's face and stepped out of Shawn's way. But not before Shawn snagged a ballpoint pen from the cop's pocket.

Shawn bent into the open car door and examined the body closely. After a moment he straightened up. "Come here, Gus," he said.

Gus didn't want to. It wasn't that he was squeamish around dead bodies, just that he found one per week was perfectly sufficient. But Shawn was glowering at him, and the EMTs were getting closer. If he was ever going to do what Shawn wanted, it had to be now, and if he wasn't, he should have started yesterday before he agreed to go to La Canada.

Gus stepped up to the car, trying not to look too closely at the dead man.

"Recognize him?" Shawn said.

Gus forced his eyes to the body. He couldn't say for sure that he'd never seen the man before, in the same way he'd never be able to guarantee he hadn't noticed a specific grain of sand. He was just an average guy with average features and average hair. It was ridiculous to think that Gus would be able to say it was the same man he'd only ever seen covered in whiteface.

"No, and neither do you," Gus said.

"What if I told you he didn't listen to his mother?" Shawn said.

"When she told him not to drive off cliffs?"

"When she told him to always wash behind his ears." Shawn took the pen and gently folded back one of the dead man's earlobes. In the hollow behind his jawbone was a thick smear of white makeup.

"That's him," Gus said. "That's—"

Shawn stomped on Gus' foot before he could say the word "mime." He glared at Shawn until he heard a voice behind him.

"That's who, Mr. Guster?" Rushton said.

While Gus was still reeling over the fact that the lawyer had known who he was all along, Shawn answered.

"That's our client."

Chapter Twenty

Henry Spencer had never had any patience for the concept of mixed feelings, and had never felt any sympathy for those who claimed to suffer them. A man made a decision and stuck to it; it was as simple as that. If you were right, you won; if you were wrong, you paid the price. To bellyache about how you were torn between two possible decisions was nothing more than a way to justify the consequences of your bad choices.

But as he stepped through the heavy wooden doors into the Spanish-style headquarters of the Santa Barbara Police Department, Henry's feeling were as mixed as he'd ever allowed them to be. He had loved coming to work in this place for so many years, and the mingled smells of bad coffee, overheating computers, and sweaty prisoners made him realize how much he'd missed walking into the station every morning ready to take up the fight in the eternal struggle between chaos and order.

At the same time, though, the same smells made him realize just how happy he was to be retired. After all the years of acid reflux, incipient carpal tunnel syndrome, and aching muscles, he'd had enough of the coffee, computers, and prisoners for one lifetime. Let someone else battle for the forces of order. He'd put in his time and now he was ready to rock.

But no matter what his feelings were, Henry had made a decision and a promise, and he wasn't about to go back on either one of them. The force needed his help with a case, and he'd agreed to give it to them. He was theirs until the case was over.

Henry was heading towards Lassiter's desk when he heard someone call his name from across the station. He turned and saw a trim woman in her early fifties, impeccably outfitted in a tailored business suit. Even though she'd had the position for several years now, and had proven herself over and over, it was still a small shock to Henry to realize that Karen Vick was the chief of this department. It wasn't that he was opposed to women in positions of leadership; it was only that he'd spent so many years railing against the incompetence of his own chiefs that he had a hard time accepting one who was as good a cop as he was.

"Chief Vick," Henry said warmly as he crossed the station to take her outstretched hand in his.

"Henry," she said again. "Is there a reason you've stopped using my first name?"

"Protocol, Chief," Henry said, giving her hand a squeeze before releasing it. "As long as I'm here in a professional capacity, you're my commanding officer. Using the title helps me to remember that."

"Then let me start by officially thanking you for your help on behalf of the department," Chief Vick said. "The good news is, I don't think we're going to need to take up too much of your time."

"Making progress?"

She glanced at her watch. "Considering Carlton and Officer Rasmussen have only been at it for a little more than an hour, I think they're doing pretty well. But I'll let you be the judge of that."

She led him through the bustling squad room to a set of glass doors backed with Venetian blinds. Henry turned the knob and pushed the door open.

Henry's first thought was that someone had set up a charcoal grill in the room and the detectives inside had been overcome by carbon monoxide gas before they knew what was happening. Carlton Lassiter and his partner, Juliet O'Hara, sat motionless in their chairs, staring ahead with cold, unblinking eyes.

The only one in the room who looked alive was the tall blond kid in the tight blue polo shirt and khaki shorts. He was standing by a white board that had been covered with microscopic scrawl, and he was pointing to one tiny collection of letters with a black Dry Erase marker.

"I then spoke to the resident who lived six doors down from Ms. Svaco," the kid was saying. "Like the neighbors to whom I had previously spoken, she reported that she was not home at the time of the murder, and thus had not witnessed anything out of the ordinary. I moved on to the next house and—"

He broke off as Henry came through the door, and his face broke into a smile of boyish glee before he got it under control. "Detective Spencer, I'm so glad you're here."

"That's ex-detective," Henry said. "What's going on here?"

"Officer Rasmussen has been detailing the investigative steps he's taken since we found the body," Lassiter said.

"With the emphasis on 'detail,'" O'Hara said.

"Emphasis like you wouldn't believe," Lassiter said.

Henry wouldn't have thought it was possible to miss the sarcasm and irritation in the voices of the two detectives. Somehow Officer Rasmussen managed. "A very great policeman once told me that the solution to every crime lies in the details."

"I can't argue with that," Henry said.

"Of course you can't," Rasmussen said. "You're the one who said it."

"For which we thank you more than we can express," O'Hara said. "If it hadn't been for that pearl of wisdom, we might be out investigating, instead of learning how many cracks there are in the sidewalk between Ellen Svaco's house and the curb."

"The number of sidewalk cracks provided the solution to one of Detective Spencer's most famous cases," Rasmussen said.

Henry had to hide a proud smile. The Haskell Smith murder had been one of his finest moments. It also had also taken place years before this kid was born. Why would he know anything about it? "Of course that case involved a safe supposedly dropped from a third-story window, so the number of cracks in the pavement was slightly more germane that it might be here," Henry said as he took a seat.

"You can't know too much," Rasmussen said.

"That may be true," Lassiter said, "but when what you know is nothing, you can just say you know nothing."

"Please," O'Hara said. "You don't need to tell us everything you failed to learn."

"But I do," Rasmussen said. "You might spot some detail that I missed. And the solution to every—"

"I think we've all got that one," Henry said before Lassiter could start throwing furniture at the younger officer. "Details are vital, but so is time. Since these two very brilliant detectives have already heard the details, why don't you give me the broad picture?"

Rasmussen stared as if Henry had just offered to turn all the station's water into wine. "You want me to present the case to you?"

"Unless Detectives Lassiter and O'Hara have a problem with that."

Both detectives quickly waved off any possible objection. Rasmussen took a deep breath and stepped to the far left side of the board. He gestured with the marker and was about to begin when Henry interrupted. "Just remember, details are crucial, but so is the overview. We need to start with the general first, then work down to the specific."

Rasmussen nodded happily at the lesson, then turned back to the board. "Victim is Ellen Svaco, forty-three years old, second-grade teacher at Isla Vista Elementary. She was single, lived alone; only immediate relative a cousin in Pasadena, waiting notification; no pets. Finances were what you'd expect from a woman in her profession: she made fifty-seven thousand dollars a year, had thirteen thousand and change in a 401(k), and a few hundred in the bank. She was friendly with her neighbors, but only on a superficial level. They really only spoke to her when she was outside working in her garden. Apparently she was partial to sweet peas, although in the fall—"

Henry cleared his throat gently. "Big picture, right?"

He was surprised to see Officer Rasmussen blush. "Right. Sorry." Rasmussen moved his marker a few inches down the board. "She was a popular teacher, and while some parents were upset over a recent field trip in which some of the children came back with poison oak, no one was angry enough to want her harmed. She sat on several school committees and—"

This time Rasmussen cut himself off without needing Henry's prompting. His marker jumped all over the board as he reeled off more facts. "No sign of forced entry at the house. Victim was strangled with some kind of cord, probably nylon, although we're waiting for lab work on that. Motive didn't seem to be robbery, as nothing was taken, as far as we can tell. The entire house was ransacked, as though the killer was either sending a message or looking for something."

"In brief, we have no motive, no suspects, and no leads. Is that what you've been trying to tell us, Officer?" Lassiter said.

"Yes," Rasmussen said.

"And it's only taken eighty-five minutes," O'Hara said.

"There was one thing that seemed odd," Rasmussen said. "Ms. Svaco had a cat box filled with litter, plus cat dishes and cat toys. They were all inscribed with a name: Fluffy. But according to all her neighbors she didn't have a cat."

"Maybe she was going to get one," O'Hara said.

"I did consider that, Detective," Rasmussen said. "But I keep thinking about something Detective Spencer once said: 'A life properly lived fits together like a puzzle. When there's a piece that won't go, that means there's something wrong with the life.'"

O'Hara glared at Henry, as if she thought he'd come up with the phrase years ago simply to prolong this meeting. But Lassiter jumped up out of his chair excitedly.

"Who can argue with that?" Lassiter said. "This is our first and only lead. You and Detective Spencer must follow it up."

"That's a general rule, but—" Henry started, but Lassiter was already leading Rasmussen towards the door.

"This could be the break we've been looking for, and you're just the man to crack it wide open," Lassiter said, pushing Rasmussen into the corridor. "You and Henry Spencer, of course."

He pulled the door closed, then turned to Henry, a pleading look on his face. "Please do this."

"You said you wanted my help solving this case," Henry said.

"I do," Lassiter said. "And getting this kid out of our way is the biggest help anyone could ever be. I'm begging you. Please."

Chapter Twenty-One

If the offices of Rushton, Morelock, and Weiss had been in Los Angeles or New York, they would have commanded the upper stories of the tallest skyscraper in the city, and Rushton's office would have been the penthouse. But Santa Barbara didn't have skyscrapers; no building in the city was allowed to rise higher than sixty feet. Instead, the firm demonstrated its power and success in the idiom understood by the locals: beachfront access.

The offices occupied the bottom two floors of a sprawling, four-story Cape Cod situated directly behind a long, curving strip of white sand and an endless stretch of ocean. At either end of the property the beach jutted out into stony promontories resembling the claws of an enormous crab; there was no way onto this sand except by boat or through the multiple guard gates along the winding private lane that ran through a dense pine forest, also part of Rushton's property. Or, of course, by helicopter, Gus noted as he steered the Echo around a vacant helipad.

Gus hadn't known what to expect when Shawn started mouthing off to Oliver Rushton, but the one thing he hadn't anticipated was an invitation to this private estate. Apparently it was Shawn's plan all along.

"You've got to figure a guy like Rushton only does business

with the biggest detective agencies in the business," he explained as Gus drove back and forth along Edgecliff Lane, searching for the promised turnoff to the lawyer's private road. "Those guys probably get him what he needs before we even get up out of bed. But on that level they're practically law firms themselves, or insurance companies. They're totally corporate, which is great when you need someone to testify in a lawsuit. But I figured that someone like Rushton grew up watching classic detective movies. Deep down that's what he thinks a private eye is supposed to be like. A tough, hard-boiled gumshoe."

"And that's us?"

"Me, anyway," Shawn said. "I don't think he saw you as hard-boiled. More like scrambled. Say, are you hungry?"

Shawn spent the rest of the drive hunting through Gus' glove compartment looking for stray Skittles that had spilled there months ago and explaining his plan for their meeting, and by the time Gus parked the Echo among a fleet of Jaguars, Mercedeses, and Maybachs, he was feeling confident about the day for the first time. Even the appearance of a tuxedoed butler at the ring of the mansion's doorbell didn't throw him off.

The butler led them down a long, dark corridor and threw open a door. Gus was nearly blinded by the sun blasting through a wall of windows looking out onto the ocean. No doubt that was the purpose of the dark hallway, he thought. To make this view even more spectacular.

The office itself was furnished and decorated in a nautical theme, from the signal flags on the walls to the ship's steering wheel in front of the windows. Just as well, Gus thought. This close to the ocean, the house felt like it was only one big storm away from being swept out to sea. Maybe that wheel would actually work.

A door in the side of the room opened. Oliver Rushton glided in and positioned himself behind his massive mahogany desk. "Please sit down," he said brusquely.

As he took his seat in a large armchair, Gus studied the lawyer carefully. For one moment when Rushton first saw the body he identified as Archie Kane, Gus was certain that he saw a flash of vulnerability in the old man. Now he couldn't imagine how that could have been. Gus might as well have been staring at a steel rod.

"Nice place," Shawn said, glancing around him. "We've been thinking about moving our offices. Mind saying what the rent is on something like this?"

Gus knew what Shawn was doing: He was channeling Humphrey Bogart. But he still had to fight off a wince. There was a fine line between cocky insouciance and the kind of rudeness that could get you keelhauled, and Shawn had never been particularly good with fine lines.

But if Rushton was offended, he didn't show it. Of course, Gus thought, if Rushton was so enraged he was about to turn into Lou Ferrigno, he wouldn't show that, either.

"You say Archie Kane was your client," Rushton said. "Do you have any evidence of that? A contract, perhaps? Or a deal memo? Even a retainer check?"

"Not that I'm free to show you," Shawn said.

"I see." Rushton reached for the phone. Gus half-expected him to order the dogs to be released. "Helen, my business meeting seems to have turned into a social call," he said into the intercom. "Feel free to put through calls."

Gus wondered if they were supposed to leave at this point. Fortunately, Shawn was no better at supposed to than he was at fine lines. He was looking around the room again, and this time Gus realized he wasn't just admiring the décor.

Shawn looked around the office and he *saw*. Saw among the framed photos one of a much younger Rushton—already in a wheelchair in his forties—shaking hands with Marcel Marceau. Saw among all the expensive nautical antiques on Rushton's desk a cheap trophy with WORLD'S GREATEST BOSS embossed on a metal plate flaking with age. Saw a plaque honoring the lawyer with an award from something called the "Second Chance for Kids Foundation." Saw a snapshot of a young mime imitating the lawyer behind his back. Saw Rushton's calendar on the desk opened to today's date, with the initials AK scrawled in the first hourly slot at the top of the page.

Shawn turned back to Rushton. "Not that I can show you," he said. "But I can tell you."

Rushton glanced at his watch. "My personal services run up to five thousand dollars per hour," he said. "I'll give you two minutes for free. Anything above that will incur the hourly charge. And people don't refuse to pay my bills."

"Archie Kane worked for you for many years," Shawn said. "Officially for the firm, but his loyalty was always with you. That's because you met him when he was a troubled youth. If you hadn't given him a minimum-wage job in your office when he was still a teenager, he would have ended up on the street trying to support himself as a mime. And we both know how far his particular set of miming skills would have taken him. Over the years he proved himself to be completely loyal and reliable, so much so that even though he never became a lawyer, he was a valuable part of this firm. Valuable, again, to you more than to the firm itself. But then, you are the firm."

"The other founding partners are dead, it's true," Rushton said.

"Archie would have done anything to protect you," Shawn said. "And when he began to realize there was someone in this firm who was using it as the base for a criminal conspiracy, smuggling stolen tech secrets, he tried to alert you. But he didn't have any evidence, and he couldn't tell you who it was, so you dismissed it as him being overprotective. Archie wouldn't let anyone do you harm, even yourself, so he started to investigate on his own. He did uncover the conspiracy, and he was planning to reveal it to you this morning. But he was careless, and they found out about him first. I suspect when the police examine that Town Car they'll discover the brake line was cut."

"I just got off the phone with them," Rushton said. "It was. Go on."

Shawn leaned back in his armchair. "The first two minutes were free. Anything above that is going to incur the hourly charge. And while people do refuse to pay our bills sometimes, it really hurts my feelings."

"Is that why you're here, Mr. Spencer?" Rushton said. "To collect a fee for the work you did for Archie Kane?"

Shawn leaned forward in his chair and punched a finger at Rushton. "Archie Kane was our client," he said. "'When a man's client is killed, he's supposed to do something about it. It doesn't make a difference what you thought of him. He was your client and you're supposed to do something about it. And it happens we're in the detective business. When one of your organization gets killed, it's bad business to let the killer get away with it, bad all around, bad for every detective everywhere.'"

"You did that well, Mr. Spencer," Rushton said. "Not as well as Humphrey Bogart, but then you didn't have John Huston directing you."

"What, does everyone have that movie memorized?" Shawn said.

Gus saw this moment slipping away. More precisely, he saw it running away, being chased by the guard dogs that Rushton was undoubtedly about to release.

"The words aren't ours, but the sentiment is," Gus said quickly. "We didn't know Archie Kane well, but we never doubted his devotion to this firm. Just about the first thing he ever said to us was that he wouldn't let any harm come to you."

"And he was wearing whiteface when he said it," Shawn said. "If he was willing to break the mime's solemn vow of silence, you know how much it meant to him."

"He was dressed as a mime?" For the first time since he wheeled into the room, Rushton allowed a flicker of feeling to cross his face. "Archie hated miming. It was his counselor at the institute who pushed him down that path. And it turned out to be a good thing for him—it's how I got to know the boy. I personally have always loved the art form. But when I hired Archie, he vowed he'd never mime again now that he had a purpose in life. And as far as I knew, he never did."

"He did it for you," Shawn said. "He died trying to protect you."

"Because I wouldn't listen to him," Rushton said.

"Because one of the people working for you is a murderer," Shawn said. "Archie Kane was the second victim; the first was a woman named Ellen Svaco, who seems to have been involved in the smuggling ring Archie was trying to expose."

"Archie warned me it was someone close," Rushton said. "One of my junior partners. Which one is it?"

"We don't know," Shawn said.

"Yet," Gus added.

"What do you need from me?" Rushton said.

"Access," Shawn said. "Instruct your people they've got to talk to us. Give us free rein for two days, and we'll give you your killer."

"I can give you something better than that," Rushton said. "I can give you a job."

Chapter Twenty-Two

Babysitting.

Decades on the force, a lifetime in detective work, and now Henry had become a professional babysitter. His sole job for the SBPD was to keep Chris Rasmussen occupied so the grownups could do the real work.

To make the day even more humiliating, every place Rasmussen had taken Henry felt like a stop any young child would want to make. They'd hit the local animal shelter to see if Ellen Svaco had tried to adopt a cat, and had to look through all the cat cages to see if there was a "Fluffy" there. They had been through half a dozen pet stores on a futile mission to see if anyone remembered the woman who'd had the name inscribed on all her cat implements. And to guarantee maximum embarrassment, wherever they went, Rasmussen would inevitably introduce himself by patting the badge printed on his polo shirt like a little boy with a tin star.

As they pulled up to one more useless stop, this one a veterinarian's office, Rasmussen gave Henry a firm chuck on the shoulder with his fist. "The brainwork is the key, but it's the legwork that makes it turn in the lock."

Henry sighed heavily. This whole day was like being trapped with a human fortune cookie—worse, because Henry had written all the fortunes himself. "I don't understand how you know all these things I've said." Henry got out of the car and waited for Rasmussen to join him at the vet's entrance. "It's not like I wrote a self-help book or anything."

"That would be great," Rasmussen said. "I'd love to own a complete collection of your wisdom."

"Where did you hear the stuff you've been parroting back to me?"

"Isla Vista Junior High," Rasmussen said as he pushed through the door to the veterinary offices.

Henry had never worked a case at any junior high school anywhere, let alone Isla Vista. And while it was flattering to think his collected works were being studied by eleven-year olds, the fact was he didn't have any works, collected or otherwise. This guy had to be playing with him.

But when Henry entered the waiting room, Rasmussen didn't seem to be playing. If anything, he was even more serious than before. He stood at the waist-high counter drumming his fingers impatiently as a young woman in scrubs wrestled with a border collie who had no intention of letting himself be weighed.

Henry joined Rasmussen at the counter. "I have to admit, I don't remember what case brought me to your school," he said. "Are you sure you have the right guy?"

"Absolutely," Rasmussen said. "Although you were there undercover."

"You've got the wrong guy," Henry said. "I never worked undercover at a school."

"Sure, you did," Rasmussen said. "You were going under the name Officer Friendly. But for me, you were Officer Role Model. Before I heard you speak, I wanted to design surfboards. Afterwards, I knew I was meant to be a cop."

Now Henry remembered. Twenty years ago he'd gotten into a shouting match with his chief over a string of robberies, and as discipline he'd been assigned to travel to the area's schools as Officer Friendly. It was a miserable assignment, and the only way he'd gotten through it was making sure to introduce Officer Friendly to Officer Bourbon every night as soon as he finished his daily lectures.

But this one kid had listened to every word. Listened and remembered. Remembered for all these years.

"I couldn't have talked for more than forty-five minutes," Henry said.

"It was enough."

Henry thought of all the things he'd tried to teach Shawn, and how few of them actually took. If only his son had been this receptive to Henry's wisdom, he'd be running a police department today. Maybe this kid wasn't so bad after all.

The woman in scrubs managed to get a reading off the scale and sent the border collie off down a corridor with an attendant, then came up to Henry and Rasmussen.

"How can I help you?" she said.

Chris Rasmussen tapped the badge printed on his shirt. Oddly, this time Henry didn't find the gesture annoying. Instead he saw the pride behind it. "I'm Officer Chris Rasmussen of the Isla Vista Foot Patrol," he said. "This is Detective Henry Spencer of the Santa Barbara Police Department. We're wondering if you have any record of a client by the name of Ellen Svaco."

"I don't know if I'm allowed to give out that information," the woman said. "Isn't there doctor-patient privilege?"

Rasmussen gave her a dazzling smile. "Only if we ask about her pet."

She smiled back warmly. Henry had to admit, this kid had something going for him.

The woman went to a large filing cabinet against the back wall and started digging through a drawer.

As they were waiting, Henry glanced around the room. It was a standard vet's office, with easy-to-clean linoleum floors, half-chewed waiting furniture, and, on the walls, pictures of grateful pets and posters warning of heartworm.

And in the corner was something Henry had never seen before. He nudged Rasmussen and pointed at it.

"Did I mention something to your class about looking too hard for information?"

"Sure," Rasmussen said. "Don't be so fixated on the thing you think you're looking for that you don't see what else is there."

"Like that?"

It was a large cardboard standee of what might have been the cutest dog in canine history. A word balloon over its head claimed it was thinking, "Fluffy saved my life." And at the bottom was a cartoon kitten and the slogan "When all else fails, Fluffy can help. The Fluffy Foundation."

The woman came back up to the counter with a helpless shrug. "I'm afraid we've got no pet owners named Svaco," she said. "Is there another name she might have used?"

"Who's Fluffy?" Henry said, gesturing towards the standee.

The woman looked confused for a moment, then realized what he was talking about. "The Fluffy Foundation," she said. "We love them. If your pet is sick and you can't afford the treatment, they'll pay for it."

"That must cost a fortune," Henry said. "Where does the money come from?"

"No one knows," the woman said. "An anonymous donor. The only thing we know for sure is that whoever it was used to have a cat named Fluffy, and he died because his owner couldn't afford treatment. So when she came into a lot of money, she donated huge amounts of it to start this foundation."

"How huge?" Officer Rasmussen said.

"I have no idea," she said.

"I do," Henry said. "Enough to kill for."

Chapter Twenty-Three

The mood in Rushton, Morelock, and Weiss' palatial conference room was somber. Even the view of the sunlight-speckled ocean seemed dimmer than it had when Shawn and Gus first took their seats.

That was only appropriate to the occasion. The firm's senior partner had announced Archie Kane's death as soon as the other five lawyers assembled around the mahogany table, and then spent the next half hour eulogizing his protégé.

But beneath whatever sorrow the people in this room might have been feeling ran another emotion. Gus could feel the tension in the air, almost smell the suspicion. And he had no question what the cause of it was.

It was him.

More precisely, it was him and Shawn. They had been sitting on either side of Rushton at the head of the table when the other lawyers filed in for the meeting. But Rushton hadn't introduced them, hadn't even spared a single word or even a glance to acknowledge their existence. It was a testament to his power over his junior partners that not one of them asked anything about the two outsiders. Most of them wouldn't even look at the detectives except in furtive glances, when they seemed to think no one would notice.

This left Gus free during Rushton's eulogy to study those

faces that were so studiously not looking at him. Three men, two women, all in their midthirties to early forties, all polished, buffed, waxed, and tanned to perfection. Gus didn't know if there was such a thing as a human equivalent to the full detailing to which he treated the Echo every six months, but if there was, these people had it done to themselves on a weekly basis.

At first Gus was so blinded by the lawyers' uniform perfection he could barely tell them apart. But as Rushton continued to speak, he began to spot differences between them. The first one who stood out was the closer of the two women. She had jet-black hair cut in bangs that fell low on her brow, and piercing blue eyes, a combination Gus suspected had not been crafted by nature. As he looked around the room, his eyes kept being drawn back to her. He tried to tell himself that it was because she had a uniquely forceful personality that overwhelmed the room even as she sat silently absorbing Rushton's words, but the fact was that she was a dead ringer for Tanya Roberts in *Beastmaster,* except that she wasn't climbing out of a sylvan pool naked. In Tanya's honor, Gus mentally nicknamed her Kiri.

Feeling he was being unfair, Gus made himself focus on the other woman in the room. At least he did until his eyeballs began to hurt. It wasn't that the short blond wasn't beautiful. He assumed she was, anyway, since everyone else in the room could have been sculpted by Michelangelo. But her hat, her dress, her shoes, her purse, even her watchband were all such a bright green they seemed to radiate light with the intensity of your average lighthouse beacon. The result was that she seemed to be surrounded by a shimmering emerald haze not unlike a fairy's aura in a Disney cartoon. He decided to call her Tinkerbell.

That made the man next to her Captain Hook. Not that he was missing a hand or had a habit of glancing nervously around the room for a ticking crocodile. But he had a wolfish, grasping look even as he attempted to convey the appropriate sorrow for his fallen comrade. Gus could practically see him laying out all the ways in which this new turn of events could be used to his advantage and how it could hurt him.

It was the man sitting next to the Captain whom Gus found most intriguing. He didn't quite fit in with the others. Sure, his skin had that perfect poreless sheen, and each of the hairs on his head was so precisely cut and shaped that Gus suspected his barber trimmed only one before switching razors, and his suit fit better than Gus' own skin and moved with his body so easily it seemed to have been woven out of mercury.

But unlike the other lawyers, this one actually seemed to have the occasional emotion, and some of these even played out on his face. There wasn't a lot of sentiment present, and in another context Gus might never have noticed anything at all. But in a group of peers who betrayed somewhat less of whatever they were feeling than a group of department store dummies, the slight twitches and frowns this lawyer displayed and then banished almost as soon as they first appeared might as well have been semaphore signals. There was only one word for a man whose every emotional response is so much bigger, louder, and more extravagant than anyone else's, so Gus decided to call him Shatner.

He'd turned to appraise the next lawyer in line when he noticed that the man had turned to stare directly at him.

They were all staring at him. Kiri and Tink and Captain Hook and Shatner and the guy who did not know he was waiting for a clever nickname. What did they want? Was he supposed to say something?

Gus realized he'd stopped listening to Rushton's speech several minutes ago. Now he tried to call up back whatever might have penetrated his ears but bounced off his brain. It was no use. He had no idea what he was supposed to do or say.

Gus could feel himself starting to panic. Under the table his knees were beginning to tremble. In another couple of seconds, he'd begin to do something he was sure no one else at this table had ever done: sweat.

Fortunately one of the lawyers who had been staring at him— a man whose white-blond hair, golden skin, and muscled physique would have led Gus to nickname him Doc Savage if he'd gotten the chance—turned to Rushton, a look of disapproval momentarily exposing his brilliant white teeth.

"We have a binding contract with InterTec and are obligated to continue paying them through the end of the year," Savage said. "If you want to terminate that relationship and bring in our own in-house investigators, we should at least wait until that commitment has been fulfilled so we're not paying twice for the same service."

Gus understood now why everyone had been staring at him. Rushton had finally gotten around to the second item of business on today's agenda, the one he had laid out for Shawn and Gus in his office. Shawn had wanted to be able to come and go at the firm at will, and he suggested that Rushton give him and Gus some kind of official cover that would entitle them to talk to the attorneys there. They could be auditors, Shawn suggested, or personnel consultants, or famous war correspondents who had taken time away from their vital service to the country risking their lives covering the global fight for freedom to write Rushton's biography. Or caterers, if that was easier.

But Rushton had an idea that was far simpler and more audacious than anything even Shawn would have come up with. He would hire Psych to be the firm's in-house investigative arm. That way Shawn and Gus could be entirely truthful about what they were doing at Rushton, Morelock, while still working undercover.

"The services are not identical, but complementary," Rushton said. "InterTec is a fine firm and essential to our growing international business. But Psych has ways of doing things that can only be called unique."

"I can think of another word for it." It was Kiri, who was glaring at Shawn with those eyes as if she really could shoot ice bullets out of them.

"And what word would that be?" Gus heard the warning in Rushton's voice. The dolphins frolicking in the ocean outside the window must have heard it. But either Kiri didn't hear, or she was so angry she didn't care.

Gus knew what the word was going to be. He'd heard it enough from people who refused to believe that his partner actually had the ability to read minds, sense auras, commune with the dead, or whatever new trick Shawn invented when it suited the situation. The word was "fraud," and Gus couldn't have resented it any more if it hadn't been true.

Gus could see the letter *f* forming on Kiri's lips. But before she could finish the epithet, she seemed to wither under Rushton's cold stare.

"Fabulous," she muttered. "And I hope that their first assignment is to uncover the truth about what happened to Archie Kane."

Good for Kiri, Gus thought. Just like her namesake, this one was clearly no mere slave girl fit only to have her clothes stolen by ferrets, but a trained warrior. In one sentence she had not only put herself directly behind Rushton, but had also managed to deflect any suspicion away from herself. Gus didn't know if she would turn out to be the one who'd killed the mime, but if she had, he now knew she would also turn out to be a formidable opponent.

"Is there anything you won't lie about, Gwendolyn?" It was Shatner, and he was looking right at Kiri. So now Gus knew her real name. "We all know what you felt about Archie, and we all know that you are as disgusted as any of us at the idea of bringing these two frauds into this firm."

There was a long moment of silence. Gus could see the various lawyers weighing the sides here and trying to choose between following Shatner's lead and saying what everyone was thinking or falling in line behind the boss. Captain Hook in particular seemed to be taking the match out at least a dozen moves and still hadn't found a convincing end game.

Shawn didn't look concerned. He stood up casually and greeted the blank faces with a cheerful smile.

"First, I want to thank you all for your warm welcome," Shawn said. "I want to thank Mr. Rushton for hiring us. And I'd particularly like to thank the gentleman who just spoke up. Because there's nothing like being called a fraud by a man who dines on human flesh."

Chapter Twenty-Four

Gus felt an odd pounding in his feet. After a second he realized it was his heart, which had plummeted all the way down there at Shawn's words and was looking for a way to break out of his body through his toes. When Rushton hired them he hadn't made any explicit threats about what would happen if they besmirched his firm, but Gus had little doubt that his retribution would be swift and horrible.

There was a stunned silence at the table. Then Shatner jumped up angrily.

"You are all witnesses to this outrageous accusation," he roared. "I demand a full retraction and an immediate apology."

"Wait a minute," Shawn said. He touched his index fingers to his temples and fluttered his eyelids; then his eyes snapped open. "Sorry, sometimes the visions come to me as metaphors, and apparently whoever is in charge of sending out vibrations today is a frustrated writer—and a bad one, too, if we can judge by the originality of his imagery. When I saw you as a man-eating killer, that was only meant to be a representation of your ferocity in the courtroom. You are widely known as a shark, aren't you?"

Gus could feel his heart abandon its efforts to bore a hole in his big toe and begin to travel back up towards his ankle. But even if Shawn had momentarily saved the day, or at least kept it from turning into a complete disaster, Shatner didn't seem mollified.

"Is this the level of insight we can expect from our new so-called psychic?" he demanded.

"'The Psych agency has a nearly unbroken string of successful cases.'" It was Tinkerbell, who was trying to look like she wasn't reading this information from the screen of her iPhone. "'They've solved multiple murders that have baffled the police, recovered items owners thought were gone for good, and made believers out of even the most dubious skeptics.'"

Gus forced himself to suppress a grin. He had just learned two valuable pieces of information. One was that Shawn had been absolutely right to pay ten-year-old Hank Stenberg to write and submit the Wikipedia page he'd just heard read back to him. More important, he now knew that Tinkerbell was no feisty rebel like her namesake. She was a calculating corporate suck-up who would say anything as long as she was sure it was what the boss wanted to hear. Gus had met plenty of this type in his other career as a pharmaceutical sales rep, and he'd had plenty of practice getting them to do what he needed. This job just had just gotten a little easier.

"Is that from the same trusted reference work that claims Jade Greenway is 'one of America's greatest lawyers' and that her annoying affectation of dressing all in green is not a pathetic plea for attention but actually 'a powerful tool in her ongoing battle for justice'?" Captain Hook sneered. "Because I read in the same entry that she admitted she dressed in green only because she couldn't remember her own name otherwise."

"That was cyber-vandalism," said Tinkerbell, who was apparently also called Jade Greenway. "I made them change that the instant it went up."

"You know she's right," Gwendolyn said. "The way she Googles herself, there's no way there's anything about her online for more than five seconds before she sees it."

This was another valuable lesson. The lawyers were bickering like schoolchildren, and Rushton wasn't doing anything to stop them. Gus was pretty sure the old man was waiting to see how Shawn and he would handle them. But it also told him a lot about Rushton's management style. It seemed to be to drop a bunch of snakes into a pit and let them fight it out among themselves.

Gus glanced at Shawn to see if he'd realized Rushton was waiting for him to prove himself. It was hard to tell, because Shawn was bent over double, his hands pressed against his forehead. It was possible he was about to utter one of his psychic pronouncements, but given the bickering around the table, it was just as possible he'd developed a terrible headache.

Then Shawn straightened up and stared at Shatner. Stared and *saw*. Saw the ragged line of white flesh near his hairline. Saw the sharp edge of the leather watchband of his Patek Philippe. Saw the puckered spot on his silk tie and the dull spots on his nails where the clear polish had chipped off.

"The wrong ocean," Shawn moaned. "It's the wrong ocean."

The lawyers snapped out of their argument and wheeled to face Shawn, who was clutching his head as if in pain.

"What is he doing?" Shatner snapped.

"I believe the metaphor has returned," Gus said.

"I see a shark," Shawn said. "He's a happy shark, although it's kind of hard to tell, since they always look like they're smiling. Anyway, he's king of his neighborhood, snacking on all the other fishes. Then one day he's scooped up in a net. When he wakes up, he's still the same shark he always was. Got the same instincts and appetites. But he's been dumped in a different ocean. All the nooks and crannies he used to hide in to wait for his prey are gone. And the waters are filled with other sharks who are just as tough as he is, but they know the place so much better. Now every mouthful is a fight for him. Every time he spots a target, one of the other sharks swoops in and steals it from him. He's getting hungry—starving, actually. And every day that goes by without a meal makes him weaker. If he doesn't find a big school of fish soon, he'll be so feeble he won't even be able to swim fast anymore. And you know what happens then? The other sharks stop preying on the local fish and turn on him."

Gus noticed that Shatner had gone pale under his tan. He sank slowly down into his seat.

"But why am I still talking about seafood?" Shawn said cheerily. "I think someone had an objection?"

"No objection," Shatner said, staring down at the table.

"In that case, I believe our business is concluded," Rushton said. "Let's take an hour to finish up last-minute details. The chopper departs precisely at noon."

Rushton waited until the other lawyers had left the conference room before clapping Shawn on the back. "I won't ask how you knew Morton Mathis was a recent transfer from the Detroit District Attorney's Office, but I will congratulate you on silencing him," Rushton said. "It gives me great confidence that I made the right decision in hiring you."

"Yes, you did," Shawn said.

Something was troubling Gus. "But I don't see what we're going to be able to accomplish here if everyone else is leaving."

"That's all taken care of," Rushton said. "There's room on the chopper for the two of you as well. This week is our corporate retreat, a time I set aside every year so that the lawyers can bond together into a family."

"I can see how well that's working," Shawn said. "They're just like every family I've ever known."

"It's a perfect time for you to get to know them, ferret out their secrets, and report it all back to me," Rushton said. "I want to know who killed Archie Kane." He touched a lever on his armrest and his wheelchair glided back from the table.

"We didn't really pack for a retreat," Shawn said. "Unless by 'retreat' you mean staying at home eating Funyuns."

"I do not," Rushton said. "But you don't need to worry about packing. Everything you could possibly want will be provided for you."

"I don't know," Shawn said. "I can want some pretty strange things."

"Of that I have no doubt." Rushton reached into the leather satchel that hung from his chair and pulled out a large manila envelope, which he placed carefully on the table. "Background information on the lawyers, and a little brochure about the retreat. And if you need to make any arrangements for your sudden absence, just dial nine on that phone. I'm afraid I block all electronic signals in my conference room, so you can't use your cells—it's the only way I can keep anyone's attention during meetings."

Rushton wheeled silently to the rear door, which opened automatically as he approached it, then closed behind him. Gus reached for the envelope, but Shawn snatched it out of his hands.

"You won't be needing any background information," Shawn said. "I've already solved the case."

Chapter Twenty-Five

When Shawn was little, Henry had a recurring fantasy that one day the two of them would partner up on the Santa Barbara Police Department. There wasn't much of a chance it would ever happen, of course. The department had strict rules against relatives working closely together. But there was nothing that made Henry happier than imagining himself and Shawn, father and son, cracking case after case together.

Then Shawn started to talk, and Henry gave up on the fantasy. But sitting in the generic accounting office that served as the mailing address for the Fluffy Foundation and watching Officer Rasmussen interview the skinny little dweeb who administered the charity, Henry felt those old feelings stirring for the first time in decades.

This is what he had always dreamed of, the relationship he'd thought possible only with blood kin. The dance between partners who could coordinate their strategy without a word. Rasmussen ran the interrogation, but Henry was able to direct him with nothing more than the slightest of looks. It was like telepathy—the real thing, not the phony version Shawn practiced.

Within minutes of their arrival in the one-man office nestled between a convenience store and a Laundromat in a down-market strip mall, Rasmussen started getting the information they needed. The Fluffy Foundation had been in operation for five years, and while it had recently begun to attract some new donors, almost all its money came from the anonymous angel who had set up the fund. That person had started the charity with a donation of fifty thousand dollars, and similar amounts came in at irregular intervals. The dweeb had been alerted to expect another gift shortly.

This sent Henry's internal radar tingling. If Ellen Svaco was indeed the anonymous donor behind the foundation, there was no trace of it in any of her financial records. And if she was about to have fifty thousand untraceable dollars to give away, that would have given someone fifty thousand good reasons to kill her. Their entire case could depend on the answer to Rasmussen's next question: Who is the anonymous donor?

Henry gave Rasmussen the nod, and the officer sat forward in his chair. "It's very important that you tell us the identity of your donor."

The dweeb pushed his horn-rims up the bridge of his nose with the tip of a pencil and cleared his throat nervously. "I'm sorry, but I can't do that," he said.

"Not even if I told you it was a matter of life and death?" Rasmussen said.

"Not without a court order," the dweeb said. "I'm just not at liberty to divulge that information."

Rasmussen hesitated for a moment, then got up. "Thank you for your time," he said. "We'll come back when we have a warrant."

It took Henry a couple of seconds to realize that Rasmussen was actually walking towards the door. Henry leaped up out of his chair and grabbed the officer before he could reach the knob. "What are you doing?" he whispered furiously.

" 'If the law doesn't respect the law, then no one will,' " Rasmussen said proudly. " 'The police officer must act with complete fidelity to the rules, or the force is nothing but a mob.' You taught me all that."

If Henry had had more hair, he would have pulled it out. For a moment he considered pulling out Rasmussen's. Instead he moved the officer back towards the dweeb's desk.

"I'm thrilled you remember my lessons so well," Henry said. "But that was a classroom situation. This is real life."

"'If our principles can't stand up in the face of an adverse reality, they aren't principles, they're just whims,'" Rasmussen said. "I've lived my life by that."

"And I'm really flattered," Henry said. "But you might want to cover your ears right now."

"Why?"

Henry marched up to the dweeb and pounded his fist on the desk. "Listen, pal," he barked, "we've got reason to believe this entire charity is a front set up to launder drug money. And that makes you a kingpin. So unless you want to spend the rest of your pathetic life in supermax, you will give us the name of your donor."

The dweeb looked like he was about to cry. Rasmussen rushed up to the desk. "That's not exactly true," he said. "What Detective Spencer means—"

"—is that you'll be lucky to get life," Henry said. "If we find evidence that some of this drug money is going to support terrorists, we'll go for the death penalty."

"It's not drug money!" the dweeb said feebly.

"We do know that," Rasmussen said.

Henry pushed him out of the way and pounded on the table. "The name! It's Svaco, isn't it?"

The dweeb gulped so hard his Adam's apple nearly tore through his throat. "Yes, the donor's name is Svaco."

Henry turned to Rasmussen and gave him a tight smile. "Here's one I probably forgot to mention in class: Make the case first; make it pretty later."

"It's no good," Rasmussen said. "We can't use that information. It's tainted."

"Except we're not putting Ellen Svaco on trial," Henry said. "We're trying to solve her murder. And this man has just given us the vital clue we need."

He patted Rasmussen on the shoulder and stalked to the door. Rasmussen stayed at the desk and handed the dweeb a business card. "Thank you so much for your cooperation. I assure you, we will arrange for a warrant so that you will not have violated your fiduciary duty to your client. Do you have any questions?"

"Yes. One," the dweeb said. "Did he say, 'Ellen'?"

"Yes, Ellen Svaco, your donor," Rasmussen said.

"I don't know who that is," the dweeb said. "The foundation's principal donor is Arnold Svaco. That's the only Svaco I know."

Chapter Twenty-Six

"**Y**ou always do this," Gus said. "You say you solved the case, and then when I ask for details, it turns out you're not even close to a solution. You've just come up with some obscure detail that half the time has nothing to do with anything."

"Because the other half of the time it has everything to do with everything," Shawn says. "And those are the ones that people remember. You can get away with a dozen wrong guesses in a row as long as you hit the last one out of the park."

"We're not in a park, we're in a law firm," Gus said. "And we're about to be away on some corporate retreat."

"Which is why it doesn't matter if I've actually solved the murder or not," Shawn said. "Because there's no way I'm staging a reveal before we get to ride on the company helicopter."

"You're going to let a killer go free so you can go joyriding in the sky?"

"So *we* can go joyriding in the sky," Shawn said. "Personally, I can't think of a better reason to let a killer go free. Except maybe if he has such a rare blood type that he is the only tissue match for an innocent little girl who will die without an organ transplant, but he won't agree to the operation unless he gets a full pardon."

"Sure, but once you set him free, how will you guarantee

he'll go through with the transplant?" Gus said. "And what if she needs a second transplant later? And what if he does give the girl the organ, but then he kills again? Do you think that little girl would want to know her life was purchased with the blood of innocents? And what if the transplant surgeon is secretly in love with the killer's wife, but she is loyal to her husband, so the doctor is planning to have something go wrong in the operation, killing the convict and making the wife available?"

"What are you talking about?" Shawn said.

"The same thing you are," Gus said. "*General Hospital* circa 1991."

"They really did run out of steam, didn't they?" Shawn said. "I mean, after you've seen Robin Scorpio befriending space aliens, how are you supposed to take it seriously when she says she's HIV-positive? Not that I ever watched soap operas, of course."

"Right, me neither," Gus said.

"Anyway, the real point is that the killer won't be getting away at all, because we'll be going with him," Shawn said. "And we know who he is."

"We do?"

"Didn't I just get done telling you we did?" Shawn said.

"You told me you did," Gus said. "But you didn't say who it was. And I'm not getting into any aircraft until you do."

Shawn let out a deep sigh. "You're taking a lot of the fun out of this," he said, but Gus' sharp gaze didn't waver. "Fine, it's Shark Boy."

"William Shatner?" Gus said, then remembered he hadn't had a chance to share his nicknames with Shawn. "I mean, Morton Mathis? How do you know?"

"The first part was easy," Shawn said. "He's wearing a watch that looks like it costs more than your car." Shawn glanced down at the Timex on his wrist. "Of course, so am I. But his looks like it costs more than a good car—until you notice that the leather strap is actually plastic. It's a cheap knockoff. His tan is sprayed on. There was a dried water spot on his silk tie where he tried to wash off a stain instead of spending a few dollars on dry cleaning, and his manicure is weeks old. He's not used to getting them, or he'd never have let it get chipped like that."

"That's how you knew he was a recent transplant," Gus said. "But what makes you think he's the killer?"

"It was the way he reacted when he thought I was reading his mind," Shawn said. "He panicked. But there was nothing I was saying that everyone in the room didn't already know. They'd all been here when he arrived at the firm; it wasn't a secret he was from out of town. And the fact that he hasn't won a big case since he got here is the kind of statistic that every lawyer in a firm like this knows. He was afraid I was going to reveal something they didn't know. Which means he's got a secret."

"Maybe he watches *Supernanny*," Gus said.

"Yes, that's it," Shawn said. "He's got bad taste in reality television. Or he's a killer with recent blood on his poorly manicured hands. Either way, we're going to be right by his side until we know for sure."

At first this sounded reassuring—at least until Gus thought it through. "We're going to be right by his side in a tiny cabin hundreds of feet in the air."

Shawn ignored the obvious implications. "And then we're going to be with him at some fabulous resort," Shawn said. "And we'll have to stick with him wherever he goes. To the pool, to the spa, to the five-star restaurant. We'll make the sacrifice."

"What makes you think we're going to some fabulous resort?" Gus said.

"It's a corporate retreat," Shawn said. "Remember the one you went on?"

Several years ago Gus' pharmaceuticals company had hosted a retreat for its entire sales force at the Four Seasons in Santa Barbara. Gus had spent three of the most glorious days of his life sipping fruity concoctions by the pool while flotillas of waiters came by to offer gleaming silver trays piled high with the best finger food he'd ever tasted. It wasn't until the end of the weekend that he realized he'd been supposed to sit through a series of seminars and training sessions, and that his failure to do so meant he'd never be invited back for another retreat.

"That was completely different," Gus said.

"Sure, a pharmaceuticals company has to spend some of its money actually making products, so they can't blow it all on their retreat," Shawn said. "What kind of expenses does a law firm have besides legal pads? Because if you buy them by the ten-pack, you'd be surprised how cheap they are. Which means they can put on one hell of a weekend."

Gus was sure there was something wrong in Shawn's reasoning. It all sounded so perfect, so appealing that there had to be a catch. But as he worked it over in his mind, there was nothing that stuck out. Maybe they had finally found something too good to be true that wasn't.

"Let's go catch a killer," Gus said.

"Right after we catch some shrimp."

Shawn tossed the manila envelope back on the table. Files scattered its length.

"Don't you think we might need those?" Gus said.

"For what?" Shawn said. "We already know who our killer is. What else could possibly be in that envelope that we'd need?"

"Maybe there's a second killer," Gus said.

Shawn glared at him as if he'd just handed him a surgeon general's warning that cocktail sauce causes cancer. Then he let out an exaggerated sigh, marched back to the table, and scooped all the files together, shoving them back in the manila envelope.

"Happy now?" he said. "You can read these when I'm checking out the previews on Spectravision."

Gus was happy. As they left the conference room, he was filled with a feeling of great contentment. This case had started out as a chore, turned into a nightmare, and now was looking like it was going to be the best job they'd ever tackled. To go on a luxury retreat and reveal a killer while they were there; people shelled out small fortunes for murder mystery weekends like that. Only this one was real—and they'd be getting paid. Gus couldn't imagine anything better.

He might have, though, if he'd noticed the other paper that had fallen out of the envelope when Shawn tossed it on the table. Unfortunately, the glossy brochure had slid along the polished surface and fallen to the floor, where neither of them saw it.

So Gus never saw the photos of the barren mountaintop, or the tiny raft swamped by enormous waves, or the string of climbers hanging from a line pitoned into a sheer cliff face. He never read the slogan "A bond that will never break." And he never saw the name of the company that had put the brochure together:

High Mountain Wilderness Retreats.

Chapter Twenty-Seven

Gus had always wanted to ride in a helicopter. If he had ever put together a list of things he wanted to do before he died, the chopper flight would probably come in no lower than number seven, right below "Win the Tour de France" and just above "Make up a list of things to do before you die."

But no helicopter ride he had ever imagined came close to this one. Because all the helicopters he'd ever imagined were drawn from some kind of objective reality. And Gus' reality never included the kind of fantasies that only the truly rich indulge in.

From the outside it looked like any large chopper. But once the passenger door slid open, Gus and Shawn were staring into the most opulent living room they had ever seen. The walls and deep armchairs were covered in a fabric woven by the only company in the world so exclusive that it became famous for keeping Oprah out. A giant flat-screen dominated the front of the passenger compartment; a Sub-Zero Wine Captain filled with every conceivable beverage nestled below it, alongside a cabinet of stemware Gus suspected was Baccarat.

What was most remarkable about the helicopter didn't become apparent until the doors had closed and they started to lift off the ground. Gus was expecting the ride to be so deafeningly loud that conversation would be impossible except for a few shouted exchanges. But the chopper's cabin was no louder than that of his Echo.

Not that the silence made conversation any more appealing to the passengers. As soon as the lawyers belted themselves into their armchairs, each pulled out an iPhone or a Black-Berry and started typing as if they were afraid their thumbs were going to be amputated as soon as they landed. If they were excited to be going on this retreat, they certainly didn't show it. None of them had even changed out of office attire, or in the case of Jade Greenway, her enveloping green aura. You'd think at least one guy would have slipped into his Tommy Ba-hamas to be ready to relax on arrival. But they might as well have been flying off to take the world's longest series of depo-sitions.

Gus was content to ride in luxurious quiet all the way to wherever they were going. He could use this time to study the files Rushton had given them. At first he was concerned that the lawyers would notice he was reading up on them and de-mand to know why. But ten minutes into the flight not one of them had even glanced up from their devices long enough to acknowledge that he was in the cabin. Gus flipped open the tray table from his armrest and started to page through the file.

It was every bit as exciting as he would have expected a law firm personnel file to be: a collection of CVs, each with a pic-ture stapled to it. Gus was hoping that Rushton might have included a little note here and there to give them some inside information, but there was nothing.

The first CV belonged to Kiri, whose real name was Gwen-dolyn Shrike. Gus was not surprised to discover that she was the firm's chief litigator. He was right when he assumed she was a warrior, even if her primary weapon was not the long-sword but the longer brief. She had an almost unbroken record of wins, and she'd thrice won the California Bar Association's Litigator of the Year award, along with two nominations for something called The Piranha, apparently handed out by the less formal Trial Lawyers League.

But it was her nonprofessional affiliations that Gus found fascinating—and a little terrifying. Gwendolyn wasn't only a

warrior in the courtroom. She'd fenced on the California state
team and had made it all the way to the nationals. She had
medals in archery, both with the crossbow and the long. And she
held black belts in three different martial arts. Gus hoped fer-
vently that Shawn was right about Mathis being the killer; he
had no desire to go up against this woman.

Suppressing a shudder at the thought, Gus flipped a page
and saw Doc Savage's bright smile beaming up at him. To
Gus' surprise, he read that Savage actually was the guy's family name, although his first name was not Doc but Kirk. His
résumé was brief and to the point: Yale Law, followed by ten
years at a New York firm, then another ten at Rushton, Morelock, as its lead tax attorney. He'd donated a lot of time to
various environmental concerns and had chaired a benefit to
clean up the bay.

Captain Hook was born Reginald Balowsky and he special-
ized in labor law, although from what Gus could glean from
the résumé, he was never actually on the side of labor. He'd
won awards from manufacturers groups and various chambers
of commerce, all of which hailed him as a "champion of
business." He didn't seem to have any outside affiliations or
interests—or at least none that would fit comfortably on a lawyer's CV.

Turning the page, Gus was surprised to discover that Tinkerbell, born Jade Greenway, was also a litigator. He had seen the
killer instinct in Gwendolyn; he could have seen it from the
helicopter if she'd stayed on the ground. But Jade seemed so
much softer and less secure than her colleague. Her outside
interests confirmed this suspicion. She did a lot of work with
pet rescue organizations, she volunteered at a local food bank,
and she'd founded something called the Society for the Preser-
vation of English Folk Songs. If Gus had had to guess, he
would have said she was a researcher, and that if she ever did
set foot in a courtroom it was to handle pro bono cases arbi-
trating conflicts between puppies and unicorns. From her CV,
though, it looked like she had taken on several multinational
corporations, and won. At least that explained why Gwendolyn
seemed to despise her so intensely; these two would be com-

peting for dominance in the same field, and Gus was pretty certain that Rushton did nothing to discourage that sort of rivalry.

Finally Gus turned to the page that interested him the most: Morton Mathis, the man Shawn had identified as the killer of both Ellen Svaco and Archie Kane. His CV confirmed what Gus already knew about the man: He was a recent transfer from Detroit, where he'd been a rising star in the District Attorney's Office. There was no indication of what had made him decide to leave the public sector or to move out to California, and his outside interests didn't provide a clue—he had been involved in a capital campaign for the Detroit Opera and had chaired a fund-raiser to produce a performance of Wagner's *Ring* cycle. But that wasn't nearly as interesting as his legal specialty at the firm. He focused almost entirely on issues of technology— not surprising, considering his undergraduate degree in computer engineering.

Shawn was right. He had to be. Morton Mathis was the only lawyer in the firm who had substantial involvement in the high-tech field. He'd have an understanding of the kind of work they were doing at JPL, and he'd know who was in the market to buy it once it was stolen. There was only one problem with the theory that Gus could see: Mathis had joined the firm six months ago. Before that he'd never worked or lived in the state. How had he made the contacts at JPL and set up his smuggling scheme so quickly?

Those were questions that could best be answered over poolside mai tais, Gus reasoned. Now that they were certain who their target was, they could take their time reeling him in, delivering him to Rushton just when the helicopter came to take them home.

Gus stashed the files away in the pocket on the side of his seat and looked out the window as the helicopter soared above Santa Barbara and then over the mountains to the east of the city. It wasn't the first time he'd seen his hometown from the air—he'd flown out of the local airport more than once— but this view was nothing like the brief glimpses you could get out of the window of a jet. They were flying level and low, and he could see everything spread out below him as if they were floating in a hot-air balloon.

Gus wanted to pull Shawn aside and whisper what he'd discovered about Mathis. But the cabin was small, and there really was no "aside" in it. And Shawn was busy doing his own research, anyway. What Gus had learned from files, Shawn seemed determined to learn firsthand: in this case, that Gwendolyn was not someone they wanted to tangle with.

"Have you been on one of these retreats before?" Shawn asked her.

Her icy blue eyes barely flicked up at him from her iPhone. "Yes."

Shawn waited for her to fill in the details, but the only filling she did was in an e-mail. "What was it like?"

This time she didn't look up at all. "I survived."

"I can see how that might be a challenge," Shawn said. "I once ate so many shrimp I had to be rushed to the emergency room."

If she appreciated his humor, she didn't show it. But she did teach Gus a little more about the luxurious appointments in the cabin. Until she swiveled her chair so that its back faced Shawn, Gus had no idea the chairs weren't fixed facing forward. He found the unlocking button below the armrest and turned his seat to get a better look out the window.

Hundreds of feet below, the ground rushed by in a blur of brown. They seemed to be flying over the Central Valley. Gus tried to calculate where they might be going. If they'd been flying with the ocean on their right, he knew they'd be heading south to L.A. or San Diego or even Baja. With the ocean on their left, he'd have guessed San Francisco or the Napa Valley. Maybe even the northern coast. Plenty of resorts in either direction. But they were clearly heading east, and the only luxury destination Gus could think of in that direction was Las Vegas. That route would take them over desert, though, and while the ground below them was dry, it was clearly farmland.

Gus was trying to re-create the map of California in his mind when he heard a voice behind him.

"I know why you're here," the voice said.

Gus swiveled his chair to see the man he had named Doc Savage leaning down into Shawn's face.

"I'm glad someone does," Shawn said. "Because I thought I was supposed to be collecting all the World Rings, but now I discover that whoever gathers them all has to be sacrificed to harvest their power, and even as a hedgehog, I can tell that's a bad deal."

Gus glanced up at the flat panel in the front of the cabin and confirmed that Shawn had turned on a Wii console and fired up a video game.

"Rushton's done this kind of thing before." If Savage noticed that Shawn was staring over his shoulder at the flat-screen, he didn't let that slow him down.

"Trapped Erazor in his lamp?" Shawn said. "Can you tell me how? Because I'm having trouble, even after turning into Darkspine Sonic."

"Setting a spy in our midst," Savage said. "That's the real reason he kept Archie Kane around all those years. It wasn't because Archie was actually good at anything, or that he ever performed a single task. He was there to make sure we knew Rushton was watching us at all times. Now he's cooked up this ridiculous story about Archie being dead, and here you are. It's this perfect little watertight story line, and we all have to pretend we believe it."

"You know what isn't watertight?" Shawn said. "The interior of a Town Car. Oh, and I guess you could add Archie Kane's nose and mouth, too."

Savage looked troubled. "You mean that story about Archie is real?"

"I don't know why you'd believe it from me if you wouldn't take it from your boss," Shawn said. "But his corpse looked pretty real to me."

Savage glanced over at Gus as if for confirmation. "Dead," Gus said.

"Then Rushton really has gone insane," Savage said after a long silence.

Gus tried to figure out what the Man of Bronze was talking

about. "Are you saying you think Mr. Rushton is responsible for Archie Kane's murder?"

"I'm not saying anything," Savage said. "But know this: We are all Rushton's pawns, even you. You may think you're above his game, but I guarantee you're not. So whatever happens in the next eight days, I will think of you two not as my enemies but as my brothers and do whatever I can to protect you."

"Will you remind me to put on sunscreen if I start to get red?" Shawn said. "Because I burn really easily."

"I will do whatever I can to keep you safe," Savage said. "And I hope, no matter what your instructions, you will do the same for me. Rushton may think this is a good time for games, but I don't."

He held Shawn's gaze for a full five seconds, then turned and gave Gus the same treatment. Then he broke off his gaze and went back to his seat across the cabin, pulled out his Black-Berry, and started thumbing.

"These guys take their retreats pretty seriously," Shawn said. "Or did the other drug reps talk like this at the Four Seasons?"

"I think one of them offered me a piña colada once," Gus said. "Then he realized I wasn't in management and couldn't help him get a promotion, so he stuck me with the tab."

"That is brutal," Shawn said. "No wonder the tan guy is so concerned about us."

Shawn turned back to the thorny problem of undoing the changes an evil genie had done in *The Arabian Nights*. Gus thought about grabbing another Wii control and joining the game, but he couldn't manage to be quite as worry-free as Shawn. He didn't understand much of what the lawyer had been hinting about, but it seemed increasingly apparent that the man who'd hired them was some kind of master manipulator. Shawn and Gus had thought they'd gotten exactly what they wanted from Rushton, but now Gus wasn't sure. What were they getting themselves into?

Gus twirled his chair towards the window as he tried to make sense of it all. But what he saw there only made him more confused. They had left the Central Valley behind them; if he craned his neck, he could see its edge far in the distance. But whatever they were flying over, it wasn't the approach to Las Vegas. There were no lights in the distance, no freeways filled with suckers speeding towards their inevitable fleecing.

What there was was . . . nothing.

Nothing, anyway, that belonged anywhere near a five-star luxury resort. There were rolling hills densely covered with pine forest. There were frequent outcroppings of granite. There were rivers and lakes, and Gus thought he saw a waterfall.

What there wasn't was any sign of human habitation. No houses. No buildings. No roads.

Gus did his best to call up that map of California in his head. If you flew out of Santa Barbara and headed east and then north, which was their trajectory as best as he could figure, you'd pass over farm towns like Lemoore and Hanford, and then you'd hit wilderness. And not wilderness like those parts of Santa Barbara where an old bungalow had been torn down but the plans for the McMansion hadn't been approved yet. This was real wilderness. Specifically the John Muir wilderness, almost six hundred thousand acres of nothing. And beyond that, more wilderness areas and two national parks, and then a lot of nothing, and then Death Valley, which was also a lot of nothing but was also hot enough to kill you in about ten minutes this time of year.

Gus would be the first to admit he wasn't a connoisseur of high-end luxury resorts, but he had never heard of one anywhere within hundreds of miles of where he assumed they were now. And even if there was one somewhere below them, it probably wouldn't have a lot of amenities, since there didn't seem to be any roads to supply them.

As Gus was trying to picture a place he'd actually want to stay in anywhere on a line between here and Toronto, the pilot's voice came over a sound system. "If you look out the left side of the cabin, you've got a great view of Mount Whitney, the highest mountain in the contiguous United States."

Gus was right about their location, but, he thought hopefully, maybe he'd been wrong about the purpose. This was probably just a sightseeing detour, a chance to give the lawyers a bit of spectacular scenery before taking them to the resort that was undoubtedly waiting for them in some civilized part of the world.

"For the person who bribed the employee at High Mountain Wilderness Retreats to get our destination and maps down the mountain, Mr. Rushton has a special message," the pilot continued. "Mount Whitney was just a decoy destination."

The chopper took a hard turn to the right. Gus had to grab the armrests of his chair to keep from falling to the floor like the crew of the *Enterprise* during a photon torpedo attack. When he'd recovered his equilibrium, he saw with horror that the ground was rushing straight up at them.

"This is your new destination," the pilot said as the helicopter lowered itself onto a rocky outcropping at the peak of another mountain. "Last stop. Everybody out."

Chapter Twenty-Eight

Henry and Rasmussen rode in silence all the way to Pasadena. Since the moment they'd left the dweeb's office, Rasmussen had spoken only twice—once to confirm that Arnold Svaco was indeed Ellen's cousin, her sole relative, and once to accuse Henry of violating every principle he'd taught Rasmussen to live by. Henry tried to retort that a policeman couldn't hope to get by with just the information he'd learned in junior high school, but one look at the pout on the officer's face told him not to bother.

Instead he spent the drive thinking through the case. He had no doubt that Ellen Svaco was the emotional force behind the Fluffy Foundation. The cat box, food, and toys in her house were all for a pet who'd been dead for half a decade; they must have constituted a shrine or a monument to his memory. But it was her cousin Arnold who was footing the bills. Why? And more important, how?

It wasn't that Arnold was rich. He made even less than Ellen had, under thirty thousand dollars a year working as a janitor for a contractor that cleaned government offices. Yet somehow in the last five years he'd managed to donate ten times his gross salary to Fluffy's memory.

So who was behind these donations—and why? Since the charity was actually paying out to pet owners, it didn't seem to be a money-laundering operation, or at least not a particularly efficient one.

And then there was the big question—why was Ellen Svaco killed? It couldn't have been for the money, because it appeared that she never had possession of it. Nothing about this case was making sense. Least of all Henry's temporary partner.

Henry pulled the car up outside a decaying bungalow in Northwest Pasadena. Its shingles were cracked, rain gutters sagging, and the lawn in front was a patch of dirt.

Rasmussen looked up from his hands for the first time since they'd left Santa Barbara. "This isn't the Pasadena Police Station," he said.

"Can't fault you on your observational skills," Henry said. "Arnold Svaco lives here."

"We need to check in with the locals," Rasmussen said. "We don't have jurisdiction."

"I don't have jurisdiction anywhere," Henry said. "I'm not on the Santa Barbara force. I'm just a private citizen stopping by the home of another private citizen to ask a few discreet questions. There's no law against that, is there?"

Rasmussen stared as if Henry had suggested executing Arnold Svaco, then dragging his body through the neighborhood behind the car. "If police don't treat each other with respect, then why should anyone else?" he said. "You taught me—"

"I know," Henry said. "But you were eleven years old at the time."

"Truth is truth, no matter what age you are," Rasmussen said.

"There are levels of complication that make sense only as you get older," Henry said. "It's like when you were little and your parents told you about where children come from. It was true, but there was a lot they didn't explain at the time."

Rasmussen crossed his arms across his chest angrily. "I didn't have parents," he said. "I grew up in foster care. I never had any kind of role model at all—until I met Officer Friendly. I thought he was honest."

In another circumstance Henry might have felt bad about disillusioning this kid. But he wasn't a little boy anymore; he carried a badge and a gun. He needed to toughen himself up, and fast.

"I'm going to knock on that door," Henry said. "You can come with me or you can drive away and visit the Pasadena Police Department alone. Up to you."

Henry left the car and went up the cracked concrete walkway. The white picket gate nearly came off in his hands when he opened it, and the porch stairs sagged alarmingly under his feet. The only architectural element on the house that seemed functional at all was the set of iron bars on all the windows. Henry rapped sharply on the warped door and called out, "Arnold! Hey, it's me!"

Henry ducked behind the doorframe just in case Arnold Svaco's answer came in the form of a gunshot. But the only sound was a creak as the door swung open under his touch.

Henry's senses went on full alert. No one installs iron bars on his windows and then leaves the door open. He waved urgently for Rasmussen to join him, but the officer looked away and pretended not to see.

Heart pounding and hand reaching for a gun that hadn't been on his hip for years, Henry pushed the door open.

Arnold Svaco's possessions didn't have a lot in common with his cousin's. Where she had almost nothing, Arnold seemed to own everything he'd ever seen in any store. There were flat-screen TVs and an elaborate stereo; there were statues in marble and bronze; there were fish tanks that looked like they'd come from the Monterey Bay Aquarium. There were four leather couches and two armchairs; past the living room Henry could see a dining room table and eight matching chairs that must have cost half of Arnold's gross yearly salary.

But there was one way in which the two Svaco households were identical. Because everything Arnold owned was smashed and scattered around the floor.

And Arnold lay in the middle of it all, dead.

Chapter Twenty-Nine

Gus' fingernails dug into the soft leather of his armchair. His muscles were screaming with pain, but he would not relax his hands. Not until the chopper lifted off again and took him out of this hellhole.

"That's a good grip you've got there," Shawn said. "If you apply a little more pressure, maybe your flesh will bond with the leather of the seat and you'll become one with the chopper. Then they'll never get you out."

"If that's what it takes," Gus said.

"But if you're going to expend all this energy to stay on board, you might as well wait until you actually need to," Shawn said. "Like when the door is open."

Gus lifted his eyes from their firm fix on the floor and saw that the door hadn't slid open yet. None of the lawyers had gotten out of their seats. In fact, they were all still jabbing away at their miniature keyboards.

Gus forced his fingers to relax and felt a wave of relief run up both arms. "They don't seem worried that they're about to be dumped out in the wilderness."

"Which is a sign that we shouldn't be, either," Shawn said. "They know Rushton a lot better than we do. He probably plays this kind of prank on them all the time. We'll sit here for a few minutes, and then once everyone has had a chance to panic, we'll lift off and head to our real destination."

Gus nodded. That made sense. It was the only thing that made sense. Because the other lawyers were just sitting there working away, as if they knew enough not to be alarmed. He loosened his death grip on the armrest a little more and felt the blood tingling painfully back into his fingers.

Until there was a thump from outside and the helicopter rocked on its skids. "What was that?" he demanded.

Shawn glanced over Gus and out the window. "Nothing."

"That wasn't nothing," Gus said. "I know what nothing feels like. It feels like nothing. That felt like something. Which means it couldn't be nothing."

"It's just the pilot," Shawn said, checking the view out the window again.

"He's leaving?" Gus said. His breath was coming in short gasps now. "The pilot is abandoning his helicopter? How can we get out of here? Does anyone know how to fly a chopper?"

"Relax," Shawn said. "He's not leaving. He's just . . ."

"Just what?"

"Unpacking."

Gus forced himself to turn his chair so that he was facing the window. The pilot had opened a cargo door at the back of the chopper and was pulling out a series of large backpacks.

"What are those for?" Gus said, not wanting to hear the answer from Shawn any more than he would accept it from his own brain.

"I believe they're called backpacks," Shawn said. "You strap them on your back and carry things in them."

"Maybe you do," Gus said, his fingers reflexively clutching the armrest again. He risked another glance out the window. The pilot was closing the cargo door. At his feet was a line of eight backpacks: seven made of beige nylon stretched over metal frames, the last in blindingly bright green.

And still the rest of the lawyers didn't seem to notice that anything out of the ordinary was happening. They kept texting away. Until the flat-screen went on in an explosion of static.

Oliver Rushton smiled warmly at them from the safety of

the TV. Gus felt an irrational burst of rage. He wanted to reach into the screen and pull Rushton through, wheelchair and all, and leave him on this desolate mountaintop.

"Greetings, friends," Rushton said. "I understand that the area you're in is one of the loveliest parts of California. I wish I could be there with you today."

"I wish you were here instead of me," Gus muttered.

"It's a constant challenge for me to come up with fun, creative, exciting retreats for this team, but I think you'll agree that this is the best one ever," Rushton said. "Because this retreat will not only test your strength, your intelligence, and your stamina, but it will also forge new bonds of friendship and trust. Here at the top of this mountain you are all individuals with your own agendas. By the time you reach the bottom, you will all be a family."

"I had a family once," Gwendolyn said. "I didn't like it much."

"So she auctioned off their organs and sold the rest off for medical research," Balowsky said.

"I made a sacrifice," Gwendolyn said, pointedly refusing to waste a glance at her colleague. "I chose to put my career—I chose to put the needs of this firm—over my own personal life. And that remains my intent. I want to work for this firm, I want to work for you, Oliver. But I don't need these people to be my family."

"I understand," Rushton said.

Gus had been assuming that Rushton's appearance was a pretaped video. But of course he was speaking to them live via videoconferencing. Which was excellent news, because it would give Gus a chance to plead his way out of this.

"But a firm can't work as a group of individuals," Rushton continued. "You need to be able to function as a team. That's why I've designed this retreat. Because, as I said, by the time you reach the bottom of the mountain, you will be a family. Or you will all be dead."

Chapter Thirty

For the first time, the other lawyers looked as if they'd realized this wasn't just another bit of eccentricity from their
boss. Maybe it was the way Rushton had emphasized that last
word. Or maybe it was the sound of the helicopter door sliding
open and the pilot stepping into the cabin. Possibly it was the
sight of the gun holstered on the pilot's thigh. Whatever the
reason, Rushton now had everyone's undivided attention.

"Sorry if that sounded a little melodramatic," Rushton
chuckled. "But these mountains are harsh, and nature is unfor-
giving. You will all have to learn to work together if you want
to find your way down."

"Or we could just use our GPS," Gwendolyn said, raising
her iPhone the way Tanya Roberts had wielded her sword
against the temple guards to free King Zed.

"Yes, you could," Rushton said. "I would prefer that you
didn't. But of course I can't stop you. When this call is over,
you'll all step out of the helicopter, and there you will find your
backpacks. Inside each pack is everything you will need for
the five-day journey down the mountain, and supplies for one
more day just in case you decide to take a little extra time to
enjoy the scenery."

"I don't mind a little nature hike." It was Savage, and indeed his muscles seemed to be on the verge of rippling right out of his body in anticipation. "But as much as I love my Bruno Maglis, they don't provide a lot of stability, ankle protection, or waterproofing. I might as well be barefoot. And that leaves me in substantially better shape than the two women who are wearing heels."

"That's an excellent point," Rushton said. "And it's been taken care of. Hector"—at this point, the pilot gave them all a brief nod to introduce himself—"has not only suitable hiking shoes, but clothes as well for all of you. Once this call is terminated, you will each be given a few moments alone to change."

There was a low murmur in the cabin. To his shock, Gus thought it sounded like gratitude, when it should have been the angry mutterings of the mob about to storm the castle with torches and pitchforks.

"One more thing about the wardrobe change," Rushton said. "Hector will take the clothes you're wearing now back to Santa Barbara, where they will be professionally cleaned and left for you in your offices. He will also take all your belongings, including any handheld devices you might have with you."

Now the muttering in the cabin sounded sufficiently angry.

"I'm not giving up my cell phone," Mathis sputtered. "I'm using that to find my way down."

"It's certainly your choice," Rushton said. "But Hector will not give you your clothes, shoes, and backpack until you have given him everything you've brought with you. If it's worth walking down in business attire to keep your GPS, I won't try to stop you. Just make sure to avoid the sharp, pointy rocks on the trail. They can go right through a leather sole. And don't worry about not having any food. I'm sure your colleagues will be happy to share theirs with you."

Mathis looked crushed. If the rest of the lawyers were surprised by any of this, they weren't letting it show on their faces. If anything, they looked slightly relieved, as if they'd been expecting something even worse. Gus wanted to grab them, to scream into their ears. Didn't they understand there was nothing worse?

"But you won't need a GPS, anyway," Rushton said with a reassuring smile. "You've got a map. A highly detailed topographical map with the fastest, safest route marked out."

"If you're giving us maps, why not let us have our GPS as well?" Savage said. "To a skilled hiker, one is as good as the other."

"I didn't say, 'maps,'" Rushton said. "I said, 'map.' One of you, and only one of you, has the map."

"Who?" Mathis demanded.

"It better not be Gwendolyn," Jade said. "Because she'll take off and leave us the first chance she has."

"Not us," Balowsky said. "You, definitely, but not the rest of us. Not as long as there's a chance she might need some help."

"It might be Gwendolyn," Rushton said. "Or it might be you, Jade. It could be any one of you. The thing is, that person is the only one who knows. And if he or she reveals that fact to anyone else, every one of you will be fired on your return."

"How would you know?" Savage said.

"Sorry, everyone will be fired except the first person to tell me about the cheating," Rushton said. "Does that explain how I would know?"

Apparently, it did, because all the lawyers were glaring at one another suspiciously.

"I don't want you to take this the wrong way," Rushton continued. "I'm not trying to kill you here. The entire point of this trip is for you to learn to work together as a team. That's why I've given the map to one person, who is forbidden to admit having it. You will all need to work together to reach a consensus on your route, and it will be up to the map bearer to convince the others of the right way to go. If you function well as a team, there shouldn't be a problem."

"And if there is a problem, we'll all be dead and you can hire new people," Gwendolyn said.

"How could I ever hope to replace your feisty spirit, Gwendolyn?" Rushton said. "No, I'm not going to let anything happen to you. In fact, nothing will make me happier than to see you all march together into the lodge at the bottom of the mountain in five days, where there will be an unbelievable celebration waiting for you. But if something should go wrong, you will not be alone. Each one of your packs has an emergency beacon that will transmit your GPS location once it's been turned on. There will be people monitoring you at all times. If one of the beacons goes on, you will all be rescued by a search party and the retreat will be over."

What does a loophole sound like? Gus was sure he heard five lawyers all diving for the same one. But Rushton wasn't done.

"And so will your careers at Rushton, Morelock," he said. "If we have to rescue just one of you, all of you will be fired. Because, again, this is about working as a team. And as a team there is nothing you can't do—especially getting down off this mountain in five days. Now, Hector is ready with your new wardrobes, if you'd like to take your turns stepping into the tent he has erected outside to change."

There was a moment of hesitation; then Savage leaped up out of his seat. "I'll go first," he said, and followed the pilot out of the helicopter. The others gave their handhelds a last longing look, then followed him out.

Gus didn't move. He was never going to move. He'd simply sit there, securely belted to the seat, until the pilot had to take off. He wasn't a part of this law firm, anyway. He and Shawn already knew who the killer was. Their job was over.

For the first time since he'd seen the backpacks, Gus risked a glance at Shawn. It wasn't that he was afraid his best friend would be as unsympathetic to his panic as he had been at Descanso Gardens; it was just the opposite. At Descanso, Shawn knew there was no real danger, and he tried to demonstrate that by acting unconcerned. Now Gus was certain that if he looked over at Shawn he'd see the one thing that was guaranteed to make him feel worse: real worry.

But Gus' state of mind seemed to be the last thing on his partner's mind. Shawn's gaze was fixed on Oliver Rushton's face. "Good news," Shawn said. "We know who the killer is."

"I'm not interested in what you know," Rushton said. "Only in what you can prove."

"We'll give you a full debrief just as soon as we're back in your office," Shawn said. "The flight shouldn't take too long, although I think we'll need to stop to use the little boys' room along the way."

"I'm afraid that meeting will have to wait until you have actual proof," Rushton said. "I need you to accompany my employees on this retreat. After all, if one of them is a killer, I'm depending on you to protect the rest."

"The best way to protect them is to bring them down in the helicopter," Shawn said.

"Apparently we disagree," Rushton said. "If only there were some way to come to an amicable resolution of our differences. Oh, wait, there is. You agreed to serve as my in-house investigative department, which means you belong to me. And if you don't take part in this retreat, I will sue your firm out of existence."

Rushton hit a button on his desk, and the screen went blank.

Gus risked another glance at his friend and this time he found exactly what he most feared: Shawn was giving him a look filled with sympathy.

"We don't have to do this," Shawn said.

"You heard what he said."

"So he sues us," Shawn said. "What's the worst thing that happens? He wins a judgment for gazillions of dollars against Psych. The firm goes out of business, and he gets nothing."

"But we are Psych," Gus said.

"We'll start a new firm," Shawn said. "If we can't call it Psych, we'll call it something else. Ic, maybe. Or Out. There are lots of things that come after 'Psych.'"

Gus felt a rush of warmth for Shawn. That his best friend was willing to sacrifice the only career he'd ever loved just to spare him some misery was overwhelming. So much so that it was even able to overwhelm his fear.

"Not a chance." Gus peeled his hands off the armrest, then used one of them to unbuckle and fling off his seat belt. "Let's get out there and kick some mountain butt."

Chapter Thirty-One

Now it starts, Gus thought. Any second now my heart rate is going to jump up, my breathing will turn into a series of harsh gasps, my pulse will become ragged and thready—and I don't even know what that means except they always say it on TV before the really bad stuff starts to happen. Then the panic will take over completely, and I'll start to run blindly. The last thing I'll feel is the empty air under my left foot as I step off that cliff . . .

There was certainly plenty of reason for Gus to panic. They were stranded in the wilderness. And this wasn't the parklike forest of his recurring dream. This was the top of a granite mountain hundreds of feet above the tree line. Wherever he looked, he saw a vast sea of wild country spread out below him, broken only by the jagged peaks of the rest of the mountain range. It would take a day of hiking just to get to the kind of green wasteland he was used to.

And Gus' rescue—his only hope for rescue—the glorious, luxurious helicopter that had brought them to this high-altitude hell, was nothing but a tiny speck disappearing in the distance. It was already indistinguishable from the enormous birds of prey that circled over the mountain—no doubt vultures waiting to pick the flesh off his broken carcass.

Gus took a breath, expecting his throat to close up and choke off his airway. To his surprise, clear, clean mountain air flowed down easily into his lungs. It flooded his bloodstream as his heart pounded slowly and steadily. It took him a moment to realize exactly what was going on here: He wasn't panicking.

Not only was he not panicking, but he actually felt better here at the top of this mountain than he had in days. The hiking shoes Hector had given him were so firm and springy that Gus had to force his legs not to start walking. His new outfit was even better. He had bright blue tees in long and short sleeves, both made of some miracle material that was supposed to wick all moisture, body odor, and, according to the label, bad karma away from his body. His shorts looked like generic cargos, but they were breathable, water- and wind-resistant, and also spent their spare time wicking bad things away. Best of all were the zippers that ran around the bottom of each leg; in his pack were extensions that would turn the shorts into long pants in case it got cold. Even the socks seemed to have been woven by wizards. His feet had never felt so snug.

And he'd taken a moment to glance through the backpack that had his name on it. There were several changes of those wonderful socks and underwear, a Swiss Army knife, a full first-aid kit, two one-liter bottles of water, and a sleeping bag and pad strapped to the pack's bottom. A fat, yellow plastic cylinder hung off a clip on the pack's frame; Gus realized this must be the emergency beacon. And then there was the food. Lots and lots of freeze-dried food. Gus had tried freeze-dried food before—his parents had hidden a stash of powdered eggs, pemmican bars, and Tang in their basement during the Cuban missile crisis, and Gus had sampled it all when he and Shawn found the stash decades later—but what he had in his pack was nothing like that. He had kung pao chicken and beef Stroganoff and shrimp Newburg and huevos rancheros. For side dishes he had peas and corn and bacon-infused mashed potatoes; desserts included fudge brownies and banana cream pie and blackberry cobbler. In their current state they all weighed just a little bit less than nothing, but once Gus added water, it would be like he had the entire buffet from a high-end Indian casino.

Gus was feeling so good it took him a moment to realize why

Shawn looked so grim as he walked over to him. It wasn't just the hazard-warning red of his high-tech T-shirt; he was seriously troubled.

"You sure you're okay?" Shawn said.

"I'm not going to let something stupid like a recurring dream get me down."

Shawn studied him carefully. "You be sure to tell me if you begin to hallucinate. Because I know how disturbing a recurring nightmare can be."

"That's the second time you've said that," Gus said. "But you never told me what your dream is."

"Let's just assume it has something to do with pudding, and leave it there," Shawn said. "Anyway, if you're really okay, the others are ready to start walking. The only thing stopping them is that they're still fighting over which of six different paths they should take."

"Six?" Gus glanced over to see the lawyers in heated debate. Even though they had all changed out of their suits and into the same kind of comfortable sportswear that Gus had on, but in varying colors, they still looked like they were arguing in front of a judge. Except, of course, for Jade, whose short, formfitting emerald dress made her look like Rima the Jungle Girl arguing with the rest of the Super Friends. "There are only five of them."

"Balowsky was fighting for the southern route, but when it looked like Mathis was going to agree with him, he changed to an eastern path just to keep the fight going for a little longer."

Shawn moved closer to Gus to make sure they could talk without being overheard. "I checked my pack," he said, "and it looks like we've got enough food for six days, just like Rushton said. Unfortunately it's going to be two weeks before these people can agree which way to go. Then it will merely be a matter of which side of the mountain to roll our bones down."

"Maybe we should just choose one and go," Gus said. "See who follows us."

"That would be a good idea if either of us had the map," Shawn said. "I have an alternative plan."

"What's that?"

Shawn fingered the emergency beacon hanging off Gus' pack. "ET phone home."

"And then ET get sued out of existence," Gus said.

"Not if we unmask Mathis as the killer first," Shawn said. "He'll run, we won't be able to catch him, and the exercise is ruined."

"Along with our agency," Gus said. "I have a better idea. We figure out which way to go, and we use the day's hike to confirm that Mathis is our killer. Then, once we've got incontrovertible proof, we use the beacon."

"You sure about this?" Shawn asked, studying Gus' face for any sign of panic, despair, or hallucination.

"I'm really fine," Gus said. "I guess being out in the wilderness is like going to the dentist. The anticipation is much worse than the reality."

"Funny, I've always found that having people jam razor-sharp pokers into my gums a lot worse than thinking about it," Shawn said. "But if you're really okay with this, then I guess it's time to start moving."

Chapter Thirty-Two

Gus slipped his arms through the straps of his backpack and shrugged it tight against his shoulderblades. Once he'd fastened the chest and waist straps, the pack balanced so well it seemed weightless, and when he stood up, it felt like it was being lifted by a skyhook. "Let's go."

They walked over to the clutch of lawyers bickering across the clearing.

"Why can't you understand this?" Mathis was saying, beads of sweat dripping down from his artificially tan hairline. "The only thing to our east is the desert. If we go down that way, we're going to die in the wilderness."

"If we don't stop before we hit Nevada," Savage said, not bothering to hide the contempt in his voice. "We're hiking down the mountain, and when we reach our destination, Rushton will be waiting for us. He knows we're not skilled mountaineers, so he's going to want us to take the safest and easiest path down. If you look, you'll see that's the eastern route."

Gus looked in the direction Savage was pointing. There was a faint trail that threaded its way through a lunar landscape of enormous boulders before disappearing into a pine forest a long way below. In other words, it looked exactly like the paths leading off in every other direction from the summit.

"What makes you think the eastern route is the easiest?"

Gwendolyn demanded. "If you have the map, you have a moral obligation to share that information with us."

"And then you'll have a moral obligation to share that information with Rushton," Balowsky said. "You're not fooling anyone."

Jade looked like she was about to burst into tears. Gus wondered if they would have a green tint, too. "Guys, we need to make a decision," she whined. "We should just strike out. If there was a wrong way, Rushton would have told us. So let's go west. Or north. No, let's split the difference and go northwest."

"It's a simple fact of natural law," Savage said, ignoring Jade as if she were a bright green mosquito. "The eastern side of this mountain gets far less rain than the western side. Less rain means less runoff, which means less erosion, which means an easier hike down."

"Hike down to nowhere," Mathis said. "When we were flying up here, I saw buildings on the southern approach. That must have been the park entrance, and that's going to be where we can expect to find other people."

"And you know this because you're such an expert on California, Mr. Detroit?" Gwendolyn said. "You do a lot of mountaineering in Motown?"

"I've got eyes and a strong desire to survive," Mathis said. "And unlike some of the people here, I'd rather be alive than see someone else die."

"Guys," Jade said again. "We don't have that many hours before it gets dark. We've got to start moving."

Again, her voice seemed to have the same effect on the others as a mosquito's whine. Shawn stepped up to the pack. "Do any of you have any balloons?" he said. "Because as long as you're putting out all this hot air we could use it to float down the mountain."

Even with that friendly opening, the assembled lawyers did not seem pleased to have Shawn join them.

"You're the psychic," Gwendolyn said. "Why don't you just beam us off the mountain."

"You know, that's a common misconception about my powers," Shawn said. "Believe it or not, I can't actually teleport anyone."

"That's the one thing I would believe about you," Balowsky said. "Oh, and that even in this vast, trackless wilderness you're a waste of space that should be used for something more beneficial to society. Like another rock."

"Yeah, I get that a lot," Shawn said. "If I could only be useful. Like the person who's got the map."

"We don't know who that is," Gwendolyn snapped. "If we did, we could be halfway down the mountain by now."

"And you'd be two-thirds of the way down, running to tell Rushton before anyone else could," Savage said.

"Let's not bicker," Shawn said. "Or maybe I should say let's not bicker anymore."

"We are having a serious intellectual argument about the proper route to take," Balowsky said. "We are adressing the issues one at a time, searching for answers to the problems they present, and coming up with a solution. We do not bicker."

"He's right," Gus said, stepping up next to Shawn. "Once you charge more than two hundreds bucks an hour, it's not bickering anymore. It's deliberation."

"Two-hundred-dollar deliberation is fine if you're suing over who is responsible for a traffic accident," Shawn said. "But when it comes to climbing down a mountain, I prefer a two-dollar map. And one of us has it."

"What good does that do us?" Gwendolyn said. "Whoever has the map can't reveal that fact. And as long as that person can't prove he or she is arguing from real knowledge and not from some half-assed Boy Scout training, there's no reason to value anyone's word over anyone else's."

"Rushton said it was so you'd learn to trust each other," Shawn said. "But I've known you all for less than a day and I know that's never going to happen. So he must have had something else in mind. Maybe we should reexamine exactly what he said."

"I believe his actual words were to the effect that if the map bearer revealed the map to the rest of us, we'd all be fired," Gus said.

"Yes," Shawn said. "If the map bearer reveals that he or she has the map, that's it. But he didn't say that anything bad would happen if someone else revealed who had the map."

"So what are we supposed to do?" Mathis said. "Tear through each other's packs?"

Gus slapped his forehead. "If only we had a psychic here who could tell us who was carrying the map."

"Why, that would be a fine thing," Shawn said. "But where would we look for such a psychic?"

"We wouldn't have to," Gus said, "if Mr. Rushton hired a psychic detective and sent him along on this trip."

"Wait a minute," Shawn said. "Didn't he do something just like that? If only we could remember who that psychic was, maybe he could help us out."

"Maybe he could help us by shutting up and letting us determine the right trail," Savage said. "Which happens to be the eastern one."

Before the arguments could start again, Shawn pressed his fingertips to his temple and squeezed his eyes shut. "I need you all to blank your minds," he said. "Don't think of anything. Let the vibrations flow."

"There's something flowing, all right, and it isn't vibrations," Balowsky said. "And my brain is never blank."

Shawn squinted one eye open and took a quick glance at Balowsky. Took a quick glance and *saw*. Saw the way his hands trembled slightly and sweat beaded the palms. Saw the pallor in his cheeks. Saw the tiniest difference in the size of his pupils.

"What's that I hear?" Shawn said to the sky. "There's something talking to me. It's a ghost. No, a sprite. No, wait, it's a spirit."

"If it isn't carrying a map," Mathis said, "tell it our smallest billing increment is ten minutes, so unless it wants to be on the hook for a sixth of our combined hourly charges, it should go away."

"No, wait," Shawn said. "Not one spirit. Spirits. Glasses of spirits. Quarts of spirits. Gallons of spirits. They're calling to one of us here. Join us, join our party. No one has to know."

Shawn opened his eyes and leveled his gaze directly at Balowsky. "I think that message was for you. You wouldn't happen to be in the habit of cavorting with spirits, would you? Because they really want to meet up with you as soon as possible, and they say that will happen much faster if you all stop arguing for one minute and let me do this."

Gwendolyn let out a snort of derision. Shawn looked over the group of lawyers. Balowsky was staring at the ground, his hands twitching more than before. Savage was gazing eastward, as if still figuring out their route. Mathis fumbled in his pack, pulled out a bandanna, and wiped the sweat that was still trickling down from his hairline. Gwendolyn was the only one who was looking back at Shawn. She met his gaze with an intensity Gus had seen only once, at the reptile cage at Santa Barbara's zoo.

And then there was Jade. Rushton had provided her with hiking clothes and boots in her trademark color, and it occurred to Gus that once they were in the woods, it would be extremely difficult to see her. But right now she stuck out like a bowl of lime Jell-O at a rock convention. She fidgeted nervously, her hands sliding in and out of the pockets of her dress, glancing furtively between ground and sky, and doing everything to proclaim her innocence short of whistling a jaunty tune.

"I'm seeing a trail," Shawn said. "It's long and it's hard. It's mysterious and confusing. But most of all, it's green."

The other lawyers turned as one to face Jade. She took a step back. "Why are you looking at me?" she said. "I don't have the map."

"Sure, you don't," Gwendolyn said. "Now, are you going to hand it over, or do we toss you over the side of the mountain and just follow the way you fall?"

"I can't," Jade said. "Even if I had the map, and you will all notice I'm not saying that I do, I couldn't possibly show it to you without our all being fired. We've got to work together to figure out the right way to get off this mountain."

"I agree with her," Savage said. "We don't need a map, anyway. We just need to work together to reach a consensus. And I vote that we all go whichever way Jade says. Who else?"

There was a moment of hesitation; then Mathis raised his hand. Balowsky nodded.

"Fine, we'll follow the green freak," Gwendolyn said. "But if she doesn't have the map, or if she does but she's so stupid she gets us lost anyway, I guarantee I will not be the first to die out here."

"Isn't it nice when we can all work together like this?" Shawn said. "Mr. Rushton would be so proud."

"Let's get out of here," Mathis said. "Which way?"

Jade looked around nervously. She glanced up at the sun, then down at the various trails that led away from them.

"Not that I have the map or anything like that," she said.

Gwendolyn groaned. "Oh, for God's sake."

"But if I had to follow my own instincts, I'd say that we should take the trail that goes to the northwest," Jade said.

She gave them all a big smile and set off down the path to her right. After a few paces she looked back to see that everyone was still standing in place. "I thought we were all following my instincts."

"Your 'instincts,' yes," said Savage. "Your sense of direction not so much. Northwest is that way."

He pointed at a trail that ran off to their left. Gus was mildly disappointed to see that when Jade blushed, her face actually turned red, not another shade of green.

"And isn't this the very definition of 'teamwork'?" Shawn said. "One of knows the directions, and another one of us knows what they mean."

The lawyers all glowered at Shawn as they trudged past him towards the northwest trail. Gus let them all start down the trail before he whispered to Shawn.

"If Mathis really is the killer—"

"He is," Shawn said.

"Fine, then he needs Jade alive until he can get the map away from her," Gus said. "And unless he's really good at hiding his wilderness skills, he needs Savage alive to interpret her directions. But does he have any reason why he shouldn't try to kill us before we expose him?"

"Only our charm and good looks," Shawn said. He hoisted his pack and started down the trail.

Chapter Thirty-Three

Of course Chris Rasmussen had wanted to run to the Pasadena Police and give a full report. But Henry'd had no desire to spend the next few hours waiting in a holding cell until the locals had determined that the bloated body on the floor had been dead for several days and that Henry and Rasmussen were unlikely to have committed the crime, so he passed on that plan. He did agree to call in an anonymous tip from a pay phone. Then he called Lassiter from his cell and filled him in on what they'd discovered. They agreed to meet at Ellen Svaco's house as soon as Henry and Rasmussen could make it back.

"That's my jurisdiction," Rasmussen pouted.

"It's your interagency task force," Henry said. "More important, it's a murder that happened to one of your citizens on your turf. If you let any ridiculous, petty concern like jurisdiction stand in the way of making that right, then you obviously didn't understand a single word I said when you were in junior high."

Henry slammed his foot on the gas and hoped the look of determination on his face would serve the same function as the cherry he didn't have to put on his hood. It did—or maybe they simply didn't cruise past any cops. Either way, they made it back to Isla Vista in less than two hours. Rasmussen sulked the entire way.

When Henry pulled up outside Ellen Svaco's house, two squad cars and a plainclothes vehicle were already parked at the curb. The crime scene seal had been cut, and uniformed officers were going in and out of the house.

Lassiter met Henry and Rasmussen at the front door.

"What have you found?" Henry said.

"Nothing directly connecting her to her cousin," Lassiter said. "Except all that Fluffy crap, of course."

"Fluffy's the key," Henry said. "I've been thinking it over on the drive back up. I think Ellen and her cousin were partners in some illegal enterprise. Arnold kept his half of the money, but she had him donate hers."

"An illegal enterprise in peaceful Isla Vista?" Lassiter said. "If only the local constabulary had noticed. Ellen Svaco might still be alive."

Rasmussen stared down at the ground and didn't say anything.

"It's the only way I can put it together," Henry said. "Still one thing that doesn't work for me, though. Officer Rasmussen spoke to all the neighbors. You'd think if she had been that emotional about losing a pet, even more than five years ago, someone would have mentioned it. It's the kind of thing that defines a person."

Rasmussen was still staring at the ground, but they could see his mouth moving. Although Henry couldn't read lips, he was pretty sure the word "jurisdiction" was muttered more than once.

"What's that you're saying?" Lassiter said.

"It's a transitory population," Rasmussen mumbled. "College town. People don't stay here long."

"Except for Ellen Svaco," Henry said. "She stayed here one day too many." He looked at Lassiter. "Did you find anything in the house?"

Lassiter sighed. "Got to give the kid credit for that one," he said. "It doesn't look like he missed anything at all. And he did come up with Fluffy, which my people might have missed entirely."

Juliet O'Hara appeared in the doorway holding a cordless phone. "Officer Rasmussen, in your background investigation did you happen to notice if Ellen Svaco had any legal troubles?"

"There was no record of any," Rasmussen said. "I would have mentioned it if there were."

"Then did it occur to you to wonder why her last phone call was to the most prestigious law firm in town?" O'Hara pressed the REDIAL button, and the phone beeped itself through seven digits. After two rings, a voice on the other end said, "Rushton, Morelock, and Weiss." O'Hara disconnected the call.

"This might have been nice to know about," Lassiter said to Rasmussen. "You didn't think it was worth sharing?"

"I didn't know," Rasmussen stammered. "I didn't think to hit the redial. No one ever told me."

Henry shook his head in disgust. Shawn might be infuriating, but he'd never have made a rookie mistake like that. "Junior high is where you start learning, not where you stop."

"What do we do now?" O'Hara said.

"Let's go back and talk to the chief," Lassiter said. "If Rushton, Morelock is involved, everything just got a lot more complicated."

"No, it didn't," Rasmussen said. "It's a murder investigation. We proceed like we would with anyone else."

Henry clapped a hand on Rasmussen's shoulder. "It's been fun, kid. But it seems like we're looking at a criminal conspiracy that could possibly involve one of the wealthiest, most powerful men in Santa Barbara. Even if I were still on the force, this would be above my level. As a civilian, I can't have anything to do with it. Isn't that right, Detective Lassiter?"

"I don't want to make any decisions before we bring the chief in on this," Lassiter said. "She's the one who's going to have to take the heat, so she'll have to let us know how she wants us to play it. But it's safe to say that this is no longer a case for a retired cop—or the Foot Patrol."

"But justice is supposed to be blind," Rasmussen said. "'As officers of the law we're supposed to follow the case wherever it takes us, without fear or favor.'"

"It's a nice thought," Henry said. "Too bad we all have to grow up sometime."

Henry climbed in his car and drove away. The last thing he saw in his rearview was Rasmussen staring after him, looking like he was going to cry.

Chapter Thirty-Four

Somebody had been putting rocks in Gus' backpack. Which was odd, because he'd spent most of the day's hike at the end of the line of lawyers, and there was rarely anyone behind him to play that kind of trick. But the pack that had seemed so light and perfectly balanced only a few hours earlier now felt like the anvil Wile E. Coyote always ended up clutching as he plummeted off a cliff. Gus could feel it pulling him down, its straps abrading his shoulders through the lightweight T-shirt he was wearing.

Whoever had been loading Gus' pack with rocks had apparently also been slipping nails into his shoes. They had seemed so comfortable the first few miles he'd walked in them, but now every step sent jagged bursts of pain through his feet.

Looking ahead at the lawyers spread out in front of him, Gus could see that most of them were suffering the same kinds of pain. Gwendolyn, who'd taken the lead right away, was still in front, but her long, confident stride had stiffened into an awkward, straight-legged march. Balowsky's entire body seemed to convulse with every third step and when he turned around to make sure he wasn't falling behind the rest of the pack, Gus could see him licking his lips compulsively, as if he might have stored a few drops of last night's vodka there. Savage was dragging, too, which would have surprised Gus more if the lawyer hadn't spent the first three hours of the hike zipping down the trail to see where they were going and then running back to report like a Labrador retriever off leash in the mountains for the first time. Jade looked like she had completely exhausted her store of pixie dust: She staggered forward as if the only thing keeping her going was the force of gravity.

And then there was Mathis. He was more of a surprise to Gus than Savage. Because Morton Mathis didn't seem to be physically exhausted. Gus was becoming an expert on analyzing people's walks from behind, and he could see the way Mathis' feet pushed hard off the stony ground with every step.

That wasn't what struck Gus as odd. Even though Mathis was a transplant from a large city, with no apparent wilderness experience, there was no reason to believe he didn't spend huge amounts of time working out, despite a physical appearance that seemed to give the lie to that idea. But what did seem inexplicably strange was the way he was pretending to be as weary as the others. His shoulders slumped under his pack, his head hung down almost to his chest. He was in every way the picture of exhaustion. A picture contradicted by the reality of his legs.

Of course it was possible that Mathis was faking fatigue simply to get away from Shawn, who had spent the last few hours hiking alongside one lawyer after another, and who was now glued to Mathis' side.

That had been the key to Shawn's plan for the day. While Gus kept an eye on the entire pack from the end of the line, Shawn would use the time to get to know the lawyers better. Not that either of the detectives had any desire to forge the strong ties of friendship that Rushton had prescribed for the entire group. All Shawn and Gus really needed was a little confirmation of what they already knew: that Mathis was behind not only the murders of Ellen Svaco and mime Archie Kane, but also the espionage plot Archie had been trying to stop.

At the beginning of the hike, Gus had managed to tell Shawn everything he'd learned from the employee files, and Shawn agreed that this was all but proof that Mathis was their guy. By the time they reached their first night's stopping point, they were certain that Shawn would have been able to get the last bits they'd need to put their murderer away for good.

But Mathis turned out to be a harder nut to crack than they'd expected. Shawn had tried to start a dozen conversations with the man, but they had never risen above the smallest of small talk, and each time, Shawn had had to move on to another lawyer without having learned anything.

Shawn slowed his pace enough to let Mathis move ahead, and then he stopped to let Gus catch up with him.

"Anything?" Gus said.

"He's smart," Shawn said. "He may be onto us."

"What makes you say that?" Gus said, a feeling of dread managing to bubble up through the cracks in his exhaustion. He forced it back down quickly. He couldn't afford to let fear get a foothold. There wouldn't be a snack bar selling ice-cream sandwiches to bring him out of it here.

"I've tossed out enough bait to land a hundred sharks, but he hasn't even nibbled," Shawn said. "I've tried to engage him on the subject of Archie Kane, but all he says is that it's a great loss to the firm and 'to us all personally.' I tried to get him to talk about the tech stuff he handles, but he insisted that so much of it was confidential that he makes a practice of never discussing any of it so as not to make a mistake. I even mentioned the Jet Propulsion Laboratory—which isn't easy to casually drop into conversation. He acted like he'd never given the place a thought."

A terrible idea hit Gus. Again, he fought to keep it from turning into panic. "What if he's not the right guy?"

"We've decided he is," Shawn said. "We put a lot of thought into that conclusion, and it seems premature to throw away all that work simply because we're having a hard time making a brilliant career criminal expose himself on the course of a nature walk."

"If by 'a lot of thought' you mean you made a snap decision based on a couple of physical and behavioral characteristics, it's hard to argue," Gus said.

"And you confirmed it through research."

"I found information that reinforced my existing prejudice,"

Gus said. "On its own, the fact that he specializes in technology doesn't mean much of anything."

They walked a few paces in silence as Shawn thought this over. "If you're right," he finally said, "we've picked the wrong suspect. And while we've been focused on Mathis, the real killer has been focused on us—and is planning to take us out."

Gus felt a cold jolt of adrenaline surge through his system. At first he assumed it was from the awareness of the danger they were in. But then he realized his body was responding to a sound his conscious mind hadn't noticed.

"What was that?" Shawn said as the sound came again.

It took Gus a second to recognize the noise that came drifting around the curve in the trail. At first he tried to figure out what kind of animal or bird made a sound like that.

Then it hit him. It wasn't an animal. It was a woman.

And she was screaming.

Chapter Thirty-Five

Before his pack hit the dirt, Gus had launched himself down the trail and towards the source of the scream. Freed from the weight he'd been carrying for hours, Gus practically flew. He could feel himself hurtling into the air with every step. He realized this was incredibly dangerous—if he landed on one of the rocks that littered the trail, he'd break an ankle, and there was no chance the lawyers would carry him down the mountain. But he recognized the voice that was screaming, and he had to help.

If it had been Gwendolyn, perhaps Gus wouldn't have reacted so strongly. But Jade exuded an ethereal vulnerability, and he couldn't stop imagining her lying dead in Peter Pan's hands as he begged the audience to clap if they believed in fairies.

Shawn was right next to Gus as they hurtled around the bend in the trail. When they got around it, they both stopped dead, shocked at what lay before them.

For the last few miles, the trail had hugged the side of the mountain on their left, and dropped off sharply to the right. But now the left side opened up into a wide meadow. A clear stream ran through it, and wildflowers bloomed yellow and red for as far as they could see.

The sight that stopped Shawn and Gus was what had been erected in the center of the meadow. Four tents, each striped in a different color, stood facing one another across a quad. Between them, a long table was set with a service fit for the White House—linen tablecloth, bone china, fine crystal, and sterling silver. A professional range had been set up a short distance away from the tents, and two young men in black slacks and white shirts stood by, while a woman in her mid-twenties, dressed the same way, unboxed a dozen bottles of wine.

Jade was standing, stunned, at the edge of the encampment. She let out another scream of joy. The other lawyers, who had taken their places around the table, ignored her.

"How did they get all this up there?" Gus knew there were other questions that were probably more pressing, but the surreal sight pushed them all out of his head.

"It's really amazing how much you can fit in one of those helicopters when they're not crammed full of egos," Shawn said. "Hungry?"

Gus hadn't thought he was. But now the air was filled with the delicate scents of sorrel soup and roast lamb, and suddenly he was starving. He started to move towards the table when a thought hit him.

"Our packs," he said. "We've got to go back for them."

"We'll go back later," Shawn said. "The food will be all gone."

"It'll be dark later. And in the morning we can't take a chance that we'll have to go back when the others are pressing on ahead."

"So we'll leave them," Shawn said. "If they're serving us meals like this along the way, why should we schlep all that dried stuff?"

"Maybe that's exactly what Rushton wants us to think," Gus said. "This is all a trick to get us to leave our packs behind, and then there's no food for the next four days."

"If he wanted us to starve, why would he put food in our packs in the first place?"

"I don't know," Gus said. "I don't really understand anything about this trip. But I know I'll feel better if I have my pack with me."

Gus could practically see the little angel and tiny devil debating on Shawn's shoulders. After a moment, Shawn nodded regretfully. "Let's get the packs."

Gus took one last longing look at the dinner table, then turned back to the trail. And walked into a wall.

At least that's what it looked like up close. Gus stepped back quickly and realized it was his pack. His pack and Shawn's. Standing behind it was an enormous figure that seemed to have been woven out of wiry red hair. The hair covered its head and flowed around its shoulders; it poured off his face in a long beard and mustache. The creature wore an old flannel shirt and filthy shorts that might once have been khaki, but now were mostly loose threads. Giant tufts of red hair poked through the holes in the creature's clothes and around the straps of its sandals.

"Don't trash my mountain," the figure said, and threw the packs at their feet.

Now that he had a clear view, Gus could see that the creature was not Bigfoot, or the Abominable Snowman, or Gossamer, the tennis-shoe-wearing monster from the Bugs Bunny cartoons. It was a man. Aside from the species, however, Gus could tell almost nothing about him. All else was hidden by the hair.

"Sorry. We were just going back for those," Shawn said. "Thanks for bringing them to us."

"Don't trash my mountain," the man said again, and then he was gone back up the trail.

"Amazing that big a guy can move so fast," Shawn said. "Of course, if he's all hair, maybe he just blew away."

Gus hoisted his pack and slung it over his shoulder, his muscles screaming in pain as the weight settled down on them again. A quick glance suggested that Shawn was feeling the same agony.

"I suppose we could just leave them here," Gus said. "We'll be able to find them in the morning."

"Do you think that counts as trashing the mountain?"

"Not as much as setting up a four-star restaurant in this meadow." This assertion came from a fourth server, who offered them a warm smile and two printed menu cards. He had curly black hair and a smile bigger than all outdoors, which was pretty big, given the context. "Hi, my name is Cody, and I'll be your server tonight. That man has been hanging around here all day shouting obscenities at us. We finally bought him off with a case of Pinot Noir. But don't worry—there's plenty left."

"Do you think he's dangerous?" Gus said.

"My usual gig is in Venice," Cody said. "He's nothing compared to the homeless guys living on the beach. Just seems fanatical about keeping the mountains clean—and who can blame him?"

"He could start with himself," Shawn said.

"Believe me, we offered him a shower along with the wine," Cody said.

"There are showers here?" Gus said.

"We've got a sauna," Cody said. He pointed at the female server, who was standing over Balowsky waiting for him to drain his glass so she could refill it. "And Maggie is a certified massage technician, if you're feeling sore. I personally recommend her scalp treatment. I think she's bringing back my hair."

Gus and Shawn must have looked puzzled, because Cody leaned over to show them the bald spot on the center of his scalp. "My agent said I should just shave my head, but I think that rules me out for leading man roles."

"I can see how that would be a problem," Shawn said.

"But my acting career is the last thing in the world you two should be worrying about now," Cody said.

"Don't worry, it is," Shawn said.

"I'd love to wash my hands before dinner," Gus said.

"The bathing pavilion is right over there." Cody pointed at a red-and-white-striped tent. "May I take your bags?"

"You may take them and keep them," Shawn said.

Cody pointed across the meadow, where the rest of the packs were neatly lined up. "I'll put them over there. We'll start serving dinner as soon as you're seated."

As Cody bent down to pick up the packs, he gave Gus another look at the bald spot, then carried the bags over to the others and went to help the other male server pour soup into bowls.

"You heard what Cody said," Shawn said. "We don't want to keep the lawyers waiting."

"You go join them," Gus said. "I'll be right there. Maybe you can get Mathis to confess and we can all go home after dinner."

As Shawn went towards the dining table, Gus headed off to the red-and-white-striped tent and pushed the flap open. It was like stepping into the spa at the Four Seasons—marble countertops, brass fixtures, and toiletries with the fanciest labels Gus had ever seen. But all that luxury paled in comparison to the scalding-hot water that gushed out of the faucet when Gus turned the tap. He lathered his hands with a jasmine-scented wash and then attacked his face with the matching defoliating scrub. Drying himself off with a plush towel of Egyptian cotton, he luxuriated in the sense of cleanliness. No matter how good dinner had smelled, he was beginning to regret passing on the hot shower. Maybe later.

Feeling more refreshed than he'd dreamed possible, Gus stepped out of the bath tent and started towards the dining table. The lawyers were involved in an argument over some obscure point of law—among the snatches that drifted over in the breeze Gus heard the words 'usucaption,' 'usufructuary,' and 'ultra vires'—and server Maggie was back standing over Balowsky with a fresh bottle as he drained the dregs from another glass. A portly chef Gus hadn't noticed before bent over the oven, pulling out a saddle of lamb.

Gus' sense of well-being began to drain away as he realized that for all the noise coming from the table, there were only four people sitting there. Mathis was nowhere to be seen.

Neither was Shawn.

Gus made a conscious effort to slow his heart rate before it started accelerating. This was probably a good thing. Shawn had undoubtedly seen an opening and taken Mathis aside to trick a confession out of him. Then he'd saunter back to the packs, flip on one of the emergency beacons, and they'd both enjoy this fabulous dinner while they waited for the helicopter to come.

That sounded like a brilliant plan. There was only one problem with it. It wasn't Shawn. There was simply no way that Shawn could bring himself to solve a case like this without an audience. If Shawn was going to expose Mathis, he'd do it in front of the other lawyers. Or at the very least wait until Gus was back to see it.

So where was he?

Gus scanned every inch of the meadow. Cody and the other male servers were polishing the plates before dinner service. The chef was carving the roast. Server Maggie was refilling Balowsky's glass.

That left the tents. There were three of them besides the one he'd just left. Gus crept over to the nearest tent, a blue-and-white-striped pavilion, and peered in. There were three low beds on the ground, complete with feather beds and down comforters. Three fluffy cotton robes hung from hooks, and there were men's pajamas laid out on a low table. But there was no one inside. Gus moved quickly to the green-and-white-striped tent. Two more beds, two more robes, and two sheer nightgowns on hooks. Clearly this tent was intended for Gwendolyn and Jade, although Gus suspected that they might both prefer sleeping alone on rocks to rooming together, no matter how splendid the accommodation. The yellow-and-white-striped tent at the other end of the camp also contained two beds and two sets of men's pajamas.

There was no one inside.

Gus came out of the tent and checked the dining table, hoping that Shawn and Mathis had reappeared there while he was checking the sleeping quarters. They hadn't.

Moving around the yellow pavilion, Gus discovered that there was one other tent he hadn't noticed before. No surprise there—unlike the grand sleeping quarters, this was a small, olive drab lean-to, probably the cheapest shelter you could find at any army surplus store. Gus approached it nervously. It was just about the right size to hide a body. He lifted the flap and peered in. And his heart stopped.

The tent was dark and close. Something lay sprawled on the ground. In the dim light it looked like a body. Gus forced himself to reach in and touch it. The form sank under his fingers.

Gus almost let out a laugh in relief. It wasn't a body. It was just a few spare pillows that had tumbled down from a stack on the left side of the tent. Gus had fallen for the same trick he'd used on his parents when he wanted to sneak out with Shawn when they were kids—he'd arrange his pillows under the covers on his bed so that when his parents looked in on him they'd see what they'd think was a sleeping boy. The only difference was that his parents had never fallen for this subterfuge— apparently a good mother could tell the difference between the child she'd borne and a cotton rectangle filled with foam—and Gus just had.

He pushed the pillows out of the way and checked the rest of the tent's contents. There were coolers filled with eggs and oranges, not doubt to be scrambled and juiced in the morning, a sack of potatoes, bags of whole-bean coffee, several restaurant-sized cans of ketchup, what looked like an entire pig's worth of bacon and a second swine of sausage, and pink bakery boxes filled with croissants, brioche, and Danishes. Gus didn't know what seemed more surprising to him—that they had brought enough food to feed the Mormon Tabernacle Choir, or that they'd flown in the pastries pre-made, instead of baking them fresh.

There were more crates stacked behind the breakfast supplies, but Gus didn't bother to check through them. None of them was big enough to hold a body. He crawled back out of the lean-to and let the flap fall shut behind him.

There was still no sign of Shawn or Mathis at the dining table. Gus forced himself to keep calm. Mathis wouldn't do anything obvious. He couldn't. He'd have to figure that Gus knew everything Shawn did. Even if he managed to get rid of Shawn and make it look like an accident—for the first time since the helicopter landed, Gus replayed that old dream image of his best friend's body broken and bloody at the bottom of a cliff— he couldn't possibly hope to get rid of Gus the same way.

Whatever Mathis was up to, Gus had to figure it out fast. The sun was dropping behind the peak of the mountain, and the shadows had disappeared. There was probably another fifteen or twenty minutes before it got too dark to see, but that wasn't a lot of time. The servers were already moving around the camp lighting oil lamps. Once the sunlight was gone, so was any chance of finding Shawn.

There was one way out. The emergency beacons. He could use one of them, send out the signal for help. Whoever showed up would be prepared to find people lost in the wilderness. It would be career suicide, but Shawn would have to find that preferable to actual homicide.

No need for that extreme measure just yet, though. Gus would give it a few more minutes, wait at least until it was dark. And if he'd heard nothing from Shawn by then, he'd do it.

Gus was moving towards the backpacks to position himself near the beacons when he caught a movement out of the corner of his eye.

He wheeled around towards the motion and saw Shawn walking away from him at the far end of meadow. He was about to call out, to wave his hands over his head and jump and scream to let Shawn know he was heading in the wrong direction. Until he noticed two small details that had escaped him in the first blush of excitement:

Shawn wasn't alone in the meadow. Morton Mathis was walking directly behind him.

And Shawn's hands were up in the air.

Chapter Thirty-Six

He was a savage jungle cat moving swiftly and silently through the tall grasses of the meadow. The sun was completely hidden behind the mountain now, and the last glimmerings of daylight were fading into dark gray. But jungle cat Gus didn't need light to find his way. He was moving on smell, on touch, on instinct.

He was going to save his friend.

As he tracked his prey, Gus tried to figure out what exactly was going on. Clearly Mathis was armed. He must have been holding a gun on Shawn. He hadn't used it yet, though. The shot would have echoed through this wilderness like an avalanche; if he wanted to kill Shawn and rejoin the other lawyers he'd have to do it silently. And that meant getting far enough away from the camp so that the others wouldn't hear even if Shawn cried out.

This gave Gus a small advantage. Mathis had to keep this quiet; Gus could yell for help at any time. Even if the other lawyers wouldn't necessarily come running, odds were at least some of the servers would try to help.

There was only one thing stopping Gus from crying out right now, and that was the fact that Shawn must have come to the same conclusion. He would have known that Mathis couldn't afford for him to shout for help—so why didn't he?

Gus crouched at the edge of the meadow and peered into the gathering darkness. Just ahead of him the ground began to slope up sharply and the wildflowers gave way to the kind of rocky wasteland they'd spent the morning walking through. Large boulders spotted the landscape, which would give Gus cover once he started to move forward again. But they were also cover for Mathis—he and Shawn could be behind any one of a dozen large enough to hide two men.

Suddenly there was a sound in the air. It sounded like voices. But where were they coming from? The stream was running off to Gus' right, and the sweet tinkling drowned out the faint sound of speech. It must be Shawn and Mathis, but Gus couldn't make out what they were saying. He cursed himself for every time he'd ever turned up the volume on his iPod to fill his brain with Mariah Carey's high notes. Didn't he know he'd need his hearing intact one of these days?

Just keep talking, Shawn, Gus thought as he maneuvered his way to the first of the large boulders and pressed himself against it. *Let me know where you are.*

For what felt like an eternity, there was nothing but silence. And then he heard Shawn's voice again. It sounded desperate, as if he were pleading for his life. Who knew how much time he had left before Mathis silenced him forever?

There was an enormous boulder up the hill to Gus' right. Shawn and Mathis were on the other side of it. Gus scrabbled around in the ground at his feet for a weapon. He came up with a stone the size and weight of a brick. It would do.

At least, it would have done if he and Mathis were Cro-Magnons fighting it out in a prehistoric age. Unfortunately a lot of time had passed since then, and mankind had invented far more advanced weaponry, including the gun that Mathis must be holding on Shawn. The rock wouldn't do Gus any good if Mathis could take him out from fifty feet away.

Gus needed one more weapon, and there was only one available—the element of surprise. He'd have to strike from above.

But for the surprise attack to work he would have to move

silently. And that was nearly impossible. The ground was scattered with loose stones, and they skittered down the hill with every step he took. He had to lift one foot, wait for the gravel to settle underneath, then find a new place for it a few inches ahead. Press it down gently, make sure there were no loose rocks underneath, and finally put his weight on it. Then he could begin the process with the other foot.

Gus had no idea how long it took him to get to the top of the boulder. It felt like hours, although the last dregs of daylight around him suggested it had been only a few minutes. He pressed his back against the boulder and listened for the voices.

"You can't just leave us out here," Shawn said.

"Watch me," Mathis said.

"You really think no one's going to figure out what you're up to?"

"That's not going to matter to you," Mathis said. "In fact, none of this is going to matter to you. And that's—"

This was the moment. Mathis was going to kill Shawn. Gus had to move now. He raised the rock over his head and leaped down from behind the boulder.

At least that's what he meant to do. But the ground around the boulder was strewn with loose rocks, and as he pushed off with his foot, the rocks slid out from beneath him. Gus went down headfirst, his face nearly slamming into the ground before he managed to get his other foot beneath him.

Gus was upright now, and moving fast, but Mathis had heard him. He whirled around, leveling the gun. Even in the twilight, Gus was sure he could see Mathis' finger tightening on the trigger as Gus stumbled towards him. Gus brought the rock back up.

"Gus, no!" Shawn shouted.

Shawn's words penetrated Gus' mind at the same instant as the tingling sensation from the shock of the rock slamming into Mathis' head. By the time he was able to process the thought that Shawn hadn't wanted him to knock the gunman out, it was too late for him to do anything about it. Mathis was sprawled out over the stony ground.

"Are you okay?" Gus gasped as he kicked the gun out of the unconscious man's hands and heard it splash into the stream in the darkness.

"I'm fine," Shawn said. "Wish I could say the same for him."

Shawn got down on his knees and felt Mathis' neck for a pulse. He looked relieved to find one.

"I've never heard you express such compassion for a murderer before," Gus said, a little hurt that Shawn didn't seem at all grateful to be so daringly rescued.

"And you never will," Shawn said. "Unfortunately, Mathis isn't our killer."

Gus gaped at him. "But he has to be. It all fits."

"And a Matchbox racer fits in a prescription pill bottle," Shawn said. "But that doesn't mean that if you dump out your mother's Darvon so you can use the bottle as a car carrier she won't get mad at you, as I think we both remember all too well."

Gus tried to make sense of what Shawn was saying. "He was holding a gun on you."

"Yes, he was," Shawn said. "In his right hand, which definitely did make our theory seem more likely. Unfortunately, what's in his left hand seems to undercut it just about entirely."

Following Shawn's gaze, Gus knelt down and opened Mathis' left hand. He was holding on to a plastic wallet. Gus took it and let it fall open. He couldn't see much in the dark, but he could feel a smooth plastic surface on one side. On the other was a shield of engraved metal.

"It's kind of hard to see in the dark, but he showed it to me before the sun went down," Shawn said. "It identifies him as Special Agent Morton Mathis, FBI."

Chapter Thirty-Seven

Gus stared down at the FBI agent, trying to will him back into consciousness. At least he thought he was staring down at Mathis. It had gotten so dark he could have been staring at a rock.

Or he could have until the rock stirred and moaned. And then let out a string of curses Gus was pretty sure no rock would ever utter.

"You're okay now," Shawn said, reaching down to help Morton to his feet. "You had me scared there. We were having a pleasant conversation, and then you just keeled over and passed out."

"Yeah, right after this idiot beaned me with a rock," Mathis said, clutching the back of his head.

"You're not supposed to remember that," Shawn said. "It's been clearly demonstrated in every movie ever made that when you're knocked out with a rock and someone tells you that you fainted, you always believe it. I think it has something to do with short-term memory. Or rocks."

"I'm really sorry," Gus said. "I saw you taking Shawn away at gunpoint and I thought you were going to kill him."

"You were wrong," Mathis said. "Though maybe not anymore."

"Oh, come on," Shawn said. "It was an innocent misunderstanding. We'll all be laughing about it in a little while."

Mathis pulled his hand away from his head and rubbed his fingers together, checking to see if they were covered with blood. Apparently they weren't. "We're not doing anything together," the agent said. "We're not laughing together, we're not crying together, and as I was explaining before Chingachgook here tried to scalp me, we're not working this case together."

Gus shot Shawn a puzzled look, which was a waste of facial muscles since it was too dark to see expressions. But Shawn knew Gus well enough to read his silence.

"Special Agent Mathis is working undercover at Rushton, Morelock," Shawn explained. "The FBI seems to believe that someone there is using the law firm as a conduit to smuggle out top-secret technology."

"Would that be the same technology that was stolen from the Jet Propulsion Laboratory?" Gus said.

"That's great. You guys figured out a piece of it," Mathis said. "Just enough to get Archie Kane killed."

"We're not the ones with guns and badges," Gus said. "We're not the ones with the entire power of the federal government behind them. We didn't even know who Archie Kane was until he was dead, let alone that he was working with the FBI."

"He wasn't," Mathis said. "I couldn't break cover with him. But I did put a little pressure on the guy, and he snapped."

"If by 'snapped' you mean dressing up as a mime and holding innocent people hostage in a public restroom, I think that's a fair assessment," Shawn said.

"I mean he tried to take care of the problem on his own to protect his mentor, and it got him killed," Mathis snapped. "I've got that kid's blood on my hands, and the only way they're coming clean is when I pop the guy who did him."

"Then we all want the same thing," Gus said.

"Not entirely," Mathis said. "Not unless you're secretly harboring a yearning for a stint at Gitmo."

"Agent Mathis," Shawn said soothingly. "Special Agent Mathis. Very Special Agent Mathis. What my rock-happy friend is saying is that we have a common goal. We all want to catch the person who committed these crimes. If we work together, we can figure it out before the rescue chopper shows up."

"There's not going to be a rescue chopper," Mathis said.

"Once we use one of the beacons, there will be," Shawn said.

"You're not using the beacons. Nobody is. One of those four lawyers sucking down sorrel soup is a murderer and a traitor. That person has given up all rights to be free in civil society. So whichever one it is, he or she is not going back to civilization except in handcuffs."

"I understand that," Gus said. "But there are three other lawyers, as well as the two of us and you, and we haven't murdered or, um, traitored anyone. What happens if we get to the end of the trail and you still haven't figured out who the bad guy is?"

"I'll sacrifice you all and myself if that's what it takes," Mathis said. "The spy is never going to walk free again."

"Say," Shawn said. "I'm not suggesting that the knock on the head has left you the slightest bit crazy or anything like that. But it sounds an awful lot like you're talking about letting five innocent people die so you can catch one criminal."

"Is that what it sounds like?" Mathis said. "Then I guess that must be what it is."

"You can't do that," Gus protested. "You work for the government. You have rules. Laws. Statutes. Regulations."

"None of which applies in the wilderness," Mathis said. "There's only one law out here. And that's me."

Chapter Thirty-Eight

Gus lay wide awake on the feather bed, staring up through the darkness at the tent ceiling. He thought back to the start of this day, when his only problem was that Shawn wouldn't share his theory of who'd killed Ellen Svaco. Somehow he'd managed to convince himself that that had been a problem worth getting worked up about.

That was before he'd found himself on a five-day nature hike with a quintet of psychopathic lawyers, one of whom was also a murderer who seemed to have no compunction about killing to keep his or her identity a secret. At least two people were already dead, and Gus couldn't imagine why the killer would feel any hesitation to continue with the spree.

But now even that seemed like the good old days. Because that killer was likely to attempt murder only if it looked like he or she was about to be revealed. Mathis, the FBI agent, had claimed he'd kill them all if he didn't unmask the killer. Which meant that someone was going to try to kill Gus, Shawn, and who knew how many others no matter which way things worked out.

There was a light snore from the bed next to his. Shawn was sleeping peacefully—as always. And he'd eaten well, too, knocking back two bowls of soup and at least three helpings of lamb, along with a couple of chocolate soufflés. Nothing seemed to bother him—not their impending doom, or the impossibility of their situation, or guilt at having gotten them into this death march in the first place. Even when Gus had told him the entire story of his long search-and-rescue mission, starting with his baffling discovery upon stepping out of the bathing pavilion, through the searches of the other sleeping quarters and the supply tent, through his treacherous journey across the rocky hillside, Shawn sounded more entertained than impressed. By the time he was done, Gus suspected he'd hit the wrong person with the rock.

He was feeling around on the ground next to him for something to chuck at Shawn when he heard noises from outside. It was a rustling, followed by the sound of a zipper being undone. It took Gus a moment to realize that it was coming from the supply tent behind them. Maybe one of the servers had decided that sleeping outside was no fun and was going to make a bed among the next morning's food.

Or maybe it was the next morning. Gus' heart sunk at the thought. He could tell through the sleeping tent's fabric that it was still dark out, but that didn't mean it wouldn't soon be time for them to be yanked out of bed. He hadn't slept at all, and now he'd have to get up and face another endless day on the march. Nothing could be worse than that.

Except what happened next.

Chapter Thirty-Nine

The walls of the tent lit up with blinding flashes of light, and the air was filled with gunfire. Gus could hear Jade screaming. This time there was no chance it was a cry of happy surprise.

Shawn sat up in bed. "What's happening?"

Another burst of gunfire lit up the tents, tearing holes in the nylon at the top.

"Is it the killer?" Gus whispered.

There was another blast of gunshot, this time from the other side of the camp. And then an answering burst from the first side.

"Not unless he's brought friends," Shawn said, grabbing his clothes from the side of his bed and sliding into his shorts.

Gus grabbed his own clothes and started to change out of his pajamas. Even as he was doing it, he didn't know why. It wasn't like the hiking clothes would wick bullets away from his skin like water. But he felt much readier for action as soon as his shorts were zipped. "Maybe he's fighting it out with Mathis," Gus said, pulling his shoes on and tying them tight.

"Mathis isn't Melvin Purvis, and the killer isn't Baby Face Nelson," Shawn said. "And a tommy-gun battle seems a little out of scale for the crimes involved here."

"Then, what?"

Shawn slithered out of his bed and crawled to the tent's front flap. "One way to find out," he said.

"Don't!" Gus whispered. "They'll know we're in here."

"There are three sleeping tents spread over a few hundred feet of ground in the middle of thousands of acres of wilderness," Shawn said. "I suspect they're going to think to look in here no matter what."

"Then let's not be here when they do," Gus said. He gestured to the far corner of the tent where two walls met the floor, then crawled over to it. He tried to lift the tent wall off the floor section, but it was so tightly sewn on it might as well have been one piece of nylon.

Outside, the air was filled again with another burst of automatic gunfire, and now in the silences between they could hear male voices barking orders.

"Get out of there!" one of the voices yelled from across the camp. "You've got one second before I blow your brains out."

"They're rounding up the lawyers," Shawn whispered as he slid in next to Gus.

"They'll be coming for us next," Gus said.

"Maybe not," Shawn said. "We're not lawyers."

"Even if that would make a difference to whoever is blowing up the camp, how are we going to prove it to them?" Gus said, still trying to tear the nylon open.

"Good point," Shawn said. "It's not like we can show them the lack of a license. The bar association should really offer certificates of non-lawyerhood."

"We can suggest that to them if we ever get out of here alive," Gus said, giving the nylon another yank. It was no use. A grizzly bear could probably tear this tent open, but thoughtless hunters had nearly wiped them out a century ago, and now you could never count on finding one when you needed him. And even if you did, he'd be more interested in knocking over suburban garbage cans than helping innocent people escape from insane killers. And when you came right down to it, that was what was wrong with nature.

"Are you all right?" Shawn said gently. "Because you look

like your brain is spinning out into some kind of reality-deflecting rant."

"I'm fine," Gus said. "At least I would be if there weren't people firing automatic weapons out there."

"Look on the bright side," Shawn said. "Soon they'll be firing them in here."

"Why do you think I'm trying to tear a hole in this tent?" Gus said.

"I didn't know that's what you were doing," Shawn said. "I thought you were using the tent wall as your blanky."

"I never had a blanky," Gus said. "Or a binky or a noo-noo, or any other stupid piece of cloth to make me feel better. And if I did, it wouldn't have been yellow, nylon, and attached to a tent that gun-wielding maniacs were about to invade."

"I do see how that could defeat the entire purpose of a security blanket," Shawn said.

"I was trying to make a way out for us."

"Oh, if that's what you want," Shawn said, reaching into his pocket. He pulled out a Swiss Army knife. "Try this. I grabbed it out of my pack. Silly me, I thought it might come in handy at some point."

Gus could have kissed Shawn. Or plunged one of the knife's many blades into his heart. It all depended on whether he decided to focus on Shawn's forethought or on the fact that he'd been sitting there for what seemed like hours watching Gus uselessly tug at the tent fabric.

Instead he pulled the longest blade out of its slot and plunged it into the nylon, then ran it along the seam between the wall and the tent. The stitching fell away like ice cream under a blowtorch, and in a second there was an opening big enough to crawl through.

"The supply tent is right behind us," Gus said. "If we can get around that, we'll be in the darkness and they won't be able to find us."

"Unless they brought flashlights," Shawn said.

Gus lifted the tent wall and wriggled through, then rolled until he hit the soft wall of the supply tent. He waited there silently until Shawn rolled against him. There was another burst of gunfire from across the camp. Gus thought he could hear Jade crying. "We've got to help them," he whispered.

"You've got the knife," Shawn said. "Go for it."

"There are at least two people with automatic weapons out there," Gus said.

"And you've got eight blades, plus a screwdriver, corkscrew, tweezers, nail file, and magnifying glass," Shawn said. "I feel sorry for them."

There was no point in glaring at Shawn in the darkness, but Gus did it anyway. "We can't just let them kill all the lawyers."

"No matter what the bumper sticker says," Shawn agreed. "But charging into the middle of a gunfight waving a magnifying glass isn't going to help anyone. Unless they're really, really big and having trouble seeing us puny humans."

"Then what do you suggest?"

"First thing, we've got to get out of here," Shawn said. "Just far enough so it's not worth their trouble to look for us too long. Then we follow and see where they take their prisoners."

"What makes you think they're going to take them anywhere?"

"Sometime tomorrow a helicopter is going to land here to take the cook and the waiters away, either back home or to the next rest stop," Shawn said. "The gunmen aren't going to want to be here when that happens."

"Unless their plan is to hijack a helicopter," Gus said.

"There is that possibility," Shawn said. "But I can think of about a million easier ways to do that. And either way, our first step is still the same. We've got to get away from here."

It didn't feel right. It felt like running away and leaving all the others to some horrible fate. But no matter how many scenarios Gus ran in his head, he didn't see one that was even half as logical as Shawn's plan. "Let's go."

Gus pushed himself up on his knees, ready to crawl back around the supply tent. Shawn grabbed his shoulder and pulled him back down.

A circle of light, the beam from a flashlight, hit the tent's back wall, then swept across its surface. A gruff voice shouted from inside. "They're not here."

Somewhere past the tent, another voice spoke in threatening tones: "Where are they?"

"I don't know. I don't know!" It was Gwendolyn's voice, and she sounded scared. After all that had just happened, it was the fear in her voice that frightened Gus the most.

"They probably ran off." It was a man's voice. Savage, Gus thought.

"Right off the mountain." That was definitely Mathis. Why wasn't he doing anything? Gus wondered, and then remembered kicking Mathis' gun into the water. "They're probably lying dead at the bottom of a ravine."

"Possibly," the threatening voice said. "Or maybe they're hiding just out of reach of our lights. Let's find out."

"That's a good idea." It was Balowsky, and there was a mild slur in his voice that Gus suspected wasn't entirely caused by fear. "We can wait until the sun comes up. Then we'll be able to see for ourselves."

"I have a better idea," the threatening voice said, and then spoke up loudly. "The two of you who are hiding out there. You have ten seconds to show yourselves. If you do not surrender to me within that period of time, I will kill one hostage. And then I will kill another hostage every ten seconds after that. One. Two."

The voice continued counting down.

Gus got to his feet.

"Are you crazy?" Shawn said.

"No, but I will be if people start dying because I didn't walk fast enough. And so will you."

"Six. Seven."

"Sometimes I hate being a decent person," Shawn said as he got to his feet.

"Fortunately it doesn't come up all that often," Gus said.

"Eight. Nine."

Shawn and Gus stepped around the edge of the yellow tent.

"Don't shoot!" Shawn shouted. "We're here."

The five members of Rushton's team were huddled together by the blue tent. Mathis had managed to change into his clothes, or maybe he'd never taken them off, but Savage and Balowsky were still in their pajamas. Gwendolyn and Jade wore robes, presumably over the sheer nightgowns that had been left for them.

Four men wearing camouflage, army boots, and black balaclavas leveled automatic rifles at the lawyers. Their leader stood in the center of the quad, aiming his own weapon at the ground where the four servers and the chef lay facedown.

The leader glanced up at Shawn and Gus, although the long, thick red hair and beard made it hard to tell exactly where his eyes were looking.

"Ten," the leader said. "Too late."

"But we're here," Gus said. "We came out within the ten seconds."

"Did I say ten?" the leader growled. "Sorry, I'm dyslexic. What I meant to say was five."

He jerked his gun up slightly and fired. A spurt of red geysered up where a server's head had been.

"No!" Shawn shouted. He ran towards the leader, with Gus right on his heels. But before they'd closed half the distance, two of the camo-men tackled them to the ground.

The leader fired four more bullets, then wiped the red off the cuffs of his pants and turned back to the lawyers.

"I warned them not to trash my mountain."

Chapter Forty

The march had gotten easier as the sun came up and Gus could see the rocks littering the trail instead of blindly tripping over them. But that only made him feel worse. When there was physical pain, when every step was a struggle, his entire mind could focus on the act of putting one foot in front of the other. Now his mind was free to wander, and it kept going back to the same place.

Gus had seen dead bodies before. He'd seen people die. But this was different. The casual executions kept replaying themselves in his mind, and he couldn't shake the image no matter how hard he tried. It seemed impossible to imagine—one second those people were alive; the next they didn't exist. Gus hoped he had thanked the servers when they'd brought him dinner last night.

The rest of the marchers were just as somber and just as silent and they walked single file along the trail. Two of the masked gunmen led them down the mountain; the other two trailed them. Where their leader was, Gus had no idea.

They'd been walking for hours now. After the execution of the chef and his servers, the gunmen had corralled Shawn and Gus with the lawyers in one of the tents. They'd allowed the ones who were still in their pajamas a minute to change into hiking clothes, and then they had all set out down the trail.

Where they were being taken, or why they were being taken there, nobody knew. Mathis had tried to ask as they were led out onto the trail, but one of their captors had informed him that the next person to utter a single syllable would be thrown off the cliff. Gus could see Mathis' hand twitching, as if reaching for the gun he no longer had, but he backed off. *Just as well,* Gus had thought. He didn't know if the kidnappers would follow through on their threat, but even if they didn't, any altercation with Mathis might lead one of them to discover his FBI credentials, and there was no way to predict what would happen then.

Although they'd all been ordered to keep their eyes firmly on the ground, Gus sneaked a look up at Shawn.. They were separated by Savage and Balowsky, whose march had started out as a hungover stagger and only weakened over the hours, and all Gus could see of his friend was his back. That was enough to reassure Gus—and to scare him.

Reassure him because Shawn was a creature of habit and reflex, and for decades any order for silence, whether from an elementary school teacher, a parent, or a police detective, would trigger an avalanche of words. Even if it was in Shawn's interest to keep his mouth shut, the command to stop talking acted on him like a rubber hammer below the knee; his response was completely beyond any physical control.

But Shawn hadn't said a word then, and he wasn't talking now. His head was down; his eyes seemed to be focused, like everyone else's, on the ground.

What made Gus nervous was Shawn's shoulders. Even from here he could see how tight, how rigid they were. Shawn was not someone who angered easily; his philosophy of life was that having fun is the best revenge for any ill. But Gus could feel the rage radiating out of those joints, and he didn't know how long Shawn could keep it bottled up. When he exploded, Gus had no idea what was going to happen, but he didn't see a happy ending for anyone.

The trail took a hard jag to the left, and Gus saw something he hadn't seen yet—a tree. It wasn't much, just a scraggly, struggling little runt, but it told him they'd descended past the timberline, the edge of the habitat beyond which trees are incapable of growing. The trail went inland from the cliff, and now was surrounded on both sides by small, scrubby bushes. Up ahead, however, the bushes were getting taller and taller, quickly turning into towering pines.

At least that meant they'd be in the shade by the time the sun reached its zenith. But it also dashed their best hope for rescue. Like Shawn, Gus had assumed that a helicopter would be arriving sometime early in the morning to pick up the servers and their gear, to bring them either home or to the hikers' next rest stop. Once the copter landed, the pilot would see the bodies, which the kidnappers had left lying in the center of the meadow, and radio for help. And no doubt start the search for the rest of the party. As long as they were out on the open mountainside, they'd be easy to spot. But once they were under tree cover, no one would be able to see them from the air.

Apparently that was their captors' idea, as one of the masked men in the lead shouted an order and forced them to walk off the trail and into the tall trees.

After a few minutes of whacking through dense brush, they stepped out into a clearing. It was an almost perfect circle of bare ground dotted with low stumps from the trees that had been cut to form it. A stone fire pit was in the center.

One of the masked men gave a signal, and Gus was slammed up against a tree. Another masked man wrapped a rope around him, tying him to the trunk, then moved on to do the same to the rest of the hostages. Gus risked a glance over at Shawn, who was tied to the next tree, only a couple of feet away. But Shawn was staring furiously down at the ground; Gus could practically hear him thinking.

When the last of the hostages was secured, the four masked men took positions around the fire pit, a small circle inside the larger ring of captives. After a long moment there was a rustling in the brush, and the red-haired man stepped out from between two large trees.

"Doesn't this look like fun!" he said, smiling cheerfully. "Nothing like a little camping trip to build team spirit."

"What do you want from us?" Mathis growled from across the circle.

"From you?" the red-haired man said. "Nothing. My brothers and I have everything we could need here. We've got the sky above and the ground below. We've got nature's bounty all around."

"Then let us go, you fat freak." It was Gwendolyn. Gus was torn between admiration for her spirit and fear that she'd get herself—and maybe the rest of them—killed.

"I said there's nothing I want from you," the red-haired man continued, as if she hadn't insulted him. "I didn't say there was nothing I wanted at all. After all, you're lawyers. If I were to sue Manning Timber because they illegally clear-cut thousands of acres of public land and you were to defend them, it wouldn't be accurate to say that I wanted something from you specifically. You would simply be the vehicle through which I would address my demands."

"You're doing this because you're mad about the Manning Timber case?" Balowsky said. "Because I think most of us would agree that that case was wrongly, even criminally settled based on false information supplied to the court about various members of the environmental organizations that brought suit. In fact, many of us voted to censure the lawyer who was in charge of that case. If you let the rest of us go, we can tell you which one that was."

"You bastard," Gwendolyn spat. "You all spent the money Manning paid us for my work. And besides, the strategy was Jade's. You go after the weakest parts of the opposition first, and then use their failure to bring down the rest."

"That's not a license to slander," Jade said. "You still need to act within an ethical framework based on respect for the other side's point of view."

"We were just doing a job for our clients," Savage said. "That's how our adversarial legal system works."

"I understand," the red-haired man said. "And I don't hold you responsible for the decision. I just want to engage your services for the next round of negotiations."

"Then use the phone like everyone else," Gwendolyn said.

"But I can save you the dime. We can't take your side in the appeal because we've already represented your opponent. If you thought it through for one second, you'd realize that, you moron."

"What my colleague means to say," Balowsky said quickly, "is that the firm of Rushton, Morelock, while not able to directly aid you in your appeal, will do its utmost to find you the best counsel possible. And if your organization is in financial straits, we would be willing to handle your legal bills, as well."

"Yeah, those death penalty cases can be expensive," Mathis said. "And since there's no chance you'd ever win, no lawyer is going to take your case without payment up front."

"Will you shut up?" Savage whispered furiously. "We're trying to negotiate a deal here."

"I don't deal with terrorists," Mathis said.

"That's really inspiring," Balowsky said, "until you remember that corpses don't deal with anyone."

"Why are you doing this to us?" Jade wailed. "We haven't done anything to you."

"As I said, you are merely the vehicle through which I am seeking redress," the red-haired man said.

"It's about time you're seeking to get redressed," Shawn said. "Because that outfit does absolutely nothing for you. And if one more thread snaps on those shorts, we're all going to wish you had killed us back at the camp."

Gus stared at Shawn, who was smiling up at the red-haired man as if he were free and his captor was the one tied to the tree.

"What are you doing?" Gus whispered furiously.

"Testing a theory," Shawn said.

"What theory?" Gus said. "That no matter how many rotten things you've done, you'll still end up in heaven?"

Shawn ignored him. "Tell me, Tubby," he said, "what's the next part of your brilliant plan? Because right now all I see is a fat guy playing dress-up and dancing around a campfire."

"Shawn, stop," Gus said, fully expecting at least a small percentage of the inevitable hail of bullets to penetrate his own flesh.

But if the red-haired man was offended by Shawn, he didn't show it. If anything, he seemed amused.

"My plan is done," he said. "I've sent out my demands, I've explained what will happen to all of you if I don't get what I want. All I have to do is wait."

"Demands?" Savage said. "We'll give you whatever you want."

"I already told you," Mathis snapped. "We do not negotiate with terrorists."

"I'm not negotiating," Savage said. "I'm giving him whatever he wants."

"I'm afraid my demands have to be settled at a higher level than this, although I do appreciate your generosity," the red-haired man said.

"What is it you want?" Jade said.

"Not much. Just the immediate and permanent end to all logging, hunting, and fishing on all federal and state lands in the country," the red-haired man said.

"You're insane," Gwendolyn shouted. "That's never going to happen."

"I really hope you're wrong," the red-haired man said.

"There must be something else you want," Balowsky begged. "We've got money. We can buy you your own forest, and then you can keep everyone from logging there."

"The immediate and permanent end to all logging, hunting, and fishing on all federal and state lands in the country," the red-haired man said, "or you are all going to die."

Chapter Forty-One

The sun was hidden by the tops of the trees, but the air near the forest floor was hot and thick, choked with dust and decaying pine needles.

Gus crawled along the ground, sweat cascading off him. He scraped away a foot of dry needles, then clawed out a small handful of dirt and dropped an acorn into the hole. He swept the dirt and pine needles back in place and crawled forward another foot.

All around him in the forest he could hear the sounds of the lawyers performing the same ridiculous, repetitive task. He was sure their fingers were blistering just like his, that their bare knees were aching and their heads pounding from the heat.

Even their armed guards looked like they were beginning to fade under the high temperatures. Their camouflage shirts were rolled up to their elbows, and their pants, unequipped with zip-off legs, were pulled up to their knees. They'd even rolled their balaclavas up over the backs of their heads to let their scalps breathe. It would have made more sense to take them off altogether, but Gus was glad they hadn't. The fact that they were concerned about being identified suggested they intended on letting their hostages go at some point.

Now that they were partially uncovered, Gus realized that

he'd been wrong about one thing. These weren't four men. Judging by the thin wrists and ankles and delicate neck, one of the guards was a woman. In normal circumstances Gus would have tried to figure a way to get her alone, in hopes of overpowering the weakest member of the team and getting away. But normal circumstances meant the weakest member wasn't carrying an automatic rifle, and that wasn't the case here.

And so he continued to crawl along the ground, dropping acorns into dry holes. This was the red-haired man's order. Manning Timber's clear-cutting campaign had cost the state hundreds of thousands of trees. Until he got his way, the hostages were going to repair that damage. They'd plant one tree for every one that had been cut.

Gus didn't know much about arboriculture, but he was pretty sure this wasn't a particularly well thought-out plan. There were already a lot of trees in this part of the forest. There didn't seem to be a huge amount of room for more to grow. And even if the older trees made room for the new sprouts, Gus suspected that before an acorn could turn into a sapling, it needed some amount of water. This ground was dry and powdery. If anything, they were probably just laying out a progressive dinner party for the local squirrels.

But the red-haired man did not seem interested in debating the logic of his plan. When Gwendolyn tried to object, he aimed his gun in the air and let out a stream of bullets. Then he turned it on the lawyer and asked if she still had any problems with her assignment.

That's when one of the gunmen brought out the sack of acorns and they all got down on their hands and knees. Ever since then, Gus had caught the occasional glimpse of one of the lawyers through the trees, but aside from that, and the armed guards who patrolled the area, he was completely alone.

Gus reached out his sore, blistered hand to scrape away another pile of pine needles, but his fingers closed on rubber. Startled, he looked up to see he was clutching the toe of a hiking shoe.

Shawn's hiking shoe.

Shawn was sitting against a tree, his legs splayed out in front of him, eyes closed as if he were taking a brief nap. When Gus squeezed his shoe, Shawn's eyes flashed open and his face brightened into a bright smile.

"Lovely day to be outside, isn't it?" he said cheerfully.

"We're supposed to be planting acorns," Gus whispered, checking over his shoulder to see if one of the guards was about to stumble across them.

"Actually, we're supposed to be catching whoever killed the mime," Shawn said. "And we're not doing that, either."

"Then what are you doing?"

"I'm thinking about a pillow," Shawn said.

"You look comfortable enough already," Gus said.

"Actually, I'm thinking about a lot of pillows," Shawn said. "To start with, I'm thinking about how many pillows we had on those feather beds back at the campsite."

"There were plenty of them," Gus said, thinking back to the way he'd sunk into the soft down as he laid his head down in the tent. If only he'd known then how much worse his life was about to get, maybe he would have tried a little harder to enjoy the night.

"Yes, there were," Shawn said. "Certainly more than enough."

"I'm glad we agree on that," Gus said. "Maybe now we could start thinking about how we're going to get away from these maniacs."

"I'm also thinking about ketchup," Shawn said.

It must be the heat, Gus thought. It was melting Shawn's brain. If a guard did show up, Gus would beg him for mercy, and for water for Shawn. "Are you?"

"Have you ever noticed it's spelled two different ways?" Shawn continued. "There's k-e-t-c-h-u-p and then there's c-a-t-s-u-p, but neither spelling matches the way the word is pronounced. You have to take the first two letters of the second spelling and put them with the last five letters of the first to approximate the word we actually use."

"Uh-huh." This was worse than Gus had feared. Shawn seemed to be in the grip of full-on delirium. If this were happening in an old movie, a couple of quick slaps across the face would snap Shawn out of it. But Gus didn't feel comfortable slapping Shawn, especially when there seemed to be so many people around who'd enjoy the opportunity to join in.

"And then there's the whole question of whether it's a condiment or an entrée," Shawn said. "I tend to come down on the condiment side of the argument myself, as I have generally used it as a complement to flavor food, rather than as a main source of nutrition. And I have to think that a chef talented enough to have whipped up that tasty dinner would see it the same way."

The mention of the chef brought the image of his death back into Gus' mind with full force. How could Shawn be prattling on like this when the man he was talking about was rotting on the ground?

"We need to get away from here," Gus said as forcefully as he could without raising his voice above a whisper.

Shawn didn't seem to hear. "So why would he bring four five-gallon cans of the stuff to our campground?"

"Maybe he was worried something would go wrong with one of them," Gus said. "Who cares?"

"That might explain bringing one extra, but four?" Shawn said. "Even if we all doused our breakfasts in the stuff, there's no way four lawyers, two detectives and one grumpy FBI agent could make it through a single gallon of ketchup, let alone twenty. And since everything they used had to be brought up by helicopter or pack mule, weight would have been a major issue."

"I promise we'll solve that mystery," Gus said desperately. "Right after we figure out how to get out of this road show version of *The Hills Have Eyes*."

"And that brings me right back to the question of pillows," Shawn said. "There were far more on every bed than we needed. So why were there stacks of extras in that supply tent?"

The whole slapping thing was beginning to look a lot more attractive to Gus. There didn't seem to be any other way to bring Shawn back to reality. First ketchup, now pillows. Gus couldn't even imagine what sort of fevered fantasy was running through his friend's brain that would lead him to connect the two.

"Shawn, you've got to focus," Gus said. "We're here in the woods; we're being held captive by murderers. You've got to stop thinking about pillows and ketchup."

"But they're the key," Shawn said.

"They're a headrest and a foodstuff," Gus said. "There's no way you can put them together to make a key."

"A pillow isn't just for resting your head," Shawn said. "You know that as well as anyone else."

It took Gus a moment to realize what Shawn was saying. Actually, it took more than a moment. It took his accepting the idea that his friend was not raving the incoherent babblings of the hopelessly schizophrenic, but was actually making a point. Once he accepted that, there was still a brief period when he had to piece together what that point could be.

And even then, he could barely bring himself to believe it.

"That can't be," Gus said. "That's just crazy."

"Crazier than holding a bunch of lawyers hostage to force the government to stop all logging?"

"It's a hard call, but just about," Gus said.

"I might have thought so, too," Shawn said. "Until I started thinking about something the fat guy said. And then I saw something that convinced me."

"What's that?"

For a moment, Shawn didn't say anything. Gus was going to ask again, but Shawn held up his hand for quiet. They waited in silence until they heard pine needles crunching in the woods to their right.

It was one of the guards. He was patrolling carefully, his gun extended, ready to mow down anyone who thought about running or fighting.

"What are we going to do now?" Gus whispered.

"Get proof." Shawn scrabbled around in the needles at the base of the tree and came up with a small, tight pinecone. "Okay, now this may be fast, so you're going to have to watch carefully."

"What for what?"

"You'll know."

Shawn lobbed the pinecone towards the guard. It flew just behind his head and thumped into a tree. The guard whirled around, leveling his gun at the source of the sound.

And Gus saw.

And Gus knew.

Chapter Forty-Two

Gus ran.

That was the plan, anyway. Gus was supposed to run through the forest making as much noise as possible and luring all four of the guards to chase him.

But several hours on his knees in the stifling air had sapped most of his energy, and the best he could manage was a brisk shuffle through the pine needles. That might have been a problem, because it could let one of the guards catch him before he'd attracted the attention of the rest of the hostages. Fortunately, while the guards might have been revolutionaries for the cause of the wilderness, they didn't seem to have any more experience than Gus in working outside in the blazing heat. As Gus shuffled, they shuffled along behind them.

Of course they couldn't afford to leave their captives alone as they gave chase. So by the time Gus found himself back in the clearing with four automatic rifles aimed at him, the lawyers were all in the circle, too. After a moment the red-haired leader puffed his way to join them.

"I warned you what would happen if one of you attempted to escape," the leader said between gasps for breath. "What happens next is not our fault. It is his."

"Actually, that's not precisely true," Balowsky said. "Not in a legal sense, anyway. California has what's called a felony murder statute, which says that if anyone is killed during the commission of a crime, no matter who is directly responsible, fault attaches to the perpetrators of the original crime."

"Another law written to protect the powerful," the leader said. "Here I am the lawgiver, and my law says whatever happens next is his fault."

"As long as you know it isn't mine, we're cool," Gwendolyn said.

The leader raised his gun. As Gus saw its bottomless black barrel pointing at him, he started to wonder how he had let Shawn talk him into this. Yes, everything Shawn had explained seemed perfectly rational at the time, but there could be a vast gulf between perfectly rational and actually true, and if Shawn had been wrong, that gulf was about to be crossed by a bullet.

"I am the lawgiver," the leader repeated as his finger tightened on the trigger.

Before the leader's gun started spitting out lead, there was a rustling from outside the clearing, and Shawn pushed his way between two of the gunmen.

"If you're the lawgiver, then tell me, is it 'ape shall never kill ape,' or 'ape shall never kill Abe'?" Shawn said. "Because I never trusted that little suck-up chimpanzee."

"What are you talking about?" the leader shouted.

"If you were truly the lawgiver, you'd understand," Shawn said. "In the beginning God created beast and Man, so that both might live in friendship and share dominion over a world at peace. But man waged bloody wars against the Apes, whom they reduced to slavery. Then God in his wrath sent the world a savior, miraculously born of two Apes who had descended on Earth from Earth's own future. And he rose up an army of Apes and gave them speech, and won freedom from their oppressors."

The leader stared at him, stunned. So did the guards. And the lawyers. Up in the trees, Gus was pretty sure, so did the squirrels.

Finally the leader seemed to shake off his surprise. He thrust his gun in Shawn's face and screamed at him, "You get down on the ground right now!"

"Did you know your stomach jiggles when you get mad?" Shawn said.

"Get down or I will shoot you!"

"I think we're done here," Shawn said. He turned to the lawyers. "You kids coming?"

Shawn turned and started towards the edge of the clearing. Gus followed him. This was the moment. Either Shawn was right or—well, if Shawn wasn't right, Gus would never find out.

"I am ordering you to stop," the leader said.

"And I'm ordering you to get down on your knees and do Moritz' monologue from *Spring Awakening*," Shawn said. "And no cheating by using the song from the musical. I want the original Wedekind. Oh, and Archie Kane sent me."

Gus sneaked a look at the lawyers. Most of them were too caught up in the impending execution to register what Shawn had just said. Most of them had looks of horror on their faces, although Gwendolyn's half-smile suggested that she wouldn't be too sorry to witness what was going to happen next.

Gus felt all the muscles in his back tense as he waited for the first bullet to strike.

But there were no bullets. The leader dropped his gun on the ground. The four guards threw their own weapons into the woods. Gwendolyn dived into the trees and came back leveling one at her former captors.

"You're all going to put your hands up now," she said.

"No, they're not," Shawn said. "Those guns are loaded with blanks."

The lawyers exchanged baffled looks. "But we saw them kill the waiters," Jade finally said.

"What you saw was an exercise in team building," Shawn said. He nodded at the guards, and all four reached up and pulled off their masks. Their faces were red from the heat, and one of them seemed to be breaking out from some kind of wool allergy. But there was no mistaking who they were. The faces were even more recognizable than Cody's bald spot had been once he pulled his balaclava off the back of his head. "As Tubs here told you hours ago. If you ever listened to anyone but yourselves, this all would have been over before it started."

"We were kidnapped by a bunch of waiters?" Savage said.

"Worse," Shawn said. "You were kidnapped by a bunch of actors."

"But we saw them," Jade said. "We saw them executed."

"What you saw was the cruel and brutal murder of innocent five-gallon cans of catsup," Gus said.

"Or ketchup," Shawn said. "Although I'm not sure there's a difference in the criminal penalty."

"And pillows," Gus continued. "Stuffed into the waiters' clothes. Amazing how a trick that never fooled my mother managed to work with all these brilliant lawyers."

"And all those psychic detectives." Balowsky nearly spit out the words.

"Didn't fool us," Shawn said. "We were just playing along."

"Playing along?" Mathis looked like he wanted to kill everyone at the clearing. "Playing along with what?"

Shawn turned to the leader. "I believe that's your line."

The leader nodded, then turned to face the lawyers and bowed deeply. Then he pulled at the beard. It peeled off his face, taking with it the shaggy red wig that covered his head, and revealing the features of last night's chef. "Ladies and gentlemen, my name is Bron Helstrom, and these are the Triton Players. I'd like to thank you personally for being such an appreciative audience for our little performance. And I'd like thank my fellow performers, Cody, Coty, Bismarck, and Miranda, without whose inspired acting I could never have hoped to pull this off. And of course our employers, High Mountain Wilderness Retreats, and the author and sponsor of today's entertainment, Mr. Oliver Rushton."

"Rushton!" The word escaped from Savage's mouth like a curse shouted after the improper application of hammer to thumb.

"He referred to our little play as a bonding exercise," Helstrom said. "Apparently you were all supposed to unite and work together when faced with a common peril. In fact, we had specific instructions to drop character the instant you all agreed on how to handle the situation."

"We could have been here forever," Jade said.

"That's why Rushton gave them a safe word," Gus said. "As soon as one of you said 'Archie Kane sent me,' the show would end."

"And we were supposed to figure that out how, exactly?" Gwendolyn said.

"Well, it would have helped if you were psychic like me," Shawn said.

Or at least smart like him, Gus thought. Shawn had explained he'd figured out the safe word the same way hackers come up with passwords—he started from the assumption that Rushton would have used words that had particular meaning to him. And while this particular set of safe words wouldn't have worked so well if Archie Kane had been along on the trip, as was undoubtedly Rushton's original plan, Shawn assumed that the old lawyer wouldn't have delivered the code to the actors until the last possible moment, to keep any of the others from finding it out somehow.

"Psychic, my ass," Balowsky said. "Rushton told you. And when we get back, you may expect to be served papers in my lawsuit over this charade. You had the ability to stop it at any time, and you refused, which makes you as culpable as Rushton."

"Do you really want to split the culpability like that?" Savage looked concerned. "My polo shirts have deeper pockets than these yutzes. We should focus our suit solely on Rushton."

"Good point," Balowsky said. "We can talk to the police about criminal charges against these two, along with the Powder Puff Players here. Anyone disagree?"

For once, there wasn't a single argument from the rest of the lawyers.

"I am moved by your concern for the small businessman," Gus said. "Not to mention touched to see how you are finally coming together to work as a team. I know Mr. Rushton would be so proud."

"But there is still one thing you need to know," Shawn said. "And that is that neither Gus nor I was ever told anything about this entire event, from the kidnapping to the safe words. We had as little idea as any of you."

"Any of you except one, that is," Gus said.

"Right," Shawn said. "Because there's no point in setting a safe word if nobody knows what it is. So that means that one of you was in on Rushton's plan all along—and chose not to tell the others, or to stop the insanity."

The lawyers glared at one another suspiciously. Gwendolyn gripped her weapon as if wishing the Blue Fairy would turn the blanks into real bullets just like she turned Pinocchio into a real boy.

"And if that's not going to get you to work together as a team, I don't know what will," Shawn said. "Now, who's in the mood for a hike?"

Chapter Forty-Three

Gus had thought the forced march down the mountain was as unpleasant as any hike could be. But back then, at least, the lawyers were all united in misery. As they trudged back up the steep switchbacks towards the previous night's campsite where they'd been forced to abandon their backpacks, Gus could see them casting suspicious glares at one another, trying to figure out which one was the traitor secretly working for Rushton.

The Triton Players, for reasons Gus couldn't begin to figure out, had gone back into character. The four servers marched in formation, rifles slung across their shoulders, behind Bron Helstrom. It would have been a more convincing performance without their leader, who did his best approximation of a military stride for as many as five steps at a time, then sank to his knees gasping for breath. In the spirit of improvisation, his troops would surround him, weapons at the ready, every time he stopped for air, but Gus could see why Helstrom hadn't accompanied them on the earlier hike.

At least Shawn was in a much better mood. His shoulders were loose and relaxed, and the spring was back in his step. His step was so springy, in fact, that Gus practically had to run to keep up with him.

"So who was it?" Gus said.

"Kristin," Shawn said.

"Who's Kristin?" Gus said.

"J.R.'s devious sister-in-law and mistress," Shawn said. "Or did you mean who shot Mr. Burns? Because that was just stupid."

"I meant who was the one who knew the safe word all along and didn't use it?" Gus said.

"Oh, that," Shawn said. "It's got to be Mathis. He had to know that as soon as the play was revealed, the rest of them would refuse to stay in the mountains any longer, and he was the only one who had any reason to keep us all here."

"Oh, good," Gus said. "We're trapped a zillion miles away from civilization with a mad killer and an insane FBI agent who now has two reasons to want us dead."

"Yup," Shawn said. He didn't seem to be troubled by Gus' assessment of the situation. He didn't seem to be troubled by anything at all.

"What are you so cheerful about?" Gus said.

"What's not to be?" Shawn said. "We defeated an armed band of terrorists and freed all the hostages—including ourselves."

"Except they weren't terrorists and we weren't really hostages," Gus pointed out.

"Which makes it even better," Shawn said. "It had all the sense of doom and incipient panic of a real kidnapping with none of the actual danger. Which means it's like riding the roller coasters at Magic Mountain, only with less danger of being hit by a stray bullet."

"We're still stuck in the mountains," Gus said.

"Not for long," Shawn corrected him. "Because as soon as we get back to the original campsite, you're going to see seven emergency beacons going off at once."

It was more than two hours before they made it back to the meadow, but as soon as they stepped off the trail Gus was delighted to see that the tents were still standing, along with the entire kitchen setup. Suddenly he realized they hadn't eaten since last night's dinner, and he was starving. Even the sight of the "dead bodies" lying in the middle of the camp—in the bright daylight, now clearly pillows dressed as waiters, with burst ketchup cans for heads—couldn't dampen his appetite.

But food was far from the first thing the lawyers were thinking of. They exploded across the meadow like sprinters at the gun, each one racing to grab one of the emergency beacons that dangled off the line of backpacks sitting next to the supply tent.

All of them except Mathis. He ran, too, and he got to the packs before the rest of them, trying to position himself in such a way that the others couldn't get around him. It might have worked, too, if he'd been three times as wide as he was tall. Or if his gun hadn't been lying at the bottom of a sylvan spring.

"Don't do this," Mathis implored the others as they grabbed for the packs. "Let's complete the retreat."

"I have finished," Savage said. He reached for a pack, but Mathis pushed him away.

"We've all finished," Gwendolyn said, grabbing for a pack on the other side of the line. Mathis made it down in time to block her. But as he did so, Balowsky sidled in behind him and yanked one of the yellow plastic cylinders off a pack.

"I'm warning you," Mathis said. "Do not open that beacon."

"Why are you so interested in keeping us in the mountains, Mathis?" Savage said.

"It was our assignment," Mathis said. "We made a contract with Rushton."

"Under duress," Jade said. "And that contract said nothing about fake kidnappings. If anyone violated the agreement it was Rushton. And since we can't launch our suits until we get back to town, it's time to go."

Balowsky took the body of the cylinder in one hand and grabbed the cap at its bottom with the other. Then he gave the cap a savage twist.

Gus realized he didn't have any idea what would happen. If he'd tried to picture it in his mind, the image would have been the cylinder Klaatu pulls out in the original *The Day the Earth Stood Still,* the one that erupts into spiny blades before an over-eager soldier shoots it out of his hand, thus preventing the president from seeing what life is like on other planets.

The last thing Gus expected to happen was what did. When Balowsky screwed off the bottom of the cylinder, three tiny pink objects, each about the size of the nail on Gus' pinkie, dropped to the grass.

"What the hell is that?" Gwendolyn demanded as Balowsky turned the cylinder over and peered in, looking for any signs of advanced electronics.

Shawn and Gus walked over and looked down at the three objects on the ground. At first Gus thought they might be pebbles, or some kind of pellet. But as he looked closer, he realized they weren't round. They were heart-shaped. He knew what these were—and they weren't about to send an electronic signal anywhere.

"I believe they're called Sweethearts," Shawn said, bending down and scooping them into his hand. "Sort of like a nineteenth-century version of the Kindle, only they never really caught on as a reading device because each piece of candy can fit only one word, so if you wanted to take *Moby Dick* on the train, you'd need something like ten thousand pounds of the things. But they're very good for delivering shorter messages, like I LOVE YOU or BE MINE."

Gus stared down at the three candy hearts in Shawn's hand. He read the words over and over again, arranging them in every possible combination, hoping against hope that there was a second way to read the message that Rushton had sent to his employees. There wasn't. There was only one way to order the hearts so that they made any sense at all.

"Or," Gus said finally, "YOU'RE FIRED, LOSER."

Chapter Forty-Four

It took only seconds for the other lawyers to tear open the rest of the "beacons" and discover that each one contained nothing but the same three candy hearts.

"There were no beacons," Balowsky said.

"No wonder you were first in your class at Moron State Law School," Gwendolyn said. "Thank you for pointing out what is agonizingly obvious to everyone."

"What's happening?" Jade wailed. "Did Rushton send us out here to die?"

"Almost everyone," Gwendolyn said. "I almost forgot our remedial student."

"Nobody's going to die," Mathis barked, his hand flicking out of habit to pull out the gun that hadn't been there in close to twenty-four hours. He moved towards Helstrom with the kind of menace only an FBI lifer can muster. "What was the plan?"

"The plan?" Helstrom said, taking a step back. "We weren't exactly going to take this show to Broadway, if that's what you mean."

"How were you getting out of here?" Mathis barked. "How were you supposed to signal Rushton when your little skit was over so he could have you picked up?"

Helstrom dug in his pocket and pulled out a yellow plastic

cylinder. He twisted open the bottom and let three candy hearts fall into his open palm.

"Mine say, HAVE FUN WALKING," Helstrom said.

Mathis looked like he was wanted to throttle someone. "This is not acceptable," he said. "I am going to get us out of here."

"What are you going to do, flap your arms really hard and fly us all down the mountain?" Gwendolyn said.

"I'm an FBI agent," Mathis said. He pulled out his wallet and flashed his badge at them.

The lawyers looked at him, stunned.

"Did Rushton know?" Savage said.

"He was cooperating in an ongoing investigation," Mathis said.

"Apparently we've found the limits to his cooperation," Balowsky said.

"So what's the FBI going to do for us?" Gwendolyn said. "Can you contact your field office and have them send a chopper?"

"I could—if I had a cell phone," Mathis said.

"That's great," Balowsky said. "An FBI agent with no gun, no cell phone, and no backup. That's almost as useless as a psychic."

"Excuse me?" Shawn said. "Are you talking about me?"

"I do believe he is talking about you," Gus said.

"And he's calling me useless?"

"He is calling you useless. And not for the first time, I believe."

"I have thousands of uses," Shawn said. "I slice, I dice, I chop. I can cut a tomato so thin it has only one side. And I get rid of the slimy egg whites in your scrambled egg."

"But wait, there's more," Gus said. Then he whispered to Shawn, "There is more, isn't there?"

"There's always more," Shawn said. "I can speak to the spirits of the mountain."

"As long as we don't have to listen," Mathis said. "We've got grown-up work to do."

"You go ahead and do what you need to," Shawn said. "We'll be quiet."

"Fine," Mathis said. "First thing we need is—"

Shawn let out a low moan that quickly ascended to a piercing shriek. "What's that, spirit of the mountains?" he howled. "You can show us the way out of here? You can send me a vision?"

"Now our lives are supposed to depend on his visions?" Balowsky said. "Can anyone picture a scenario in which we're not all dead?"

"What's that?" Shawn said loudly, cupping a hand to his ear. "You say you already sent me a vision of the way out of here? And all I need to do is reach out and touch it?"

Shawn stretched his hands out in front of him and took one staggering step forward.

"You might want to step out of his way," Gus said. "When he's possessed by a vision, he might as well be a zombie."

But the lawyers were in a huddle and barely glanced up from their conversation. Only Gwendolyn could be bothered to expend the necessary energy to express her contempt with a sneer. Until Shawn lurched forward and started to run towards them, his eyes still squeezed shut, arms waving furiously in front of him.

Gus cleared his throat loudly. "A zombie in an old George Romero movie," he said. "The ones that stagger along slowly. Because the zombies in newer movies go so fast they might run right off a cliff."

Shawn slowed down immediately, sneaking a quick peek through squinted eyelids to make sure he wasn't about to plummet to his doom. He wasn't, although he was close to a fatal impaling on the daggers Gwendolyn was shooting out of her eyes.

Shawn corrected his course and staggered towards the packs. His body jerked left and right, then fell forwards onto the one bright green pack in the line. He shoved his hand under the top flap, dug around in the freeze-dried food and the clothes, and came out clutching a fan-folded piece of paper.

"Thank you, spirit of the mountains," Shawn said to the sky, then looked at the topographical map he was holding. "As I said, I have a vision of the way to get out of here."

"That's mine!" Jade squealed. "Oliver Rushton entrusted it to me. No one else is supposed to look at it, or even know I have it."

"I stopped caring about what Rushton wants a while back," Balowsky said. "Something about seeing my life about to end gave me a new perspective on things."

"Give me the map," Mathis commanded.

"So you can destroy it?" Gwendolyn said. "We haven't forgotten you were the one who didn't want us to use the beacons."

"I've changed my mind," Mathis said. "You can use them all you want. But I need that map."

"We all need the map," Savage said. "Don't you understand? We're all in this together. There's no reason to bicker here. We are stronger together than we are divided. We'll all go down the mountain together, and we'll live as a group. If we bicker, we'll all die."

"That sounds familiar," Gwendolyn said. "Oh, wait, it's the same crap Rushton was spewing when he sent us up here. Makes me wonder whose side you're on."

"I'm on my side," Savage said. "Which means I'm on all our sides. Because we have only one side. What other agenda could there possibly be?"

The lawyers all cast furtive looks at one another, as if trying to ascertain their colleagues' motives. Until Shawn let out another moan.

"O, spirit of the mountain," he cried, waving the map up at the sky. "Do not tell me about these other agendas. Don't say that one of us refused to use the safe word to free us from the terrorizing acting troupe, proving that his or her loyalty remains with Rushton. Don't insist another one of us wants us to stay here until he's caught his suspect. And please, please don't whisper in my ear that there are people among us who would be happy to let the majority get lost in the mountains if they thought it would advance their own position to arrive far in advance of the others."

Shawn pressed the map to his forehead, then dropped his hands to his sides and called out to Helstrom, who was inventorying food supplies with his acting troupe. "You guys got a menu figured out yet? Because I'm good with anything that doesn't require ketchup."

He turned back to see the lawyers all staring at him. "What's up?" he said to them.

"What did he say?" Gus said.

"Who?"

"The spirit of the mountains."

"Oh, nothing," Shawn said. "Apparently I didn't leave him anything to talk about."

The lawyers looked away, disgusted, and went back to arguing among themselves. Except for Mathis, who marched up to Shawn.

"I am ordering you to surrender that map," Mathis said.

"Just as soon as we're done with it," Shawn said.

"You are going to let a murderer escape," Mathis said. "And I will see that you are charged as an accessory after the fact."

"My mother always said don't be afraid to accessorize," Shawn said.

"I think that was Tim Gunn," Gus said.

"Really?" Shawn said. "I keep getting those two confused."

Mathis' face, already red with sunburn, crimsoned even more. "You'd better know what you're doing."

"I don't see why," Shawn said. "I never have before, and it's worked for me so far."

Across the camp, a bell rang. Bron Helstrom was summoning them to the table. The smell of charbroiled steaks hit them right after the clang of the bell.

"I think that concludes the conversation part of this evening's entertainment," Shawn said. "It's time for food."

Chapter Forty-Five

"**O**f course," Shawn said once he and Gus were back in their tent, safely nestled among the down pillows and feather beds, "when you're with a bunch of lawyers, the conversation portion of the entertainment is never truly over."

Gus couldn't argue with that—except maybe over the part about entertainment. He hadn't found anything amusing about the conversation that had taken place at the dinner table. Well, maybe the beginning, when the lawyers were so intent on cramming as much food as possible into their mouths that their cogent legal arguments, witty retorts, and dire personal insults were all reduced to a mess of indecipherable consonants and the occasional projectile of beef lingually launched across the table.

But once the appetites had been partially sated and etiquette had been restored to the group, the conversation quickly spiraled down into paranoid accusations and angry threats.

For the most part, Shawn and Gus stayed out of the table talk. For one thing, this meal, although much more quickly put together than last night's, was even better than the one from the night before. Neither of them felt compelled to use their mouths for anything less pleasurable than eating.

And of course Shawn and Gus didn't have to contribute to a discussion of who would hold on to the map. They would, and there didn't seem to be any compelling reason to change that situation.

Even now that everyone had retired to their tents, Shawn and Gus could still hear isolated pockets of bickering coming from across the camp as a killer argument occurred to one of the lawyers just before they all fell asleep.

Gus waited until several minutes had passed since the last triumphant exclamation, and then he whispered to Shawn, "So what is our plan?"

"Sleep," Shawn muttered.

"Yes, we'll go to sleep in a minute," Gus said. He was exhausted, too, but he knew he'd spend a much more pleasant night if he had an idea what to expect in the morning. "But first, what's our plan?"

"Sleep is our plan," Shawn said.

"How can sleep be a plan?" Gus said.

"It can't, if you keep talking," Shawn said, pulling his pillow around his ears. Within seconds he'd started to snore.

Gus lay awake trying to work out options for the next day. But even before he could form bullet points in his head, he was snoring, too.

When he woke up, the sun was streaming through the light nylon of the tent. And he discovered that Shawn's plan was not bad at all. He felt infinitely better than he had the night before. He rolled over to see that Shawn was already up and dressed.

"I can't believe I've been using a regular bedroom," he said, pulling on his shoes. "A tent in the mountains is so much better. In fact, I'm going to have one installed in my own place as soon as we get back home."

Gus felt all his good feelings swirling away. It took him a moment to figure out why. And then it hit him. It was that last phrase: as soon as we get back home.

"That brings up an important question," he said. "About the whole 'as soon as we get back home' thing. And that is: how?"

"Well, once we're off the mountain, it shouldn't be a problem at all," Shawn said. "We left your car at Rushton's office, but I'm sure we can get someone to give us a ride over there. Worst-case scenario, we can get a cab from the police station, if Lassiter won't arrange for a squad car to drive us. Do I smell pancakes?"

Shawn started out of the tent, but Gus jumped up and grabbed his arm. "Once we're off the mountain?"

"I don't think we can get Lassiter to send a squad car all the way up here," Shawn said. "Yes, he owes us for all the cases we've solved, but I don't think he'll be willing to spring for the extra mileage."

"Maybe I didn't phrase my question precisely enough," Gus said. "When I asked how we were going to get home, I meant how we were going to get home from here. Which would include the sub-question of exactly how we were going to get down from this mountain."

"The way I see it, we have two choices," Shawn said. "We can set out on a hard, grueling trek through the blasted wasteland, facing the constant threat of thirst, hunger, bears, or desperate villains protecting their illegal marijuana fields."

"You mean hike down," Gus said.

"Or we can stay here and gain weight," Shawn said. "I'll go whichever way you want. We can think about it over bacon."

Gus had known Shawn long enough to realize that if he didn't feel like explaining, nothing was going to make him do so, not even the hundreds of lightning strikes Gus was wishing down on him from the heavens. He followed Shawn out of the tent and to the table and allowed one of the waiters—it was either Coty or Bismarck; Cody was off juicing oranges, and waitress Miranda was nowhere to be seen—to slide a plate of fried eggs, bacon, and hash browns in front of him. There was a small bowl of ketchup in the center of the table, but as much as Gus usually liked to put the stuff on his potatoes, somehow he couldn't bring himself to do so today.

As they ate, the table began to fill up. Gwendolyn was first to arrive, and Bismarck or Coty presented her with a plate. A few moments later, a smiling Balowsky took a chair, and almost immediately was presented with a brimming mug of coffee by Miranda, who seemed to have materialized out of nowhere.

"It is a grand morning, isn't it?" Balowsky boomed cheerily. "I feel like I've been sleeping on a cloud."

"Is that what you call it?" Gwendolyn said. "I've never seen one up close, but I always assumed a cloud would be a little less bony."

"Pierced to the heart," Balowsky said, clutching at an imaginary arrow through the organ. "Your great wit has claimed another victim. Just like my great—"

"Hi, everybody," Jade said as she came shyly up to the table. "I hope everyone slept well."

"If we didn't, it's only because we found something more relaxing to do," Balowsky said.

To Gus' surprise, Jade seemed to be blushing as she took her seat. She stared down at the tablecloth, apparently trying to hide a smile.

"Funny," Gwendolyn said. "I wouldn't have thought you had all that peaceful a night."

"Really?" Jade was staring at the table even harder now. "What would make you say something like that?"

"I thought you were having a nightmare."

"You weren't there," Jade said. "You were sleeping outside."

"Under the stars, that's true," Gwendolyn said. "But I walked past our tent when I got up to use the bathroom in the night, and I could have sworn it was rocking."

"Must have been the wind," Jade mumbled as Savage strode up to the table, the grin on his face a double of Balowsky's.

"Wind is the word for it," Gwendolyn said. "And now that we've all answered the call of the wild, maybe we can start to talk about how we're going to get the hell out of here."

Shawn pushed his plate away and stood. "I'm glad you brought that up," he said. "I've got a plan."

"How nice for you," Gwendolyn said, then turned back to the lawyers. "We need to formulate a strategy, and then—"

Shawn lifted his empty plate and dropped it on the table with a crash. "As I was saying," he said, once all the lawyers had turned in his direction, "I have a plan. More important, I also have the map. So unless your strategy includes growing wings and flying off this mountain, you might want to pay attention."

"Actually," Gus said, "even if they did grow wings, the map would still come in handy."

"My partner makes an excellent point," Shawn said. "Although if you were going to grow wings, you might get a homing sense, too."

"We'll listen to your plan," Balowsky said. "Just as long as we don't have to listen to any more of this drivel."

"I can live with that," Shawn said, then turned towards the stove, where Helstrom was gathered with his waitstaff. "You need to hear this, too. You're stuck here with the rest of us."

Helstrom came over and stood at the head of the table. Cody, Coty, and Bismarck joined him. Miranda went over to where Balowsky was sitting and leaned against him. He slipped an arm around her thighs.

"As you may have noticed, we have been stranded on top of this mountain," Shawn said. "It seems to me we have two choices. We can send an expedition to get the hatch open, or we can take our chances with the Others. But I'm still concerned about the polar bear and the cloud monster. Plus, what are we going to do when Claire's baby is due? I don't know nothing about birthing no babies."

"What hatch?" Gwendolyn said.

"What Others?" Balowsky said.

"None of this makes any sense at all," Jade said. "It's like you're taking concepts at random and jamming them together, hoping your audience will do the work of making sense of them."

"You know, that's exactly what I yell at the TV every week," Shawn said.

Gus could see that the lawyers were getting restless. Jade was staring deeply into Savage's eyes, while Balowsky was practicing his Rolfing techniques on the small of Miranda's back. Gwendolyn was absently playing with the spreader she'd taken from the butter dish as if planning how she could sharpen it into a shiv.

Gus stood up next to Shawn. "Please, we need your attention for just a few minutes. Shawn—focus."

Shawn fluttered his eyes, then reared back as if he'd been slapped. "Sorry, apparently the spirit of the mountain stepped out and left the spirit of the island in his place," Shawn said.

"And that spirit just says anything that will keep the story going on for another week, no matter how little sense it makes. The spirit of the mountain, on the other hand, is extremely specific about what needs to be done."

"Like you sitting down and shutting up?" Gwendolyn said.

"You know, it's funny," Shawn said. "As I look around this table, everyone here seems to have made a new friend except you. Why do you think that is?"

Gwendolyn fingered the spreader as if calculating the exact speed and trajectory she'd need to propel it so that it would lodge in Shawn's trachea.

"As I was saying," Shawn said. "We are stuck up here and we need to formulate a plan."

"Why don't we just walk down the mountain?" Savage said. "That's what we all signed up for."

"Not all of us," Helstrom said.

"I say we wait," Balowsky said. "Rushton may be an evil old bastard, but I don't believe he's insane. If we don't show up on time, he'll send choppers up to look for us."

"Quite possibly," Shawn said. "And I know that I'm eager to risk my life on a gamble that the man who hired a troupe of actors-slash-waiters to play terrorist and kidnap us all isn't insane."

"And one actor-slash-chef," Helstrom said. "We're not all waiters here."

"That's a good point," Shawn said. "And it's good to have a chef with us as long as we're stuck up here. It will be especially useful when our food runs out and we have to start eating each other. Bron will be able to cook us up in ways so that we all taste like chicken."

"Chicken is one of my specialties," Helstrom said.

"Good to know," Gus said. "Say, Chef, how many days' worth of food do we have up here?"

Helstrom did a quick count of the people sitting and standing around the table. "Let's see, there are eleven of us," he said. "We might be able to stretch it out through tomorrow night's dinner, as long as we don't eat a big lunch."

Something was wrong in those calculations. Gus knew it,

but he couldn't put a finger on the problem. And Shawn was moving on.

"Plus we've got the freeze-dried food in our packs, which should be enough for each of us for six days," Shawn said. "As long as we don't mind watching Bron and his staff starve to death while we feast."

"We can pool our resources," Savage said. "We're expected in four days. If we're not in by then, they'll have choppers up the next day."

"Except that Rushton gave us all extra rations in case we wanted to take a little extra time to enjoy the scenery," Gus said. "Does that really sound like your boss to you?"

It didn't—not to anyone at the table.

"I knew he was up to something," Balowsky said. "But even I never dreamed it would be this diabolical."

Gwendolyn jammed the blade of the spreader into the table. "That bastard," she said. "He knew it was going to take at least six days to get down the mountain."

"Probably seven," Shawn said. "Six with full food, and one last day on empty, just to put the fear into you all."

"I can gather seeds and nuts," Savage said.

"Apparently," Gwendolyn said with a glance at Jade. "You're already halfway there."

"We've got to get word down," Shawn said. "Then they can send up the rescue team."

Savage nearly jumped out of his seat. "One of us needs to hike down to summon help," he said. "I'll volunteer."

"And then you can have a good laugh on us with Rushton when you get there," Gwendolyn said. "For all we know, you're the one who had the safe word."

"I'm thinking of a word now," Savage said. "But it's not a particularly safe one."

"Two people have to go," Gus said.

"How about Jade?" Savage said. She blushed furiously.

"Because we know she won't do absolutely anything you ask her to do," Gwendolyn said.

"There were some things . . ." Savage said.

Jade blushed even more deeply. "It was our first date."

"The second can wait," Balowsky said. "Sending the two of them would be worse than letting him go alone. At least he wouldn't be stopping every five minutes for some quality time."

"Unless we gave him a mirror," Gwendolyn said.

Gus shot Shawn a look—his partner was losing control again. And there was something else nagging at Gus. He wished he could remember what it was.

Shawn clutched his forehead. "What's that, O spirit of the mountain? You say the wilderness asks for the mighty huntress to accompany the great woodsman?"

"Tell the spirit to put a sock in it," Gwendolyn said. "I'm not spending a week alone on a trail with Captain Nature."

"It's not a bad idea," Balowsky said. "If either one of you turns out to be Rushton's spy, the other will never let him get away with it."

"Or her," Savage said.

"It's not me," Gwendolyn said.

"I'm not thrilled about this," Jade said. "But if they run out of food, Gwendolyn can kill something."

"Then it's settled," Shawn said. "With two people gone, we should be able to stretch the food to cover the rest of us. But to make sure this is absolutely fair, we should take a vote. Everybody in favor of the plan?"

The hands of the waitstaff and the chef were up before Shawn finished his sentence. One by one the lawyers raised their hands until the only one without an arm in the air was Gwendolyn.

"Whatever," she said.

"That's it, then," Shawn said. "Eleven to nothing."

Gus suddenly knew what was wrong. "Twelve," he said.

"No, I just counted," Shawn said. "Four waiters, one guerrilla commando, four lawyers, and the two of us. That's eleven."

"There should be five lawyers," Gus said. "Or at least four lawyers and one grumpy FBI agent."

The realization hit them all at the same time, but it was Jade who spoke first. "Where's Mathis?"

"Don't look at me," Gwendolyn said. "I didn't feel the need to hook up with the nearest loser last night."

"Who was sharing a tent with him?" Shawn said.

"I was," Savage said. "But I chose to sleep outside last night."

"As did I," Balowsky said.

"Has anyone been back in that tent this morning?" Shawn said.

Savage and Balowsky shook their heads. Everyone turned to stare at the blue-and-white-striped tent assigned to Mathis.

"This is ridiculous," Gwendolyn snapped. "He's probably in there sulking because we wouldn't all do what he wanted us to."

"Or he's left," Jade said. "Set out into the wilderness on his own."

"He wouldn't get far," Savage said. "He might be the reincarnation of J. Edgar Hoover, but in the mountains he doesn't know which way is down."

"He didn't leave," Gus said. Mathis was willing to see them all die in the wilderness before he'd let his suspect get back to civilization. If there had been a second person missing, Gus could have believed the Fed had taken him out. But there was no way he would simply walk away from the rest of them now.

"Statistically, we don't need his vote," Shawn said. "But in case there's an inquiry from the Robert's Rules of Order people, we should try to include him."

As the others watched, frozen, Shawn got up from the table and walked to Mathis' tent.

"You're missing breakfast," he said before he pulled open the flap. Then he stopped and stared.

"What is it?" Gus said.

"Well, the good news is we don't need to save any bacon for him," Shawn said.

Gus jumped up from the table and ran over to the tent, followed by all of the lawyers. They pushed around Shawn so they could get a good look.

A good look at Mathis lying peacefully on his feather bed. And at the kitchen knife protruding from his chest.

Chapter Forty-Six

Chris Rasmussen stalked the mean streets of Isla Vista. He'd loved this town, but now it seemed soiled to him. There had been a criminal conspiracy underneath its manicured lawns, eating at the roots of the community like a gopher destroys an entire field of grass.

How had he missed it all? Had he been so busy writing jaywalking tickets he had let the real villains go free? Had they been laughing at him all the time?

However it had happened, he could not let it stand. He'd called Lassiter repeatedly, offering his services, but the detective had said the task force was closed and had hung up on him. No doubt Lassiter was busily figuring out a way to pretend these murders had never happened. He was up against forces greater than himself—and he was folding.

Henry Spencer had understood that. Rasmussen saw it all now. The great detective could tell that the fix was in, that when the rich and mighty got involved, the pursuit of justice took a backseat to the protection of power. That's what he had been trying to tell Rasmussen at Ellen Svaco's house. That's why he walked away from the case. Detective Spencer thought he was protecting his new protégé.

But Officer Chris Rasmussen neither needed nor wanted protection. He wanted to do his job. His duty. He wanted to see the guilty punished and the innocent protected. That was all that mattered to him.

In a way he was touched by Henry Spencer's desire to shelter him. He supposed the thought was that if Rasmussen walked away from this, he'd survive to protect and serve another day.

But the law didn't work like that. You couldn't simply choose which criminals you'd stop and which you'd let go. Once you started down that path, there was no way back. You weren't the law anymore. You were just a hired thug with a badge silk-screened on your chest.

Years ago Rasmussen had rousted a bunch of students who were drinking on the beach long after closing. He confiscated their beer, smothered their campfire, and wrote them all tickets. Normally during an encounter like this he expected some mild-mannered abuse. But this time had been different. The kids were polite, even pleasant. And one of them had offered Rasmussen a bit of wisdom he'd treasured ever since: "The law, in its majestic equality, forbids the rich as well as the poor to sleep under bridges, to beg in the streets, and to steal bread."

That was the way Chris Rasmussen had always enforced the law, and the way he always would. When a crime was committed, it had to be investigated and the guilty punished, no matter who it was. Maybe the Santa Barbara Police Department didn't work that way. But that wasn't going to stop Chris Rasmussen. He had his badge and he had his gun, and that was going to be enough.

Chapter Forty-Seven

Just a few hours earlier, Gus had wanted nothing more than for the bickering among the lawyers to stop. Now that it had, all he wanted was for it to start again. What had replaced it was so much worse: a hostile silence marked only by suspicious glares and the tromping of feet on the forest floor.

They were marching down the same trail they had taken before. It wasn't just Savage and Gwendolyn. It was all the lawyers, along with Shawn and Gus.

Shawn's plan had been a good one. It would have sent the group's two strongest hikers down the mountain, almost guaranteeing they'd make it to a rangers' station. Even if one of them had been the smuggler or Rushton's spy, the other would have made sure the mission was carried out. And best of all, it removed two of the most annoying bickerers from the campsite, ensuring that the rest of them could enjoy the time they spent waiting for rescue.

But that plan couldn't work once they found Mathis' body.

"We have to face the truth," Shawn said. "One of our group is a murderer."

"You don't know that," Savage said. "For all we know it could have been one of them." He waved a hand at the acting troupe, who were huddled together as far from the lawyers as they could get without leaving the safety of the camp.

"Save it for the courtroom," Balowsky said. "There's no jury here to taint."

"It wasn't one of them," Shawn said.

"How can you rule them out so definitively?" Savage said.

"Do you even know their names?" Shawn said.

"I know Miranda," Balowsky said. "And I can vouch for her whereabouts all night."

"Which by some astonishing coincidence gives you an alibi, too," Gwendolyn said.

"That never occurred to me," Balowsky said. "But I suppose you're right."

"The fat chef is named Bram Tchaikovsky, or something like that," Savage said. "The rest of them have some kind of cowboy names."

"Exactly my point," Shawn said. "These are anonymous, faceless figures. Redshirts, actually."

"They're wearing white," Jade said.

"It doesn't matter what color their clothes are," Shawn said. "You've got your three stars and one major guest player beaming down to the planet along with one security officer you've never seen before. Who do you think is going to get mowed down by space Nazis before the opening credits?"

"They're wearing white and they're still alive, while Mathis is dead," Jade said. "What you're saying doesn't make any sense at all."

"He's trying to say they're bit players," Gus said. "We don't really know them except for the limited function they perform in the camp. We haven't been able to differentiate them in any substantive way, and they are, for all intents and purposes, interchangeable. So there's not much point in assuming that one of them is the killer."

"Are you saying that you are ruling them out as suspects because they lack sufficient entertainment value?" Savage said incredulously.

"Absolutely," Shawn said. "Do you think it's too early to start thinking about lunch?"

"We can't just sit down and eat lunch when there's a killer among us," Jade wailed. "One of us is dead. Don't we care at all?"

"We sat down and ate breakfast when there was a killer among us," Shawn said.

"We didn't know," Balowsky said.

"One of us did," Shawn said. "Which brings up an important point. We need to rethink our plan."

"It seems to me that the only change we need to make is to accelerate it," Savage said. "Gwendolyn and I should leave immediately."

"That's a good idea," Shawn said. "If these two are our only hope of survival, we want them on the trail before the killer can get to them."

"Unless," Gus said, "one of them is the killer."

"That would be a problem," Shawn said. "Because if one of them killed Mathis, then it would only make sense for that person to kill the other hiker and escape, as we all starve to death waiting for a rescue that will never come."

"Go ahead, say it," Gwendolyn demanded. "You mean me."

"It could be Savage," Shawn said.

"Standard English usage is to use the male pronoun when talking about someone whose gender is not known," Gwendolyn said. "When you avoid pronouns altogether, you really mean 'she.'"

"Female pronoun there has a point," Gus said.

"I can prove it wasn't me," Gwendolyn said. "Because I wouldn't have used a knife. I could have snapped his scrawny neck with my bare hands or smothered him with a pillow. Hell, I could have jammed a finger through his eye socket into his brain and he'd have been dead before he noticed I was in the tent."

The other lawyers moved a step away from Gwendolyn.

"Well, that certainly sounds like the declaration of an innocent person to me," Shawn said. "Who's for sending her out on the trail with Savage? Show of hands?"

Not a hand went up. Not even Gwendolyn's.

"What if one of them isn't the killer?" Balowsky said. "Then do we just stay here waiting to be picked off one by one?"

"There's no reason to assume the killer is going to strike

again," Shawn said. "Of course, since we have no idea why *that person* killed Mathis, we have no way of predicting what *that person* will do next."

"There are other pronouns beside 'he' and 'she,' " Gwendolyn said. "For example, there's 'I.' And then of course there's '*you*.' How do we know you aren't the killer?"

"She's right," Savage said. "We don't know anything about you two."

Shawn looked hurt. "What do you want to know?" he said. "I'm an open book. With pictures. And a table of contents. An index. Pull me off the shelf and check me out. And you don't even have to reshelve me when you're done. There are metal carts placed in the aisles for your convenience. Which is actually kind of annoying if you're looking for a title and someone has stuck it on the cart and no one's gotten around to putting it back in its place."

Gus could see the lawyers getting restless again. And worse—suspicious. If Shawn kept talking this way, it wouldn't be hard for the real killer to plant a suspicion in the minds of the others.

"Morton Mathis infiltrated Rushton, Morelock six months ago," Gus said. "We joined the firm only a couple of days ago. Whoever he was hunting there, clearly it wasn't Shawn or me."

"We don't know he was searching for any of us," Gwendolyn said. "All we have is your word on that. For all we know you were the criminals he was hunting all along, and you came along on this trip just to kill him."

"And a darned good plan that would have been," Shawn said. "So many criminals are able to plot the perfect crime, but when it comes to the getaway, that's where they slip up. So we designed a murder in which getting away was impossible from the beginning, so there was no chance of it going wrong."

The logic of Shawn's argument, or at least the complete lack of it, seemed to quell the lawyers' suspicion of the two of them. Gus took advantage of the opening.

"Grab your packs," he said. "We need to get going."

"Before lunch?" Shawn said.

"No lunch for us," Gus said. "We need to leave the fresh food for the Triton Players. They'll stay here until we can get a helicopter up to them."

"All of us?" Balowsky said. "What if I want to stay here with Miranda until you come back?"

"What if you want to stay here until we're gone, then kill all the actors and make your escape in the wilderness?" Savage said.

"Then at least there would be five fewer actors in the world," Gwendolyn said. "Mathis wouldn't have died for nothing."

"Gus is right," Shawn said. "We all go or none of us goes. And if none of us goes, none of us is getting back home."

There was grumbling from the lawyers. Grumbling and more suspicious looks. But then Savage marched over, swung his pack up on his back, and fastened the straps. "Let's go," he said. "Those trails aren't going to hike themselves."

One by one the lawyers put on their packs and headed towards the trail. Gus took a moment to tell the actors what was going on and give them a chance to join the trek down the mountain. Either Coty or Bismarck—Gus still couldn't say which was which—looked like he wanted to come along, but troupe loyalty outweighed the desire to flee the meadow, and since there was no way the chef would make it past the first day, they all decided to wait for rescue. If nothing else, Helstrom reasoned, the owner of the costume shop where they had rented their terrorist outfits would report them missing if they didn't return the clothes in a few days.

Shawn, in the meantime, had been going through Mathis' pack and dividing the packets of dehydrated food between his load and Gus'. When Gus came up to him, he swung his pack up on his back. "Race you to the bottom?" Shawn said.

Chapter Forty-Eight

There was a pain in Gus' left foot. At least that's where it started every time he took a step. A dull, throbbing ache pounding across his sole, it pulsed a few times, then traveled up through his ankle to his calf on its way to his knee, where it knocked around for a bit before traveling up through his thigh. It stopped only when Gus lifted his foot. That's when it started on the other side.

How long had they been hiking? Gus had no idea. They had set out before eight in the morning, and the sun was well past midpoint in the sky by now. He could have checked his watch to see what time it was, but he'd misstepped while maneuvering through a stony patch of trail, and a rock had gone out from under him. He'd managed to keep his head from slamming into the ground, but only by using his watch to check his fall. At the time it had seemed like a fair trade-off, to smash the watch's face in order to protect his own, but about now a spell of unconsciousness—even a permanent one—was sounding pretty appealing.

Gus was once again taking up the rear position in the line of hikers. He'd volunteered for the job at first because he liked the idea of being able to see what everyone was doing. It was much harder for any of them to sneak up on him that way.

But after all these hours, strategy didn't have anything to do with his positioning. He just wasn't keeping up, not even with Balowsky, who had started off limping and complaining about rocks in his shoes, but who had picked up his pace as the trail steepened. He had no idea how long it had been since he'd seen Gwendolyn. Maybe she'd managed to cut six days off the hike and was already down at the bottom. Or maybe she had run up ahead to dig pits and cover them with brush, so that the rest of the hikers would all fall to their deaths impaled on sharpened stakes. About now, even that sounded preferable to walking for most of another week.

For what felt like hours, Gus had been hiking behind Savage and Jade, who whispered and giggled together like the newest couple on the junior high school campus. Gus had had to slow his pace in order to get out of earshot after he accidentally overheard them giving legal-jargon-based nicknames for the parts of each other's bodies.

Then something had gone wrong between the two of them. Savage said something, and Jade stiffened angrily. He tried to apologize, but she slapped him hard across the face and accelerated away from him. He marched along sullenly for a moment or two, then broke into a jog to go after her. They disappeared around a switchback, and Gus hadn't seen them again.

At first Gus hadn't minded being alone. Under the blazing sun it was easier to let his mind focus on nothing but making sure that each foot hit solid ground at every step.

But after a couple of hours the trail took that familiar turn, and scrub brush started appearing along the wayside. Within minutes Gus was entering the pine forest.

That shouldn't have been a problem, he kept telling himself. He'd been here already, and there had been no feelings of panic, no flashbacks to his familiar nightmare, no hallucinations.

At the time, though, Gus had had plenty of more pressing issues to worry about. There was something about the prospect of imminent murder at the hands of insane terrorists to keep you from thinking about being lost in the forest. Now that threat was gone, and as much as he tried to convince himself he needed to stay wary in case the Triton Players were actually a front for a real terrorist band, and they had just been pretending to be innocent actors to throw off suspicion until they could make their move, he couldn't help feeling that the trees were pressing in on him.

Part of the problem was that they were. As the trail moved farther into the woods, it was growing narrower. Now it was just a slender track, sometimes completely obscured by heaps of brown pine needles. If he took his eyes off it for more than a second, if he lost his concentration and drifted off the path, would he ever find it again? Or would he be hopelessly lost, like he was in the dream, lost and chased by some hideous unseen monster?

Gus fought to keep these thoughts out of his mind, but it was getting harder and harder. The pain in his feet and legs was keeping him anchored to reality, but he could feel the ropes starting to fray.

He followed the trail around an enormous tree, only to find Shawn sitting against the other side of it nibbling at a granola bar.

"Can you believe people actually fight to protect this kind of wilderness?" Shawn said, getting to his feet. "Go ahead, try to tell me it wouldn't be better without a Burger King every couple of miles."

Gus stopped. "How far ahead are the others?"

"They're spread out over a mile or two," Shawn said. "If it makes you feel any better, even Gwendolyn was looking like she really needed a sylvan pool to splash in."

"It doesn't," Gus said. He took a step forward and felt the pain run up his leg.

"It should," Shawn said. "We need these people to be at least as exhausted as we are."

"Small chance of that," Gus said. "Why?"

"Because it's our only chance of survival," Shawn said. "We need the killer to be tired so that he or she starts to make mistakes."

For the first time in hours Gus didn't feel the ache in his legs. He didn't think about the horrors of being lost in the wilderness.

"Mathis was the threat to the killer, and Mathis is dead," Gus said. "Why kill again?"

"Because as long as any of us is alive, Mathis is still a threat," Shawn said. "If the world knows he was murdered, they'll also know it had to be one of us. And once they start investigating, they'll figure it out. It may take a while. If it's Lassiter on the case, it may take decades. But they will figure it out."

"But if we all disappear in the wilderness, no one will ever know what happened." It was so obvious that Gus couldn't believe he hadn't realized it before. "The killer is presumed dead along with the rest of us. The only difference is we're all rotting out in the woods, while he or she is smuggling that chip out of the country."

"I'm going to follow Gwendolyn's lead here," Shawn said. "Let's just call the killer 'he' from now on, and remember we don't know the real gender. Because if we have only hours left to live, I don't want to spend precious seconds of my life saying 'he or she.'"

"Fine," Gus said. "He's going to kill us all. He'll have to kill all the actors, too."

"He's got time," Shawn said. "Even if Rushton isn't playing games, no one's going to know anything's wrong for at least four more days. It will take another forty-eight hours before they send out the search parties. And they're not going to find anything, if the killer is smart."

"So what do we do?" Gus said.

"As I see it, we've got a couple of options," Shawn said. "First, we could kill all the lawyers before they can get to us."

"I'm going to pass on that one."

"Just as well," Shawn said. "I don't really have enough energy for a mass killing. It looks so easy when you see it in the movies, but when you start figuring all the logistics, all the luring the victim into a secluded location, then hiding the body, and then getting ready to start all over again with the next one, it gets to be a lot of work."

"Why wouldn't you just drop behind them on the trail and shoot them all at once?" Gus said.

"You mean like you?"

"Yes, Shawn," Gus said wearily. "That's the real reason I've been taking up the rear. Because I am actually the killer, and I plan to eliminate all the lawyers. On the off chance I ever catch up with them, of course."

"You have to admit, it would be a great twist," Shawn said. "No one would ever see that coming."

"No one ever saw that Tommy Lee Jones was killing Laura Mars' models, either," Gus said. "And for the same reason: It's really stupid and makes everything that comes before it ridiculous."

Gus pushed himself off the tree and started walking down the trail, trying to ignore the pain in his feet and legs. Shawn caught up with him within three steps. Or almost caught up with him; the trees grew so close here there was only room to walk single file.

"Okay, okay, forget the twist," Shawn said. "We'll focus on finding the real killer, even if it turns out to be the most obvious suspect."

"You mean Gwendolyn?"

"Of course not," Shawn said. "She's a trained killer, a natural hunter, and a born predator. She'd murder us all as soon as look at us. Sooner, probably, if she knew how bad you looked right now."

"Which makes her the most obvious suspect," Gus said.

"Maybe in that bizarro universe you live in," Shawn said. "She's so obvious she couldn't be the killer. Not if we're going to maintain any self-respect as detectives."

Gus tried to ignore the throbbing in his head, which was beginning to pulse in rhythm with the pain in his legs. "So when you say 'the most obvious suspect,' you really mean the least obvious suspect, who is most obvious by virtue of not being obvious at all."

"Now that is some respectable detecting," Shawn said.

"Who are we talking about?" Gus said.

"I'd think it would be obvious."

Gus tried to glare back at Shawn, but all he could see behind him was the edge of his own pack. "I don't want to have this conversation anymore," he said.

"Okay, I'll tell you, but only because you're tired and cranky," Shawn said. "Jade Greenway."

Gus stopped so suddenly that Shawn walked into his pack, nearly knocking them both over. He steadied himself against a tree as Shawn came around to face him. "What makes you say she's the killer?" Gus said.

"Jade is perfect," Shawn said. "She's quiet and kind of shy and seems pretty easy to intimidate, at least compared to the rest of this bunch. She's the only one who ever expressed remorse over Mathis' death, even if it was expressed more as a confirmation of her own moral superiority than as any actual sense of grief. And she always wears bright green, which makes her unbelievably easy to see, especially if she tries to hide in this dusty brown forest."

"Everything you're saying is an argument for why Jade Greenway isn't the killer," Gus said.

"Exactly," Shawn said. "You don't get a lot less obvious than that. Which all adds up to make her the obvious suspect."

"If you're living in a nuthouse," Gus said. "Or a Joe Eszterhas movie."

"I'm going with the nuthouse," Shawn said. "Unless Jade and Gwendolyn throw off their tops and start dancing around the trees."

Gus could feel his legs beginning to tremble beneath him. Since his only choice was to fall over and die right here or start walking again, he set out along the trail. He could hear Shawn crunching through the pine needles behind him.

"Okay, fine, don't believe me," Shawn said. "But when she sneaks up on you in the night, and you have only one second to cry out before your life is over, I hope you'll have the common decency to use that time to say I was right."

"I'll keep that in mind," Gus said. "In the meantime, whether it's Jade or Gwendolyn or Savage or Balowsky or even Joe Eszterhas, how do we keep the rest of us alive for the next few days?"

"I've been working on a plan," Shawn said. "To start with, it's absolutely crucial that the six of us stay together at all times. As long as we're all in each other's sight, there's no way the killer can start to pick us off one by one."

"That is a good plan," Gus said. "I do see one little hole in it, though."

"It's true that the killer could tell everyone their shoes are untied, and then when we all bend down to look, in that instant he strikes," Shawn said. "I recommend we keep our laces tightly tied at all times."

"The killer could still drop to the back of the line, pull out a gun, and take us all out," Gus said. "With these packs on, it's almost impossible to see anything that's behind you."

"I've got a two-pronged solution to that," Shawn said. "The first prong is you, although I've always considered you more of a tine. You'll stay at the end of the line at all times."

"How do I keep someone from dropping behind me?" Gus said.

"Whatever you've been doing so far has worked just fine," Shawn said. "You've been dead last since we started out."

Gus stopped short, braced himself against a tree, then waited for the satisfying thwock of Shawn's nose hitting his pack. Then he moved on again. "Until now," he said. "You're behind me as we speak because you chose to wait for me. Couldn't the killer do exactly the same thing?"

Shawn rubbed his bruised nose, then started off after Gus. "That's what the second prong is for," he said. "And in this case the prong is a rope, which wouldn't be very useful if we needed a pitchfork, but is pretty good as a way to keep us from getting killed."

"You're going to tie us all together?" Gus said.

"Mountain climbers do it," Shawn says. "That way if one person falls off a cliff, he doesn't have to worry about the others making fun of him after he's dead, because he'll drag them all down with them."

"I don't think that's the actual purpose," Gus said. "But it's not a bad idea. If we can get the others to go along with it."

"Oh, we will," Shawn said. "And even if we don't, the exercise will serve a useful purpose. It might even reveal the killer."

"Because the killer won't want to be roped together with

us," Gus said. "So the one who fights hardest against the idea is our murderer."

"Except that he knows that we'll be thinking that," Shawn said. "So he might try to throw off suspicion by being the first and most energetic supporter of the plan."

"Or maybe he'll know that we're thinking that way, too," Gus said. "And he'll stay neutral during the entire debate and let the others fight it out."

"Exactly," Shawn said. "So all we need to do is look for the one who is for, against, or neutral about the plan, and that's our killer."

This part of the plan didn't seem promising to Gus, but he did like the idea of their all being roped together. It would keep the killer from being able to pick them off one by one. And even better, it would rule out any possibility that he himself would get separated from the pack and become hopelessly lost in the wilderness. In all the times he'd had that nightmare, not once had he been bound to a group of bickering lawyers in it.

"Sounds good," Gus said. "It would be even better if there were any lawyers around here to tie ourselves to."

"Don't worry," Shawn said. "We'll catch up to them pretty soon. I remember from the map that there's a fork in the trail a couple miles ahead. And since I'm the only one who's got the map, the others are going to have to wait for us to know which route to take."

Gus nodded, even though there was no way Shawn could see his head bobbing with the pack between them. For one moment, Gus felt the terror oozing out of him..

And then, just as suddenly, it came rushing back.

Somewhere up ahead a woman was screaming.

"Did you hear that?" Gus said.

"It's Jade," Shawn said. "And I don't think she just discovered another campsite."

Gus' feet started to run before his mind was even aware it had sent out the signal. Pain ricocheted up his legs with every step, but he ignored it. He'd heard Jade scream twice before— once had been a cry of delight at the discovery of Bron Helstrom's outdoor restaurant; the other had been a shriek of terror when she was kidnapped by Helstrom's killer commandos.

But this was worse than either of the others. There was something particularly piercing about this scream. Gus didn't know what could have frightened Jade more than being rousted from her tent by four armed, masked men, and deep down he never wanted to find out. But if she was in danger, they were all in danger, and it was his duty to save her and the rest.

Gus rounded a bend, and now he heard something else—the sound of water crashing far below him. Right in front of him, the ground dropped away in a steep cliff. Far below, a churning river plummeted over a waterfall and down a series of white-water rapids.

It wasn't the sight of the drop that filled Gus with horror, or the pale faces of Gwendolyn, Savage, and Balowsky as they stared down at the river.

It was the pack. The bright green pack hanging off a tree branch upside down, spilling its contents down the cliff.

It was Jade's pack. And Jade was nowhere to be seen.

Gus could feel Shawn pressing up beside him as he moved to join the lawyers.

"I heard her scream," Balowsky. "I ran back as fast as I could."

"We all did," Savage said. "We were too late."

"One of us wasn't," Gwendolyn said.

Shawn and Gus peered over the cliff's edge to the white water pounding far below. The contents of Jade's pack were churning under the pounding of the waterfall. Gus could see packets of freeze-dried food bob to the surface, then disappear again. And something else. Gus wanted to believe that the flash of bright green was nothing but a large leaf from some kind of tree they simply hadn't noticed along the way. But he knew there were no green leaves here; all the trees up the river produced only needles. That flash of green could be only one thing: Jade's dress.

Shawn stared down at the dress until it disappeared under the water. "I guess she wasn't so obvious after all," he said.

Chapter Forty-Nine

There was a fire. Gwendolyn had built a stone ring, then laid dry wood and kindling in it, demonstrating an understanding of woodsmanship that would have put a troop of Boy Scouts to shame, although she used the lighter from her pack instead of rubbing sticks together to produce the first flame.

The fire was meant to provide comfort, as well as to allow them to heat water to rehydrate their dinners. And its warmth was certainly welcome. Although the day had been uncomfortably hot, once the sun went down the temperature started to plummet, and now it felt like it was close to freezing.

But comfort was the last thing the fire was bringing Gus. Its jumping, flickering light gave their campsite the look of the main set in a slasher movie, and it turned the people sitting around it into malevolent specters. Even Shawn, who sat directly across the campfire from Gus, looked like an evil troll. Savage and Balowsky were on Gus' left side and Gwendolyn on his right; apparently neither of the other lawyers felt comfortable being too close to her.

They had been sitting like this for what felt like hours, sitting and staring at one another. Waiting for someone else to make a move. To reveal himself as a threat.

Because there was no doubt now that they were all on the killer's hit list. Balowsky had tried to convince the others—or maybe himself—that Jade's fatal plunge could have been an accident. After all, he'd pointed out, the trail jagged away from the cliff's edge at the last possible moment. If Jade had been too tired to pay attention to where she was walking, if she'd even been hiking with her eyes half closed, as he'd found himself doing, she could have marched right off the mountain.

Gus had thought it would have been nice to be able to believe that. But when Shawn looked around the place Jade had fallen, he noticed a small smear of blood on a nearby tree. She'd been hurt before she went over the cliff, and if she had been sleep-hiking, the pain would have woken her up. And there was no way she could have stumbled from the bloodied tree and off the trail.

Shawn didn't communicate his findings by pointing out the blood. Instead he received a telepathic communication from Jade that came in the form of verse one from the Red Hot Chili Peppers' song "Green Heaven." But none of the other lawyers felt like arguing the point. Two of them accepted that their colleague had been murdered, and the third knew from firsthand experience.

They had spent the rest of the day hiking together in silence. At least they were in silence once Savage had run out of ways to say, "Why didn't I stay with her? Why did I let her go off on her own?" and Gwendolyn had run out of ways to tell him to shut up.

By the time the sun was disappearing behind the mountain, they'd reached a small meadow split by the river. It had enough flat ground to lay out their sleeping bags, and they could refill their water bottles in the morning. Gwendolyn and Balowsky set out to gather firewood, while Shawn, Gus, and Savage set up the camp and collected the stones for the fire ring.

That was the new rule: No one was allowed to wander off alone. The killer would not be allowed the chance to strike again.

They'd been sitting in front of the fire for what seemed like hours when Gwendolyn started to fidget. She crossed her legs, then uncrossed them and crossed them again. Finally she got up and started to move outside the ring of firelight.

"Where do you think you're going?" Balowsky said.

"Where do you think?" she snapped.

"For all I know you're going to step behind a tree, whittle sticks into spears, and start picking us off one by one," Savage said.

"You've got the first part right," Gwendolyn said. "I am going to step behind a tree. But what I do after that is a lot more urgent and a lot more useful than killing any number of you."

She started towards the forest again. Until a rock thumped into the ground at her feet.

"The next one doesn't miss," Savage said. "Do not take another step."

"Do you want me to pull down my pants right here?" she said. "Because I can't guarantee my stream isn't going to run right into the sleeping bags."

"You can go," Shawn said. "Just take someone with you."

"That's a good idea," Gwendolyn said with mock brightness. "We gals like to go to the bathroom together, anyway. I'll just take one of the other girls with me. Which one should I take?"

Savage stared sadly into the fire, either thinking fond thoughts of the girlfriend to whom he never got to say good-bye or wishing he'd murdered the other female lawyer first. After a moment, Balowsky got to his feet. "I'll go," he said.

"Like hell you will," Gwendolyn said.

"He promises not to peek," Shawn said.

"You've got that right," Balowsky said.

"I'd find that easier to believe if I didn't have to wash off the slime tracks from his eyeballs every time I wore a low-cut blouse to the office," Gwendolyn said.

Shawn took a burning stick from the fire and handed it to Balowsky to use as a torch. "It's this easy," he said. "Either you take Reggie with you, or you sit there and pee in your pants. I know which I prefer, but we'll leave the decision up to you."

She glared at them all, then turned back to the woods. "Come on, then," she said to Balowsky as she disappeared into the darkness.

Gwendolyn and Balowsky were gone for hours. Or maybe it

was seconds. In the darkness Gus couldn't keep track of time. He was about to propose that the rest of them go out and search for the missing lawyers when the nearest trees were lit by the orange glow from a torch.

Gwendolyn tossed the flaming brand into the fire.

"Where's Reggie?" Shawn said. His hands closed around a rock as he waited for the answer.

"Maybe he tried to kill me and I had to knock him out in self-defense," Gwendolyn said. "Or maybe I made him turn his head and then slit his throat with a sharpened twig."

Around the campfire, everyone stared at her, waiting. Until they heard the sound of legs crashing through underbrush and Balowsky stumbled out of the woods behind her.

"Or maybe his legs are even slower than his mind," Gwendolyn said, and took her place by the fire.

"I figured as long as I was out there I might as well take care of my own business," Balowsky said. "So I turned my back on her for one second. And when I turned back, I saw the torch disappearing into the woods."

"Your prostate problems are your own," Gwendolyn said. "I was cold."

"Enough!" Gus shouted.

They all turned to look at him. Shawn looked particularly concerned.

"We can't keep bickering like this," Gus said. "We're just using up all our energy in meaningless backbiting. Meanwhile the killer is plotting how to take us out."

"That's not entirely true," Shawn said. "I mean, unless you or I turn out to be behind it all, then the real killer is using up his energy in meaningless backbiting, too. So it's not all bad."

"It's bad enough," Gus said.

"It could be worse," Shawn said.

Now the lawyers all turned to stare at him.

"How?" Gwendolyn asked in a tone that was less a question and more a dagger aimed directly at him.

"We're all sitting around this fire not knowing which one among us is the person who has been systematically picking us off," Shawn said. "Now imagine that while we're sitting here,

Reggie's head falls off his body, grows spider legs, and runs away into the darkness."

The silence following Shawn's remark was the quietest Gus had ever heard. Even the fire stopped popping and sparking for a moment.

"Well," Shawn said cheerily as he stood and stretched, "this is fun, but I'm going to bed. Who wants first watch?"

"I'll take it," Gus said. He didn't think he was going to sleep anyway, not with the image of the monster from *The Thing* in his mind. And if he did manage to doze off, there was a bigger threat. The dream.

"I'll stay up, too," Savage said. "Two people on watch at all times, right?"

"Right," Shawn said. "You and Gus go first; then in six hours wake Reggie and Gwendolyn."

"What about you?" Balowsky demanded.

"Can I help it if we have an odd number of potential victims here?" Shawn said. "If the one of you who is trying to kill us had done a better job today, we could divvy up the watches a little more fairly."

Shawn took the two steps from his seat to his sleeping bag, lay down, and started snoring within seconds. Savage and Gwendolyn followed him to their own beds.

The next few hours passed surprisingly quickly for Gus. If Savage was the killer, he was doing an excellent job of pretending to be terrified. And while Gus envied Shawn just a little bit for his ability to sleep so easily, he was also happy that he hadn't felt tired since they discovered what had happened to Jade. He knew that the next day's march was going to be long and hard, and much more so if he didn't get any sleep tonight. But he liked being awake. He liked being able to see what was going on around the fire—or what wasn't going on.

When Balowsky's watch alarm went off and he woke up Gwendolyn and Savage so they could take their turn, Gus relinquished his job without much enthusiasm. He felt so much safer here by the fire. But he went to his sleeping bag and closed his eyes, and when he opened them again the sun was breaking over the mountains.

Except as the sun rose, it didn't seem to give off any light. It shone hot and yellow in the sky, but the campsite stayed dark. Gus sat up in his sleeping bag to ask the others if they saw what he was seeing.

The others were gone.

Chapter Fifty

It wasn't even nine o'clock yet and Heidi Sansome was already having a terrible day. She'd slept through her alarm and had been so freaked about being late she was nailed for a speeding ticket on the way to work. That got her to the reception desk ten minutes late. She'd be lucky if she wasn't fired before lunch.

And to make everything worse, there was this ridiculous lifeguard in her waiting room. At least he was dressed like a lifeguard. He kept pointing at an insignia on his shirt and insisting he had something to do with feet, then demanding to speak to Mr. Rushton immediately. She'd explained a dozen times that Mr. Rushton saw no one without an appointment, which she would be happy to schedule for him. He just pointed at his chest and insisted he needed to see the boss now.

Heidi pressed the red button on her phone for the fifteenth time. Where the hell was security? They should have had this nut out of here ages ago.

Finally a side door banged open and Fritz the security guard came through. "What seems to be the trouble here?"

Well, duh, Heidi thought. It's the crazy lifeguard with the foot fetish. She was about to point out the obvious when she noticed that Fritz's hands were up in the air and his face had gone white.

Heidi turned to see that the lifeguard had pulled out a gun and was aiming it directly at Fritz.

"I want to see Mr. Rushton," he said. "Now."

Chapter Fifty-One

The others hadn't been gone long. Gus reached over and touched Shawn's sleeping bag. It was still warm. And the fire was blazing in the ring, a pot nestled among the embers heating water for instant coffee and freeze-dried eggs.

Gus looked back at the sun. It had climbed in the sky and it pounded him with its heat. But it still didn't seem to give off any light. The only illumination in the campground came from the flickering fire. Shadows jumped, danced, laughed at the edges of the camp.

"Shawn?" Gus whispered. Beyond the reach of the firelight something rustled in the underbrush. Gus tried to peer into the darkness, but he couldn't see anything. "Shawn?" he whispered again, but there was no answer.

Where had Shawn gone? Where had they all gone? And why had they left him here alone? He bent down to check one of the sleeping bags and his hand came back sticky and feathered. There was a gash in the bag, and as Gus stood up, the feathers flew out of the tear and swirled around his face. He shook his hand to get the feathers off, but they wouldn't fall. He slapped at them, and his hand came back red with blood.

The gash in the sleeping bag was bleeding.

This wasn't possible. Even as his rational mind was being consumed with terror, Gus knew that a nylon shell filled with duck feathers couldn't bleed. And that meant this couldn't be real. He had to be dreaming. He had to be dreaming *that dream*. All he had to do was wake up.

Gus squeezed his fist until his fingernails were digging into his palm. Then he looked down at the sleeping bag. It was still oozing blood. He looked up at the sun.

The sun was oozing blood, too.

There was another rustling in the bushes behind him. Gus turned to see who was coming after him. *What* was coming after him. A branch tore off a tree and fell to the ground and a hand reached through the opening in the tree trunk. Except it wasn't a hand, it was more like a—

Gus woke up. His eyes flashed open. The sun was coming up over the mountains, and it was actually shining light down on the campsite.

Shawn was sitting by the fire mixing something in a metal Sierra Cup with a plastic spoon.

"I keep stirring and stirring," Shawn said when he noticed Gus was awake. "But this still doesn't look like eggs Benedict." He tilted the steel cup so Gus could see the yellow-and-white soup floating inside.

Shawn was here, but the lawyers were all gone. As he crawled out of his sleeping bag, Gus searched the camp for any trace of them. "Where is everybody?"

"Bathroom break," Shawn said. "They worked out some system where the three of them go into the woods together so no one actually has to look at anyone else. Or something." He took a sip of his eggs and grimaced. "If I ever come up with a brilliant moneymaking scheme that revolves around eggs Benedict you can drink with a straw, talk me out of it."

Gus wanted to grab Shawn by the shoulders until his head fell off, grew spider legs, and ran away. How could he be thinking about anything so trivial right now?

There was a rustling from the bushes. Before Gus had time to formulate the image of the creature in his head, the three lawyers stepped out into the camp. Savage and Balowsky stayed a step behind as Gwendolyn walked up to Shawn and reached for his pack.

"We've taken a vote," she said. "We've decided to share control of the map."

Shawn nudged the pack out of her reach with his foot. "I voted that if Quaker Oats was going to release a new flavor of Life cereal they should go for chocolate instead of maple-and-brown-sugar," he said. "They seemed to think that my vote didn't count, especially since they never had an election."

If Shawn had hoped to distract Gwendolyn into a discussion of the Quaker Oats company's unfair decision-making process, he was disappointed. "We don't trust you and your little sidekick."

Gus should let that go, he knew. There were monsters in the woods. They couldn't start fighting among themselves. But he found himself taking a step forward, his hands clenching into fists. In the last few days he'd been held hostage first by a mime, then by a group of actors. He'd been stranded in the mountains and forced to hike a bazillion miles to save his life. He spent half his energy fighting to stay alive and the other half struggling against blind, irrational panic. Through it all he'd remained pleasant and polite. And what was his reward? To be insulted by a lawyer—a lawyer! Worse—a lawyer with a thirty-four percent chance of being a mass killer. He wasn't going to take it anymore. "I am no man's sidekick," he said.

"I didn't say you were a man's sidekick," Gwendolyn said. "I said you were his."

"That's it," Gus said. "The last straw."

Somehow Shawn didn't seem to share his anger, even though the barb had been aimed primarily at him. "I guess that makes you the camel's back," Shawn said. "That could come in handy on the rest of the hike. Which is what we should really be saving our energy for."

"I'm ready to hike as soon as I can see the map," Gwendolyn said.

"You want that map?" Gus said. "You can come through me to get it."

"Because that would be a long and exciting fight," Shawn said casually. "After all, she's only the Master of Sinanju looking for an excuse to scoop your brains out through your nose with her pinky finger. And you never came in lower than second when we played Rock'Em Sock'Em Robots."

"We've got to have this out now," Gus said.

"That's a good idea," Shawn said. "I mean, it's not like they came up to us and deliberately tried to get us mad so that we'd start a fight, giving them an opportunity to kick our asses and take the map from our cold, dead hands. And when I say it's not like that, I mean it's exactly like that."

The blood pounding in Gus' ears was almost enough to drown out Shawn's logic. Almost, but not quite. He dropped his hands and felt the blood surging back into his fingers as they unclenched. "So by not fighting, we win," Gus said. "It's like a Zen thing."

"Wax on, wax off," Shawn agreed.

"That is the lamest excuse for wussing out on a fight I've ever heard," Balowsky said.

"Almost as lame as letting the girl do your fighting for you while you hide behind her?" Shawn said.

"Even lamer," Gwendolyn said. "They know who their strongest warrior is."

"I know I do," Shawn agreed. "If there's one of the three of you who's tough enough to toss Jade off a cliff, I'd vote for you."

"And yet the other two want to give her the only map out of here," Gus said

"Nice try," Savage said. "But we can work that out between ourselves once we've got the map. Now hand it over."

Shawn picked up his pack and slipped it over his shoulders. "Tell you what," he said. "We'll be the ones going in the right direction. You get moving, and we'll call out the turns."

He headed out of the camp between two tall trees. Gus shouldered his pack and followed. There was a moment's whispered discussion among the lawyers, and then Gwendolyn led the others quickly through another stand of trees and around so that they were positioned in front of Shawn and Gus.

"You're going to give us the map," Gwendolyn said.

"You couldn't trick us into a fight; you're not going to out-smart us," Shawn said. "There's no way we're going to give it to you."

"Except that there are only two of you," Savage said. "And there are three of us."

Savage took one menacing step forward. But as his foot hit the ground, something snaked through the litter of dried pine needles and seized him around the ankle. Before anyone could move, the snare tightened on his foot and flung the lawyer upside down high among the top branches of the trees. Gus heard a meaty thump as Savage's head collided with the trunk. Gus peered up. Way above them, he could see the tiny, broken figure of the lawyer dangling limply from the rope.

"I guess that makes us even again," Shawn said. "Shall we start walking?"

Chapter Fifty-Two

After leaving the investigation, Henry had thought he'd go back to rock and roll camp. He'd driven most of the way to Ojai beating out his drum solo on the steering wheel. But he couldn't focus on jamming right now; his mind was completely preoccupied with a double homicide, and he knew that even though he wasn't officially involved, he couldn't just let it alone. So he made a U-turn as soon as he passed the end of the divided section of Highway 33 and headed home.

He'd spent the next day working the phone and the computer trying to find any information on the case. He'd even popped into police headquarters, but Lassiter and O'Hara were out in the field, and no one knew when they'd be back. Of course he could have called their cells and offered his services, but he knew what they'd have said: He was retired.

The long and fruitless day landed him exactly one piece of information—the janitorial contracting service Arnold Svaco had worked for had a contract to clean, among many much less interesting places, the Jet Propulsion Laboratory, and Arnold had been working there almost exclusively for years. Maybe that meant something, although Henry had no idea what. He left the information on Lassiter's voice mail, just in case.

The next day was the last session of camp, and when he woke up Henry decided he'd go back for the big jam session finale. The case was still pushing the beat out of his mind, but after wasting all of yesterday, he decided he could leave the police work to the working police.

He was getting into the car for the drive to Ojai when his cell rang. He answered. And heard the last two words he ever expected to hear since his retirement:

Hostage situation.

Henry blew through a half dozen red lights on his way to Edgecliff Road, but by the time he got to Rushton, Morelock's mansion offices, the parking lot was already filled with police cruisers. He jumped out of his car as Lassiter rushed up to him.

"How bad is it?" Henry said.

"How bad can it get?" Lassiter said. He started towards the mansion, assuming that Henry would keep up with him. They blew past the front door and continued along the exterior of the building.

"What does he think he's doing?" Henry said.

"'Bringing justice to an unjust world,'" Lassiter said. "Or something even dumber. You can ask him yourself. He's been demanding to speak to you."

There was a window open at the far end of the building. Lassiter stopped short, but gestured for Henry to walk up to it.

Henry peered into the open window. The room was enormous, the size of Henry's whole house, and furnished in nautical antiques. Across a huge desk Henry could see an elderly man in a wheelchair. He'd never met Oliver Rushton, but he'd seen enough pictures in the paper to recognize him. Standing over the lawyer was Officer Chris Rasmussen. He was pointing a gun at Rushton's head.

Henry had to think fast. He should have formulated a plan of action on the drive down, but the situation was so insane he couldn't bring himself to believe it until he saw it for himself. Now he had to improvise.

"Officer Rasmussen," he said with as much authority as he could muster. "Report."

"I came to interview Mr. Rushton," Rasmussen said, snapping to attention. "He was unwilling to speak to me, so I was required to use force."

"That's very good thinking, Officer," Henry said. "Excellent initiative. Then what?"

"He still won't talk!" Rasmussen wailed, sounding close to tears. "I've been asking and asking, but he won't tell me anything! And I keep trying to remember what you told us about interrogation techniques, but I forget!"

"It's okay, Officer," Henry said. "I don't think we covered that in class."

"You're just saying that to make me feel better!"

Henry could see Rasmussen's hand shaking; he was clearly about to snap. Rushton, on the other hand, looked completely in control.

"I've tried to explain to the officer that I haven't heard of the woman he's inquiring about," the lawyer said. "I'm willing to look at a picture, if you have one."

"She called you!" Rasmussen shouted.

"She called my offices," Rushton said. "As I've explained, many people work here, and she could have been calling for any of them. Or she could have misdialed. I have offered to let you go over my phone logs for the day in question, to see if her call shows up. What else can I do?"

"You can tell the truth!"

"I am telling the truth," Rushton said. "The sad fact is that one of the lawyers in the firm might well be involved in these crimes. That person may have killed one of my own employees. As soon as the lawyers return from their retreat, I promise to urge them to cooperate fully with your investigation."

"You're stalling!" Rasmussen's finger was tightening on the trigger. Henry had to do something fast.

"Officer Rasmussen, you will stand down now," he commanded.

"I can't!" Now there were tears in Rasmussen's eyes. "This is all my fault, Detective Spencer. Ellen Svaco was involved in some kind of crime ring in my own town, and I missed it. And I missed the redial thing, too. You tried to teach me, but I was too stupid to understand any of it, and now I've messed everything up. I've got to make it right!"

"This isn't the way, Officer," Henry said. "You can't fix one crime with another crime."

"That's what you said when I was in school, but how do I know this isn't something that's much more complicated in grown-up life? Nothing is like it's supposed to be!"

Rasmussen was about to explode. Henry had to do something fast. He wanted to dive through the window and knock the gun out of his hand. He wanted to tell the officer what a fool he was making of himself. If it had been Shawn in that room, he would have.

But of course his own son would never have been in such a ludicrous position. For all that Shawn pretended not to listen to Henry's advice, the fact was he always absorbed the important parts. He had allowed Henry to mold him into a man. Chris Rasmussen had never had anyone to do that for him.

"Officer," Henry started, then softened his tone. "Chris. We had forty-five minutes together twenty years ago. Forty-five minutes with a crowd of other children. And you took that brief meeting and built your entire life around it. Do you have any idea how proud that makes me?"

Henry could see sunlight glinting off the tears in Rasmussen's face. "Proud?"

"I'm only sorry I wasn't able to be there for you all along," Henry said. "I wish I had. I always wanted a second son. I hope you'll allow me to consider you that now."

Rasmussen's hand trembled furiously. And then the gun dropped to the floor.

"Clear!" Henry shouted, and the office was full of police officers in body armor. Henry's last sight of Rasmussen was just a scrap of flesh buried under a mountain of black uniforms.

Henry was about to rejoin Lassiter when Rushton called his name. He turned back to see that the lawyer had moved towards the window.

"I hope you meant what you said about cooperating," Henry said to him.

"My devotion to the cause of justice is as strong as yours, even if we express it in different ways," Rushton said. "I suspected that something was wrong in my firm, but until today I didn't realize just how bad it was. And that concerns you as well."

"Me?"

"I heard you mention you have a son," Rushton said. "He's a detective, isn't he?"

"Technically," Henry said, feeling a cold shiver of fear run down his spine.

"Then there's something you need to know."

Chapter Fifty-Three

This time there was no chance that Gus was going to lose sight of the rest of the hiking party. Shawn hadn't even needed to bring up his notion of roping them all together; no one moved out of anyone else's view. Gwendolyn and Balowsky walked together, staring at each other. At one point, Gwendolyn, her eyes fixed firmly on Balowsky's face, hit a rock with her foot and tripped. She fell to the ground, rolled, and popped back up—never looking away from the other lawyer.

Even though there were two people on watch all night long, one of them had managed to slip away in the night and set the trap that took out Savage. If the killer could strike this quickly and this invisibly, what hope did the rest of them have?

From their place at the end of the pack, Gus and Shawn examined Gwendolyn and Balowsky. They both seemed completely consumed in studying each other for treachery.

"One of them is a pretty good actor," Shawn said. "I wonder if Helstrom needs a new member in his troupe."

"If only I had shared my watch with someone besides Savage, since he clearly wan't the killer," Gus said. "I would have known if whoever was staying up with me had sneaked off to set a snare. That would have narrowed the suspect pool down to one."

"How much could you actually see when you were on watch?" Shawn said.

"I could see you sleeping," Gus said. "I could see you sleeping peacefully all night long."

"You mean you could see whatever was in the direct firelight," Shawn said.

"That, too," Gus said. "But mostly I could see you sleeping."

"Yes, the clever and subtle dig has been heard and now acknowledged," Shawn said. "But my greater point was that it was really dark in the camp. If Savage had slipped away on your watch, are you sure you wouldn't have seen him?"

"I'm pretty sure he wouldn't have stepped into his own snare," Gus said.

"You're getting awfully literal all of a sudden," Shawn said.

"I'm getting scared," Gus said. "No, I take that back. I am scared."

"Okay, there's a killer out there picking us off one by one," Shawn said. "But look at the bright side. One more murder and we'll know for sure who it is. And that's halfway to safety right there."

"Unless one of us is the victim," Gus said.

Shawn stopped to think this over, as if the thought had never occurred to him. "That would be a problem," he said. "Because if the killer took out you or me, that wouldn't bring us any closer to knowing who it is."

"And because I'd be dead," Gus said, panic rising in his chest. "Or you would. Or we both would."

"That wouldn't make any sense," Shawn said. "If we were both out of the running, then there wouldn't be any question who the killer was. No, the next murder has to be a single, unless said killer is willing to take all three out at once."

"What if she is?" Gus said.

"She?"

"Oh, come on," Gus said. "Only Gwendolyn could have set that trap. She's the one with all the jungle lore at her fingertips. She's the one who is obviously willing to kill without even blinking. And she's coming after us next."

"It's a good argument, but if we guess wrong—"

"I'm not guessing," Gus said. "I know. I know from my dreams. Because the thing that's chasing me is always female. I just never realized until right now that it was a female human."

"This is based on your dream?" Shawn said. "Haven't you learned anything from working for a fake psychic-detective agency?"

"I know something has been trying to warn me of this day for almost as long as I've been alive," Gus said. "I know that I've lived what happens next again and again—and I've never survived it."

"If you give in to panic and superstition, we are never going to make it home," Shawn said. "We need to be intelligent. Rational."

"Says the psychic," Gus said.

"Exactly," Shawn said. "We can get away with almost anything by claiming I'm psychic—because people aren't intelligent and rational. They believe that stuff. We don't."

"Then maybe you should start using that brain of yours," Gus snapped.

"I am," Shawn said.

"You're using your feet," Gus said. "You're using your mouth. But you're not using your brain. You're walking along this trail, waiting for the killer to reveal herself, gambling that her preferred method of doing so won't involve our decapitation. But what you're not doing is the one thing you do well—putting together a series of microscopic clues and solving the case."

Shawn stopped, scowling angrily. "Have you considered maybe I'm doing this for you?"

Gus stopped, too. "You're keeping me stranded in the wilderness with an insane killer for my own good?"

"Immersion therapy," Shawn said. "You've got to get over this bizarre, superstitious fear of a silly dream."

"Even if it kills me."

"At least you'll be cured," Shawn said and started down the trail.

Gus grabbed the top of Shawn's pack and pulled him back.

"Don't you dare blame this on me," he said through clenched teeth. "People are dead. We could be dead. You can't be doing this to help me with my recurring dream. Even if you do have one of—"

Gus broke off, realization dawning on him. Shawn saw it coming and tried to get away.

"If that's the way you feel, I apologize," Shawn said as he took a step down the trail again.

But Gus wouldn't let go of his pack, and Shawn was jerked back like a marionette whose puppeteer suffered from Parkinson's. "You never told me what your recurring dream was," Gus said.

"It's really not important now," Shawn said. "If you want me to solve this crime now and leave you emotionally crippled, then that's what I'll do."

"*This* is your recurring dream," Gus said.

"Don't be ridiculous," Shawn said. "This is *your* recurring dream. See? Wilderness? Lost? Big scary monster in the trees?"

Again Shawn tried to get away, and again Gus held him back. "In your recurring dream, people are dying, there's a killer right in front of you, and you can't figure out who it is," Gus said. "That's your deepest fear, isn't it?"

"I have no idea what you're talking about," Shawn said with a complete lack of conviction.

He did. Gus could see it in his eyes. Shawn was afraid, and it wasn't of the killer. He was afraid of a vision he'd seen in a dream over and over again. Gus let go of his pack and took him by the shoulders.

"You can do this, Shawn," Gus said. "You know you can. I know you can. It's just another case, just another set of clues."

"It's not!" Shawn said loudly enough for Gwendolyn and Balowsky to hear—and to stop walking. He moved in closer to Gus and whispered, "I don't have clues here. I don't know who the killer is, and I won't until one of them is kind enough to eliminate the other one from suspicion."

"You only think there aren't any clues," Gus said. "But there are. There have to be. You've seen them, you've heard them. You just didn't notice at the time. But they're all in your head.

All you have to do is put them together. And you've got to do it now."

Shawn still looked shaken. "Why now?"

"I've seen you solve enough crimes to know that there are two elements you need before you can swing into action," Gus said. "You need the clues—and you need an audience. If you wait much longer, there won't be anyone left to be stunned by your revelations. And then you might never be able to pull it together."

Shawn looked up the trail at Gwendolyn and Balowsky, who were staring back at them. "They're not much of an audience."

"Next time we'll book the State Theater," Gus said. "Right now this is what we've got. So go dazzle 'em."

Shawn took a deep breath. Then another one. Then he plastered a broad smile across his face.

"Wait up, guys," he called to the lawyers. "Let's take a break and unmask a killer."

Chapter Fifty-Four

The reveal wasn't going well, Gus could tell. It had started out strongly. Shawn was full of his usual bravado as he launched into an explication of the case's known facts. But even as he was finishing up the saga of their ordeal at Descanso Gardens, Gus could feel he was losing momentum—and with that, his audience. Even the revelation that the gun-toting mime was actually their late colleague Archie Kane didn't elicit more than the slightest gesture of impatience from Gwendolyn and Balowsky.

"So everything Rushton told us about you was a lie," Gwendolyn said. "That's a shock. Can we start walking again?"

"We're just getting to the good part," Shawn said, a hint of desperation in his voice.

The trouble was, Gus knew, he wasn't getting to the good part. Gus had listened to enough of these summations to understand their structure. Shawn would lay out what seemed like a string of facts known to everyone, apparently at random. What his audience wouldn't understand until it was too late was that there was nothing random about the selection. Shawn would pick out the precise pieces of information that built up, step by step, to his conclusion. As a technique, it was flawless. Even when Shawn was wrong—something that happened along the way before he hit the ultimate solution in the occasional case—the summation itself never was. The chosen clues would always lead inexorably to the determined conclusion. If that conclusion was wrong, it was simply that Shawn had selected the wrong pieces or put them together in the wrong way.

But this time was different. Shawn didn't have a destination in mind, so he had no guide in choosing his clues. He was spewing out everything he'd seen, heard, and done over the last week, in the desperate hope that he could pick a pattern out of it. Gus suspected the lawyers had no idea how much Shawn was struggling, because they'd never witnessed the master at work. He could still put on an entertaining show. But Gus knew it was just a show, and he found it painful to watch.

"Yes," Shawn said. "Rushton lied to you all. For good reason. He suspected that one of you had killed Archie Kane. Or—"

He broke off, trying to figure out where to go next. Gus gave him a nod of encouragement.

"Or did he know?" Shawn said. "Know because he was working with the killer all along?"

"Why do you need a driver's license to buy liquor when you can't drink and drive?" Balowsky said. "Why are their interstate highways in Hawaii? If you want to play rhetorical questions, we can be here until the mountain crumbles into sand, and then we don't have to worry about walking down. Unless we're murdered first."

"As if that's something you're worried about," Gwendolyn said.

"Standing next to you, I am," Balowsky said. "Why don't you just get it over with? I'll even let you have your favorite target."

He turned his back on her—and then whirled around quickly to see if she was aiming a knife at it.

Gus looked at Shawn. Wasn't he going to stop this? But Shawn wasn't paying attention to the bickering lawyers. He didn't seem to be paying attention to anything outside himself. He stared off into the far distance, the beginnings of a smile on his face.

"Shawn?" Gus said.

"Rushton brought us into the conference room apparently so we could learn what you all were like," Shawn said. "And you didn't disappoint. Gwendolyn Shrike attacked immediately, only to retreat when there was clearly no hope for victory. Kirk Savage hid behind legal technicalities. Morton Mathis was scared we'd reveal his real identity. Reggie Balowsky sat back and waited to see who was going to win before he chose a side. And Jade Greenway, poor, sweet Jade Greenway, bravely stood up for us."

"Bravely!" Gwendolyn almost spat the word. "Is it brave to suck up to your boss?"

Gus stared at Shawn. What was he doing now? What he was saying still seemed like a stall, but there was confidence in his voice and a glint in his eye that hadn't been there when he started the reveal.

"Not to speak ill of the dead or anything," Balowsky said.

"The only reason you don't speak ill of the dead is because you can't do them any more damage that way," Gwendolyn said.

"Personally, I'm all in favor of sucking up to the boss," Shawn said. "Of course, that may have something to do with the fact that I run my own business and I end up sucking up to myself. Which isn't really as easy as it sounds. Anyway, there's sucking up and there's sucking up. It's one thing to lavish praise on your boss's new pet detectives. It's another thing to do it before you even know they exist. This is the point where you ask what I'm talking about."

If it was, neither Gwendolyn nor Balowsky was taking advantage of the opportunity. They were glaring at each other, unmoving.

"I've had enough of you to last a lifetime," Gwendolyn said. "So if you're going to try to kill me, go ahead."

"No point pretending with me," Balowsky snarled. "We both know I didn't do it, and that only leaves you. And I'd like to see you try it now."

Balowsky opened his hand, revealing the Swiss Army knife he had palmed. It was opened to its largest blade, and the three inches of forged steel trembled in Gwendolyn's direction. Gus didn't see her move, but somehow she had a large rock in her hand, which she was holding up as a club.

"They seem pretty busy," Shawn said to Gus. "Maybe you should ask what I'm talking about."

"Do you know?" Gus said without taking his eyes off the lawyers.

"You should try me and find out," Shawn said.

The bright tone in Shawn's voice gave Gus a small hope. Maybe they could get of this with a minimum of bloodshed.

"Okay, Shawn," Gus said. "What are you talking about?"

"You sure you don't want to lecture me here about how I always drag these things out and make you ask questions instead of just giving you the answer?" Shawn said. "Because I figure we still have a couple of minutes left."

"Before what?" Gus said, a shiver of dread going up his spine.

"One question at a time," Shawn said. "So let's get back to the first one, and the answer involves Hank Stenberg. Which is really remarkable, because this is not the first time that kid has helped solve one of our most baffling cases, and he really is kind of a tard. But if he hadn't written that Wikipedia entry on us, we never could have figured out the truth."

"Why, did he put the solution to our final case in there?" Gus said, beginning to wonder if Shawn had simply lost his mind.

"How could he?" Shawn said. "We couldn't tell him what was going on in the mountains because we have no way to contact him, so he'd have to be up here with us to know about it. And even if he was, he couldn't access Wikipedia, because there's no cell service and no Wi-Fi up here. So how could anyone access Wikipedia in a place where there's no cell service and no Wi-Fi?"

Gus tried to slog through the layers of verbiage Shawn was spewing out to find the point. He even managed to keep himself from chiding Shawn for the inappropriate use of the slur "tard" as he searched for the point. What difference could it possibly make to point out that there was no Wi-Fi up here, especially since no one had a cell phone? And yet Shawn seemed to think there was something significant about the availability of Wikipedia in the mountains.

Something began to click in Gus' brain. It wasn't here Shawn was talking about. It was about receiving information where there shouldn't be any signal. He knew this meant something, but he couldn't quite place it.

He turned to Shawn, expecting to see the triumphant grin that would accompany Gus' admission that he needed Shawn to carry the explanation out another step. But Shawn wasn't smiling at him. In fact, he wasn't looking anywhere near Gus. He wasn't looking at the lawyers, either, even though they seemed to be frozen in place.

Shawn was staring off into the woods, his attention riveted to a space between two large trees.

"What are you looking at?" Gus asked.

Shawn didn't take his eyes off the space. "I think I was wrong."

"It doesn't really matter," Gus said. "You haven't explained what you were talking about, so I'll never know if you change your mind now."

"Not about the killer's identity," Shawn said. "I'm right about that. But when I said we had a couple of minutes, that was all wrong."

Gus felt a flash of fear run up his spine. "Couple of minutes until what?"

"And I was wrong about something else," Shawn said. "And this is the big one. I told you to fight your fear. I told you not to give in to panic. That was absolutely backwards. You need to panic. You need to panic right now."

"I don't understand," Gus said.

"Look around you, Gus," Shawn said sternly. "There's nothing here but trees and sun and mountains and cliffs. You're alone in the wilderness and there's no one who can help."

"Stop it," Gus said. The panic was rising now. Even though Gus was clearly not alone, his brain was having an increasingly difficult time convincing his muscles of that fact.

"It's your dream finally coming true," Shawn said. "You're going to die and there's nothing you or I or those two freaky lawyers can do to stop it."

Gus squirmed as a spasm of terror flowed through him. His feet pawed at the ground as if trying to shake off the shackles of his will and start running blindly. "What are you doing?"

"There's nothing any of us can do to stop it," Shawn said.

Gus' head was spinning, or maybe it was the ground. He tried desperately to hold on to reason. "Stop what?"

"That." Shawn pointed at the gap in the trees. For a moment, Gus saw nothing. And then it was there. Just a flash, barely enough to settle on his retinas, but Gus saw it and he understood what Shawn had been trying to tell him.

Just a flash, but that one flash told him everything he needed to know. That one flash of bright, brilliant green.

Chapter Fifty-Five

Gus ran.

The branches tore at his arms, the jagged rocks dug into his feet, his lungs screamed in pain as he gasped for breath. At least it wasn't night, as it had been in the dreams, but the trees were so dense they nearly blocked out the sun completely.

How long had he been running? It could have been hours; it could have been months. He had no idea where he was; the trail was a distant memory. At first he'd tried to remember landmarks so he could find his way back if he survived, but rational thought was the first cargo he'd jettisoned as he realized he needed to go faster.

And where was Shawn? They'd started running at the same time, along with Gwendolyn and Balowsky, and for a little while they were all together. But somehow they had split up, apparently on the philosophy that Jade couldn't track four targets at once. At the time, that sounded like a good idea. No matter how many times he reordered the priority of their deaths, Gus always found himself near the bottom of the list. Shawn would be an intellectual threat to Jade, Gwendolyn a physical one. So Jade could pick them off, then take her time going after Balowsky and him.

It was only after he heard her footsteps behind him that he

remembered Jade's philosophy—take the weakest one down first, and then use that failure against the stronger. No matter how fast he moved, how cunningly he changed direction, she was always there.

How was this possible? He'd had this dream so many nights in his life, and every time the thing chasing him was a hideous, demonic monster. That's one reason he'd been so fast to assume Gwendolyn was the killer, because she could fit that description.

But Jade Greenway rescued puppies and kittens. She preserved English folk songs. Unless she was preserving them to hum while she ate those rescued pets, this was not the portrait of a cold-blooded killer. What right did she have to be complex?

Gus could see the plunge just ahead of him, the cliff falling off hundreds of feet to a roaring river far below. There was plenty of time to stop or turn away, but no matter how hard he willed his feet to change direction they kept pounding inexorably towards the edge. He pummeled his thighs, tried to throw himself to the ground, grab hold of a tree, anything to slow himself down. Nothing worked. His feet kept propelling him forward.

It was the moment he always knew would come. It was the end. He felt his foot take one last step and hit nothing beneath it but empty air.

He was going to die. But at least there was this. At least now he understood why his body insisted on taking him off the cliff. It was because he couldn't run anymore, and because he wouldn't let the killer who was chasing him have the satisfaction of finishing him off.

A hollow victory, but as much of a victory as he could hope for, Gus thought. But as his left foot began to come down on open air, something happened that never happened in the dream.

In the nightmare, he didn't know what was chasing him or why. But in reality he knew it was Jade Greenway, and he knew why—she was a crook who was going to use their deaths to help her escape. In the dream Gus felt only terror and hopelessness. But now there was something else.

There was anger.

If he went over this cliff, then Jade would win. If he didn't go over the cliff, she'd probably kill him easily, and she'd still win. But Gus would not let that happen without a fight.

As his right foot, still propelled by his momentum, began to lift off the ground to join its mate in space, Gus stretched out his arm, reaching for a branch that hung out over the chasm. His fingers closed around the limb.

And then they opened again. The rough bark tore at the skin of his palm as the branch slid through his hand.

Gus was falling. Part of his mind tried to calculate exactly how long it would take for him to hit the rocks so many hundreds of feet below.

But the other part still refused to give up. He reached out blindly and his hands hit a root that had grown out of the cliff face. He grabbed it tight and felt the pain blast through his palms to his shoulders as he stopped his fall.

Gus let himself hang for a moment, allowing the pain to fade a little. Then he looked up. His head was about a foot below the cliff's edge. He scrambled with his toes for a foothold, but the cliff fell away inwards and he couldn't touch it. He tried to pull himself up, but his arms were so shocked with pain it was all he could do to dangle helplessly.

He heard something moving at the top of the cliff. Before he could do anything, there was a flash of green and Jade stepped to the edge.

"Let me help you." She crouched down to her knees and extended a hand. "Take my hand."

"So you can drop me?" Gus snarled. "I don't think so."

"If you're holding on to my hand, I don't see how I can drop you," Jade said, looking puzzled. "Also, why would I want to?"

"For the same reason you killed Archie Kane and Morton Mathis and Kirk Savage," Gus said. "To cover up your conspiracy to sell stolen technology from the Jet Propulsion Laboratory."

She gave him a little frown. "If that were true, it wouldn't be very smart to bring it up right now," Jade said. "It would be much wiser to tell me how delighted you are to discover I'm alive, and to pretend you have no idea I'm the killer. That way I might actually help you up, thinking that you weren't a threat."

"You need us all dead," Gus said. "It's the only way to convince the world that you died out here, too, so that no one will bother to look for you."

"Unless you've got this whole thing figured out wrong," Jade said. "Has it occurred to you that Morton Mathis wasn't the only one who was investigating Rushton, Morelock? A crime that big brings in lots of agencies. Some are secret, even from the FBI."

Gus tried to put this together. Was it possible? Could she be some kind of federal agent? It seemed so unlikely. And yet if it were true, it would solve all his problems.

And those problems were getting worse by the second. Because his hands were beginning to slip off the root. He wouldn't be able to hang here for more than a few more seconds.

"Prove it," Gus said.

"I didn't exactly bring my badge, unlike that idiot Mathis," Jade said. "It's kind of a tip-off on a deep-cover operation. But if I'm the mad killer you think I am, why didn't I take you out when you were all together on the trail?"

"I don't know," Gus said. "Why did you chase me through the woods if you didn't want to kill me?"

"I was trying to save you," Jade said. "It's dangerous to run blindly around here. You could even step off a cliff. Now, come on, give me your hand."

She reached down for him. He didn't trust her. But he couldn't refuse. His hands were slipping. She was his only chance. He unclenched one hand from around the branch and stretched up until his fingers met hers. Then he reached a little more and grabbed her wrist. "Now, pull!" he shouted.

She reached down with her other hand, but this one wasn't empty. She was holding a small plastic box in it with two tines across the top. She pressed a button on its center and a crackle of electricity shot between the tines, then pressed it against the hand Gus was using to hold on to the root. "This will only hurt for a second," she said.

Jade's thumb reached for the fire button on the taser. Before she could hit it, her body gave a jerk and she tumbled off the cliff.

Gus managed to free his hand from hers as she fell. He tried to grab the root, but before he could reach it, Jade seized his ankle with both hands, nearly yanking him down with her. They dangled over space from his one hand as the taser exploded into shards on the rocks far below.

Shawn's face peered over the cliff's edge. "That's the trouble with going after the weakest opponent first," Shawn said. "You leave the stronger ones out there to go after you."

Gus thrust his free hand at the root, but he couldn't reach it. He kicked his ankle to keep Jade from pulling him down. But she wouldn't let go, and he was beginning to.

"Help," Gus called to Shawn.

"Just hold tight," Shawn said.

"Oh, thanks," Gus gasped, his hand slipping off the root. "That hadn't occurred to me. Maybe you want to come down here and show me how to do it right."

"No need to get hostile," Shawn said.

"I'm dangling a million feet in the air by one hand with a mass killer on my ankle and I can't hold on," Gus said. "If that isn't a reason to get hostile, I don't know what it is."

"How about when you've TiVoed *Law & Order,* but the show runs a minute past the hour and gets cut off, so you never get to hear the pithy phrase that ironically sums up everything you've just seen?" Shawn said while getting down on his knees and reaching his hand out to Gus.

"My God," Jade called from below. "Do you two ever shut up?"

Shawn ignored her and said to Gus, "Say, would it be insulting your sense of initiative if I suggested you might want to reach up and take my hand?"

Gus tried. His arm flailed and his fingers brushed Shawn's hand.

"Grab his hand, you idiot!" Jade called.

Gus took a deep breath and pulled with every bit of strength in his body. He stretched out his hand, slashed through the air with it . . . and made contact. Shawn's fingers wrapped around his wrist.

"This works much better without the taser," Shawn called down to Jade. "You might want to take notes for next time."

Shawn closed his free hand around Gus', then began to pull. For a moment, Gus felt himself moving slowly upwards. Then the movement stopped.

Then they started to slide back down.

"You're going the wrong way!" Gus shouted.

"I'm slipping!" Shawn shouted back. "You're too heavy."

Gus tried again to kick his ankle free. Jade only held tighter.

"What about Gwendolyn and Balowsky?" Gus said. "Can they help?"

"I'll be sure to ask them if they happen by," Shawn said.

Gus and Jade dropped another inch before Shawn managed to stop himself from sliding.

"Jade," Gus pleaded. "You have to let go. We're all going to die if you don't."

"Seems to me I have a tiny chance of surviving if I hold on, and none if I let go," Jade said.

"Surviving so you can get the death penalty," Gus said. "Isn't it better to let go nobly?"

"Possibly," Jade said. "But it's even better if I live and get away."

Gus felt one of her hands release his ankle. Before he could kick the other one away, she reached up and grabbed his calf. Then she let go of his ankle and used that hand to clutch his belt.

"What are you doing?" he shouted.

"She's climbing up your back," Shawn said. "I think she's going to use us as a ladder and once she's up top, kick us both over the edge. You've got to do something!"

"Like what?"

Jade was grabbing Gus' collar now, and the shirt pulled tight against his throat. He gasped for breath.

"I don't know," Shawn said. "Maybe you could let her know how well this worked out for Ricardo Montalban at the end of *The Wrath of Khan*?"

Gus could see Shawn's lips moving, but he couldn't hear the words. "What did you say?" Now he could barely hear his own words.

Jade's hand was on Gus' head now and pressing down. He couldn't see up anymore, but he knew she'd reach Shawn's arm quickly, and then she'd be at the top—and they'd be at the bottom.

"I said *The Wrath of Kahn*," Shawn bellowed.

Gus still couldn't hear him.

"Kaaaaaahhhhhn!"

It was no use. Gus still couldn't hear Shawn over the pounding sound that filled his ears. The pulsing, pounding, blasting sound, and the pulsating whooshes of air that were threatening to slam him into the cliff.

Jade's feet were on his shoulders now, and Gus could raise his head to look for see the source of the noise.

It was Henry Spencer, and he was reaching out a hand to Gus.

This was it, Gus thought. The final hallucination before he died. Then a strong arm reached out and grabbed him and pulled him away from the cliff's edge.

Away from the cliff's edge and into the hovering helicopter.

Chapter Fifty-Six

The trees towered over them, and the last glint of the setting sun burned orange before it disappeared behind the mountains. Gus leaned back against a huge oak and let out a happy sigh.

"This is the life," he said.

"See?" Shawn said. "How long have I been telling you there's nothing to fear about being in the wilderness?"

Shawn got up from his lawn chair and grabbed another hot dog off the hibachi, slapping it inside a bun already liberally smeared with condiments—including ketchup.

"As long as there are no psychotic lawyers chasing you."

"I don't think that's going to be happening anytime soon," Shawn said. "Unless you define soon as sometime longer than forty-to-life."

That was the term the DA had offered Jade in exchange for taking the death penalty off the table, and she had accepted. Her only demand was that they find her a maximum-security prison where she'd be allowed to wear at least some small amount of green.

Gus was astonished the prosecutors were willing to give her that much. Once they started digging, they discovered she'd been smuggling tech secrets out of the country for years. Arnold Svaco was actually the third mole she'd had at JPL, although he was by far her favorite. Passing the information through his schoolteacher cousin made it that much harder to connect Jade to any crime.

She might have kept up her espionage for years if it hadn't been for Archie Kane's protectiveness towards Rushton. Once he started investigating, Jade knew he'd never stop. And when Ellen Svaco called her at the firm, in a panic, to say she was being followed, Jade realized Archie was about to unmask her. So she stopped him. First she killed both Svacos to make sure they couldn't inform on her; then she dealt with Archie.

Still, she couldn't know how much Archie had told anyone else. She needed to disappear. A company retreat gone disastrously wrong seemed like a good way to make that happen. And since Rushton's retreats were famous for their difficulty and unpleasantness, no one would have any reason to suspect he wasn't responsible. She'd kill all the lawyers and slip away in a car she'd arranged to have left in a parking lot at the base of the mountain. Maybe a body or two would be recovered over the years, but there would never be a reason for anyone to assume hers hadn't been eaten by scavengers.

"So I was thinking, Rushton let us keep the backpacks, why not use them?" Shawn said. "You and me, a quick trip to the top of some mountain?"

"Did you have a mountain in mind?" Gus said warily.

"Normally I'd suggest the mountain of fries at BurgerZone," Shawn said. "But something's come up and it seems like a good time to get far out of town."

"When?"

"Now. Run!"

Shawn jumped to his feet, but before he could get away there was a rustle from behind the tree.

"Not so fast." Henry had come into his backyard with another tray of hot dogs for the grill.

"I'd love one, but I'm stuffed," Shawn said. "Besides, Gus is desperate to get up the mountain before the season ends."

"What season?" Henry said.

"Um, mountain season?" Shawn said. "Okay, fine. Let's have it."

"Let's have what?" Henry said.

"The thing you haven't said all night," Shawn said. "The thing you've been dying to say every second of every day since you plucked us off that cliff."

"That Shawn broke his promise," Gus added helpfully. "That he promised to stay out of the case, but ended up right in the middle of it."

Henry looked baffled. "I wasn't going to say that."

"You weren't?" Shawn said.

"You said you'd stay out of the Ellen Svaco murder case, and you did," Henry said. "You were following a separate and distinct case, which just happened to dovetail with mine. And good work on that, by the way. You managed so save some lives."

Shawn stared at him, searching for the trick. "What's the trick?" he said finally.

"No trick," Henry said. "I'm proud to have a son who listens to his father—and who knows when not to."

Gus could see Shawn taking that statement and turning it over in his mind. Poking it, prodding it, dissecting it—and still finding nothing insincere about.

"Thanks," Shawn finally said. "I guess we can stay to have another hot dog."

"You sure about that?" Henry said.

"Absolutely," Shawn said.

"Definitely," Gus said.

"I'm glad to hear that," Henry said. "Because speaking of listening, I've got some for you to do right now. I've decided to put the band back together, and you boys are our first audience."

"Oh, no," Shawn moaned.

"Oh, yes," Henry said. "And there's no way to weasel out of this one."

He thrust the plate of hot dogs into Shawn's hand and headed off to the garage. He threw open the door and climbed behind the drum kit he'd set up there. Ralph, Fred, and Sid all picked up their instruments and plugged them in.

Shawn tossed the hot dogs on the grill and he and Gus strolled over to the garage just as the band started to play.

"What do you know," Shawn said. "Apparently I will get fooled again."

Acknowledgments

I know it says in the beginning of this book that this is a work of fiction and that any resemblance to persons living or dead is entirely coincidental. I just want to point out here that that's particularly true in the case of the Isla Vista Foot Patrol, which in real life is a highly regarded law enforcement agency staffed by members of the UCSB Police, Santa Barbara County Sheriff's Department, and the California Highway Patrol.

As always, I am greatly indebted to *Psych* masterminds Steve Franks, Kelly Kulchak, and Chris Henze for entrusting me with these wonderful characters.

About the Author

William Rabkin is a two-time Edgar-nominated television writer and producer. He has written for numerous mystery shows, including *Psych* and *Monk*, and has served as showrunner on *Diagnosis Murder* and *Martial Law*.